She Be
Damned

She Be Damned

A Heloise Chancey Mystery

M.J. TJIA

PanteraPress

great storytelling

Published in 2017 by Pantera Press Pty Limited
www.PanteraPress.com

Please send all permission queries to:
Pantera Press, P.O. Box 1989 Neutral Bay, NSW 2089 Australia or info@PanteraPress.com
A Cataloguing-in-Publication entry for this book is available from the National Library of Australia.

ISBN: 978-1-921997-88-4 (Paperback)
Cover Design: Chris Wright
Typesetting: Kirby Jones
Author Photo: Red Boots Photographic
Printed in Australia: McPherson's Printing Group

Pantera Press policy is to use papers that are natural, renewable and recyclable products made from wood grown in sustainable forests. The logging and manufacturing processes are expected to conform to the environmental regulations of the country of origin.

For Mum, who introduced me to Christie,
Marsh, Allingham and Sayers

"A superb Nemesis in crinoline,
bent on deeds of darkness and horror"

Mary Elizabeth Braddon, *Eleanor's Victory*

Prologue

Pain bursts through Nell's abdomen, so intense it wrenches her awake. But she can't seem to open her eyes, her eyelids are too heavy.

He's muttering to himself. There's a jangle of metal.

The stench of vomit is strong, and the back of her thighs are wet.

She watches his shadow through her eyelashes as he moves around the room. She wants to struggle, get away from this awful pain but her wrists are tied to the arms of a chair. Her feet are bound, wide apart, in stirrups, and a terrible lethargy weighs upon her body.

He positions himself between her legs.

The piercing agony starts up again.

She wants to scream to him to stop, but she's too weak. And in any case, there's something crammed into her mouth, something metallic. Sharp.

He murmurs soft words to her. He tells her he'll be merciful. That the opiates he'd injected into her arm are strong. Presses a wad of cloth, bathed in something sweet, something acerbic, to her nose, her mouth. As she drifts off she thinks of how kind he is. She is thankful.

Chapter One

The bedroom door closes softly behind him. I then hear the front door close.

Thank Christ. I sit up in bed and rub at the crick in my neck. I've been lying in the same decorous pose for some time, pretending to be asleep, conscious of his admiring gaze. Two hours ago, while it was still dark and he'd snored and farted on his own side of the bed, I'd taken a pee and chewed on mint washed down with water so my breath was fresh when he woke. I'd reclined, eyes closed, amongst my silk pillows, one arm flung above my head, mouth gently clamped shut. I lay slightly to the side, so that the fullness of my cleavage was accentuated. My sheer night dress fell away to reveal one rosy nipple, which tautened in the crisp morning air and I'd wondered if he would take it into his warm mouth, willed him to, almost squirmed with the anticipation of it, a giggle spiralling up my chest. But I hadn't initiated anything. I was the sleeping kitten, the sleeping beauty, after all.

My night dress slips to the floor as I step out of bed and I look at my reflection in the dresser's mirror, tilting my head from one side to the other. I pull my tousled dark hair forward, so that only the lower curve of my breasts are visible. Running my fingers over the small triangle of hair between my legs, I wish it was a shade lighter, so that I could colour it yellow or blue. That would amuse my lovers. I pose for a moment, a cross between the Greek nude I'd sneaked in to see at the Exhibition of '51, and the girls ironically named Chastity and Faith in the photographs I keep in the bottom drawer of the nightstand. I pivot to see the reflection of my pale bottom. I hate it, I'm embarrassed by it. It's small and firm. I will never be a *Grande Odalisque*. I want it to be rounded and heavy like the base of a vase. I want his fingers to be able to knead it like it's biscuit dough.

Taking a step closer to the mirror I scrutinise my face. I'm vain, and I am not vain. I know I'm beautiful, but I know my beauty is to be utilised, tended. The winged eyebrows, the high cheek bones, and the full bottom lip that I pout as I gaze at myself. The colour of my eyes are changeable, depending upon my mood, or maybe even upon how much wine I'd enjoyed the night before; sometimes they're as smooth as a hazelnut, other times flecked with gold. They are perfectly set off by my heart-shaped face, so I'm told. 'Shimmering pools of melancholy, making thy heart ache'. Isn't that how that ridiculous poet had described my eyes? More like 'shimmering pools of colic, making thy middles ache'. I grin, a deep dimple puckering my left cheek. I own my face, but so do others. I'm almost famous, infamous. When I think of this I feel a flutter of excitement in the pit of my stomach, but I also feel a little sick. I've worked towards this for a long time, even before I knew what could be achieved. And of course, now I have other strengths to work with besides this beauty. I have more to trade than just my body.

I hurry into my dressing room and tug on the bell pull. Wrenching open the door I call for Amah to come and help me dress. We will have company soon.

I'm already tying the ribbon on my silk underwear when Amah Li Leen enters. She's a plump, middle-aged woman from the East. She's wearing a plain, white blouse and black skirt, and her shiny black hair is coiled into a low bun. I never cease to be irritated by how she dresses. We've often argued about it. I want her to dress in colourful sarongs from Malaya or those heavy Chinese smocks with the mandarin collars. I want her to fit in with the Oriental décor of my house. Furniture and art from the Orient are very much in style at the moment, and many men, especially those in shipping and diplomatic work, admire how I've decorated my rooms. So she could at least look the part if my guests are to catch a glimpse of her. But she won't. She says she doesn't want to stand out, although it's almost as if her sober apparel accentuates her almond-shaped eyes, her bronzed skin colour.

"What is Sir Thomas visiting for, Heloise?" she asks as she helps me shrug into a sheer chemise. The faint cadence of a Liverpool accent is discernible in her speech.

"His missive just said something about a number of suspicious deaths in the Waterloo area."

"Why does he think this would be of interest to you?"

I gasp as she tightens my corset. "I am hoping he wants me to investigate."

"Ridiculous," she mutters, helping me step into a voluminous, crinoline hoop. "Nearly as ridiculous as this contraption."

Amah's skirt is far narrower than what's fashionable. "I would be mortified to be seen in your skirt, Amah."

"Well, I'm used to it, aren't I?"

I laugh. "That's a lie. If it were not so cold here, you would wear much less." I look for an answering smile from her but, not receiving one, I sit down at my dressing table. Tears smart in my eyes as Amah Li Leen brushes and pulls my hair into loops, tutting that there is no time to curl the ends.

"What will you wear today?" she asks, as she moves to the dressing room that houses my vast collection of gowns.

Gone are the days of wearing the same gown until it's stiff with grime and drudgery – that one I had of grey batiste, bought for a song from the Belgian girl grown too large in the belly, that hid stains yet showed sweat under the arms or, later, the blue silk, which was more expensive but acquired the shine of poverty and overuse. I don't even want to think of the creased, brown sheaths of leather I wore as shoes. The sour reek that wafted from my feet, embarrassing, distracting, as I grimaced with feigned pleasure pressed against a brick wall.

"How about the new lilac one with the orange-blossom trim?"

"I think maybe the dove-grey would be better for a meeting with Sir Thomas," says Amah. She comes back to the dressing table carrying the heavy gown across both her forearms and deposits it onto a plush armchair.

I frown slightly. "I suppose you're right. But I will wear the crimson petticoat beneath it."

She pulls the petticoat, then the dress, over my body. Although it does not reveal my shoulders, it is gathered at the waist and cut low over my breasts. I dab perfumed powder across my neck and bosom.

"Maybe just a little lace at the front," I say, smiling. "I don't need to show so much flesh for the work Sir Thomas offers me."

I go to add something gay to my apparel, a flower or a feather, but there's a hard rap on the door knocker and I can hear Bundle, my butler, on his way to answer it.

I'm clasping down the sides of my gown to fit through the doorway when I notice the stiff expression on Amah's face. I squeeze her arm and lean down to kiss her on the cheek. "One day we'll be back in the sunlight."

I'm surprised to find two men in my drawing room. Sir Thomas Avery I know well. He is a man of maybe forty-five years, a little shorter than me, with thick, frizzled mutton chop sideburns. He steps forward and takes my hand in greeting. He then introduces the stranger standing by one of the windows which overlooks the street below.

"This is Mr Priestly," he says.

The other man doesn't approach me but bows his head. "Pleased to meet you, Mrs Chancey," he says.

His lips widen a little, but he makes no real effort to smile. A thin frame and large ears preclude Mr Priestly from being a handsome man, but he is well, if soberly, dressed and gentlemanly. His eyes flick over my figure and then, with more leisure, he looks around my drawing room.

His gaze follows the pattern of the Oriental rug, the scrollwork on the mahogany side board and the richly damasked sofas with intricately worked legs. He takes in the assortment of Chinese blue and white vases in the dark cabinets and the jade figurines on the mantelpiece. Finally his gaze rests on the large mural that adorns the furthest wall. A painting of a peacock, sat on a sparse tree branch, fills the space. The peacock, a fusion of azure, green and gold leaf with a regal crown of feathers, displays its resplendent train so that the golden eyes of its plumage can be admired. It might be a trick of the light and artistry, but the peacock's tail feathers seem to quiver.

"How very... exotic," he says.

He moves towards the fireplace and studies the painting in the gilded frame above it. The portrait is of a young woman dressed in Javanese costume. Her hair is pulled into a low bun, silver earrings decorate her lobes, and she holds a white flower behind her back. Richly decorated batik is wrapped around her breasts, and a tight sarong swathes her lower body.

"Is that you?" he asks me, surprise in his voice.

"Yes." I stand by him and look up at the portrait. "My friend Charles Cunningham lent me the fabric for the sitting. His father brought the lengths of silk and batik back from Java, after one of his assignments with Raffles. Such beautiful, earthy colours, aren't they?"

Mr Priestly steps a few feet away from me. "I'm afraid I don't follow this fashion for aping savages."

I feel a prick of resentment at the insult to my drawing room and portrait – the insult to me. But I learnt long ago to hold my temper in check, I have learnt to behave with decorum, for I no longer work in a Liverpool back-alley. Smiling sweetly as I lower myself and my wide skirts carefully onto the sofa, I say, "Oh, don't feel bad. Not everyone can be *a la mode*, can they?"

Sir Thomas clears his throat loudly. "Maybe we should discuss the purpose of our visit, Mrs Chancey."

"Yes, let's," I answer, patting the sofa cushion next to mine. "Please have a seat."

Sir Thomas sits down and looks at Mr Priestly expectantly. However, rather than speak himself, Mr Priestly gestures for Sir Thomas to proceed.

"Well, Mrs Chancey," says Sir Thomas. "I have come to ask you to do a spot of work for us again."

"Wonderful. Who will I need to be this time?"

Sir Thomas smiles. "Certainly your prior experience as a stage actress has benefitted us, Mrs Chancey. And it is true. We do need you to do some covert investigating for us."

One of Sir Thomas' many businesses includes a private detective agency. Although he has a surfeit of male detectives, he has found it very difficult to find females willing or able to sleuth. Having both the willingness and ability, I've worked on and off for Sir Thomas over the last eighteen months. I've posed as a sewing woman to gain access to a noble house, I've rouged and revealed myself as a street prostitute in order to spy on a group of young men and I have even performed as a harem dancer in order to reconnoitre at a foreign embassy.

Sir Thomas clears his throat again. "Yes. Well, maybe the task we ask of you this time will not be so enjoyable, I'm afraid."

He glances at Mr Priestly, who nods him on.

"As you know, we are investigating the deaths of several women in the Waterloo area."

"How did they die?" I ask.

Sir Thomas waves his hand. He won't go on.

Mr Priestly stares hard at me for a few moments. "Sir Thomas assures me I can broach any subject with you, Mrs Chancey."

"Of course," I smile. He means because I'm a whore, of course, but I won't let him think his sting has broken skin.

He turns and gazes out the window as he speaks. "It seems that each of these women – well, really, they were prostitutes – had terminated a pregnancy and died soon after from blood loss and infection."

"Well, unfortunately that happens far too frequently."

"That is so, but luckily the body of the last prostitute who died in this manner was taken to the hospital to be used as a specimen, and they found that..." He glances over at me, his eyes appraising.

"What?" I ask.

"They found parts of her body missing."

"What parts?"

"Her uterus was gone, but so were her other... feminine parts."

Revulsion curls through my body and I feel the pulse of an old wound between my legs. I glance at Sir Thomas whose eyes fall away from mine.

"What makes you think her death is connected to the other deaths in Waterloo?"

"It was the fourth body they had received in this condition in the last seven weeks."

"What? And was it not reported to the police?" My voice rises in disbelief.

Mr Priestly shrugs. "Well, they were only prostitutes, after all. At first the hospital staff thought they were the victims of amateur hysterectomies, but when they found that each of the women was also missing..."

"Missing...?" I shake my head a little, hoping I'm not about to hear what I think is coming, although a part of me, tucked away beneath the horror, wonders how he'll describe it.

Mr Priestly straightens his collar. "Apparently all their sexual organs were missing. Inside and out. I am positive you know to what I am referring, Mrs Chancey."

I can't help but press my knees together. I nod.

"Accordingly, it became apparent that there was a pattern to these deaths," he continues.

"And what do the police think now?"

"Obviously someone in the area is butchering these unfortunate women, whether accidentally or in spite is uncertain.

However – and it's not surprising – the police don't want to waste too much time investigating the deaths of prostitutes when the rights of decent, law-abiding Londoners need to be protected."

Indignation sharpens my thoughts, but I command my body to relax. After all, what else is to be expected? If I'm to mix in polite society I need to mimic their ways. I force a languid smile to my face, eyes narrowed, as I watch Mr Priestly. "So, what on earth do you want to look into these deaths for? If the police are not interested, why should we be?"

"A friend of mine heard of these cases and has become immensely interested. It is on behalf of my friend that I have engaged Sir Thomas' services."

"And why has your friend become so interested?"

Mr Priestly takes his time seating himself in an armchair, crossing one leg over the other. He scrutinises my face for a few moments before answering. "My friend has a special concern. It is for this reason we ask for your assistance."

"What is this special concern?"

"My friend is a respectable gentleman, well known to his peers. A short time ago he found out that his daughter was in an unhappy condition. She is not married." Mr Priestly pauses to let the awful truth of his statement sink in.

"Ah, I see. And what did he do?" I ask.

Mr Priestly frowns. "Naturally he disowned her. He allowed her to pack some of her belongings and had her taken to a convent near Shropshire."

"Naturally," I repeat, my voice dry.

"Yes, but she did not make it to Shropshire. She bribed the coachman to take her to a hotel in Charing Cross, and from there she has disappeared."

"Do you know why she wanted to be left at that hotel?"

"Apparently her... the other party... was staying there. He is a Frenchman." He nods, as if this fact alone throws light on the cause of her predicament.

"But nobody knows where she is now?"

Sir Thomas takes up the thread of the story. "At first Mr Priestly required my men to look into her activities at the hotel, but upon questioning Monsieur Baudin, we learnt she had left his care most swiftly."

"I suppose he did not want her now she was in trouble?"

"Something like that, it would seem. Since then he seems to have flown the coop," says Sir Thomas. "My detectives have since found out that the young lady took a cab to Waterloo where she spent a little over three weeks in a boarding house before moving into another well-known establishment nearby."

"What establishment?"

Mr Priestly purses his lips for a moment. "A house of ill-repute, it would seem. She moved to an abode owned by one Madame Silvestre."

"Ah yes, I'm aware of her services," I reply, thinking of how it's been many years since I have had the pleasure of the old cat's acquaintance. "Do you need me to fetch her?"

"If only it were that easy. It seems she has since disappeared. Nobody knows where she has gone."

The sudden realisation dawns on me. "Are you concerned that she too has been mutilated?"

"We are not sure what has become of her," says Sir Thomas. "Madame Silvestre might just be hiding her, or maybe the young lady has moved on to another place."

"Or maybe she is one of the butcher's victims," says Mr Priestly. He withdraws a card case from his pocket and carefully takes out a small photograph. He hands this to me. "Eleanor Carter."

The likeness is of a very fair, young woman. Her face is small and serious and the bodice of her gown is buttoned tightly to the base of her throat.

"How old is she?" I ask.

"She is only seventeen. She is quite small and pretty – this photograph does not do her justice," says Mr Priestly. "My friend is worried for her safety."

"He might have thought of that before he threw her out onto the street," I say, before I can help myself.

Mr Priestly's brow lifts as he looks across at me coldly. "Although it is out of the question for her to return to her familial home, naturally my friend is troubled. He would like to see her ensconced safely at the nunnery."

I glance from Sir Thomas to Mr Priestly. "You want me to find her?"

Sir Thomas sits back into the sofa and extends his legs out before himself. He studies his shoes as he says, "Well, as you now know, I have already had my detectives scouting for information on Miss Carter, but they have failed to find her."

"And you think my womanly touch might avail?" I ask, amused.

Sir Thomas resettles himself again. "As simple questioning has not sufficed, we wondered if you could possibly discover Miss Carter's movements with more covert methods."

"Such as...?"

Mr Priestly makes an impatient motion with his hand. "You seemed interested in picking up the mantle of another character again, Mrs Chancey, and that is what we are asking of you. I believe it won't be too much of a stretch for you, for we would like you to pose as a..." he glances at Sir Thomas, "a 'gay girl', I think they're called."

I stop breathing for a moment as annoyance flushes through my body. It's true that I posed as a street prostitute for Sir Thomas, but that was just a lark, and it's also true that in the dim past I'd worked in many places, both good and bad, but I choose not to think of that now. So, for this absolute pig of a man to refer to me as a mere gay girl makes me angry. I'm no longer a lowly *grisette*, willing to flatter or implore my way to a few more pennies or ribbons while I try to hide my desperation.

I lift my chin. "You want me to pose as a prostitute?"

"Precisely."

"At Madame Silvestre's?"

"If they would have you, certainly," says Mr Priestly, his voice even. "What better place for you to be situated in order to find out where Miss Carter is?"

I heave myself up from the sofa and stride to the bay window. My skirt bumps a side-table causing a figurine of a Chinese goddess to totter. Go back to work in a brothel, for the sake of a little detection? I'm not so sure.

Sir Thomas puts his hands out entreatingly. "Mrs Chancey, not only can you investigate the disappearance of Miss Carter, you can also look into the other deaths. You can try to find more information about the monster who is harming these women."

"Who knows?" interrupts Mr Priestly. "You could even pretend to be pregnant and see where that takes you."

"Be your bait, you mean?" I ask, my voice flippant.

"Whatever it takes, Mrs Chancey, whatever it takes." Mr Priestly slips his fingers into his gloves. "You may put it about that Miss Carter is a young relative of your own, but in no way must her name be connected back to my friend. Sir Thomas will take care of the case from now on. I am sure you will be remunerated…" he glances around my sumptuous drawing room, "as grandly as possible."

I turn from the window, the smile on my face fixed. "I don't work for Sir Thomas for the money, Mr Priestly. I have my own independent means. I follow inquiries for Sir Thomas purely for the pleasure of it, and in this I would find no pleasure. I'm afraid I will need to decline your kind offer."

He stops pulling on his remaining glove and eyes me for a few, long moments. "I must assure you that I do not request you to take this case – I insist you take this case."

"Insist? You cannot make me take this case, Mr Priestly."

"Mrs Chancey, I know the local magistrate, Sir Herbert Brimm. I know for a fact that he and others are interested in your mysterious activities in the Limehouse area. One word from me and you will be examined by the local police and the doctor in their employ."

I can feel anger drain the colour from my cheeks and my fingers quiver with adrenalin. I've heard of this movement to examine prostitutes for contagious diseases. He would menace me with this detestable law that terrorises prostitutes and offends even righteous women? He would dare threaten me with a disgusting doctor probing my body for sickness?

"That will never eventuate, Mr Priestly. I know far more important and powerful people than you."

"Ah, you must mean your protector," replies Mr Priestly. "Tell me, how would he like an examination of your private life smeared in the newspapers for his wife and esteemed friends to see? Think of his poor children. Be sure, Mrs Chancey, the damage can be done before he is able to assist you."

I grip my waist, my fingertips digging into the unyielding corset. My popularity with patrons is closely tied to my discretion. It has always been so. But in this trembling moment of rage I have nothing to lose. "Do it then, sir. Do your worst," I say, struggling to keep my voice low.

Sir Thomas steps between us, his hands raised. "Please, Mr Priestly, there's no need for these threats." He turns to me. "Mrs Chancey, surely we can come to an agreement on how you can investigate this in a manner with which you are comfortable. We really do need your assistance."

I look into Sir Thomas' flushed, kind face and then shrug one shoulder. "Allow me to think it over. And if I do decide to proceed," I glare at Mr Priestly, "I will only deal with Sir Thomas."

"That suits me perfectly," says Mr Priestly. He leaves the room without bidding farewell.

Sir Thomas thanks me profusely and presses my hand goodbye between his clammy ones. "I will be in touch." He follows Mr Priestly to the front door as swiftly as his short legs will take him.

From the window I watch the men descend the few front steps down. I make sure to stand a little behind the silk drapes so that they can't see me. Stopping on the last step Mr Priestly turns to Sir Thomas and says, "What on earth do you think a little dollymop like her can achieve?"

"She's done some very good work for us..." Sir Thomas protests. The rest of the conversation is drowned out by the arrival of their carriage.

I stand very still for a few minutes, watching the carriage pull away, until I sense someone behind me.

"What are you thinking?" asks Amah. "Are you wondering how you will investigate this dreadful affair?"

I turn my head slightly, and meet her eye. "No. I am considering in what way I will repay the precious Mr Priestly for his insults."

Li Leen

I watched her through the peacock's tail again today. She really is beautiful. She stands so tall, so straight and her nose is little, not flat like mine. I used to be beautiful when I was young and lived by the sea in Makassar. Because we were richer than most I had gold bangles that jangled on my wrists and gold rings in my ears. My hair was black then, only black, without the stripes of white that line my hair now. I never pulled my hair back, I allowed it to drape over my left shoulder and rest on my breast as I counted out buttons or weighed the fruit for customers in our produce store. Oh yes, I was beautiful. The men of Makassar admired me, as did the Dutch men, but no one ever asked for my hand.

She would find it hard to believe that I once was beautiful too. She only sees me as I am now. People notice her when she walks past. They even follow her sometimes. I am anonymous. Nobody watches me. So I watch her.

Sir Thomas admires her; why else does he continue to employ her in this manner, so that she needs to use the skills she has learnt outside the bed? He is twice her age, yet he blushes when he speaks to her. But that Mr Priestly, the one with the big ears, I did not like how he looked at her when she was not noticing. He looked at her long and hard, but like he hated her. And when she turned to him again he smiled that sour smile of his. I am not quite sure what he said that made her so angry, but I hope she is careful. He is dangerous, that man.

Chapter Two

I watch the front of Mme Silvestre's house from my carriage. It's a bleak evening, the gas lamps shedding only hazy light. The terraced house looms tall, its exposed, dark bricks gloomier than its painted neighbours. I'm really loath to leave the comfort of my warm carriage to re-enter this world I'd left several years past, but I know I must. It's the only way forward.

I adjust my bodice to push up the fullness of my bosom. I pat my hair to make sure it is neat, and press a finger lightly to my mouth to ensure the rosy lip rouge is still in place. Looking once more up at the house I notice the sash curtain on the lower window twitch, allowing a sliver of light to appear. Someone has noticed my presence.

I hop down from the carriage with the help of my coachman. He's a small, wiry man dressed in the tight-fitting black and red silk livery I'd chosen for him a year beforehand.

"Thank you, Taff," I say as I step over the mud in the street to the pavement. I clutch my skirt and petticoats high and stand on tip-toe to keep my slippers from the muck. "Can you wait for me here with my baggage? I might be a while."

"Of course, Miss Heloise," he says, his voice gruff. "I won't go no further without a word from you. These be'm rough parts we are in."

I pause for a moment and peer into the gloom. I can see why Taff thinks this area is rough. The road is full of dirt, and the stench of horse manure and rotten food is strong. Most of the passers-by are slow and dishevelled, some smelling of gin and piss. The muckers across the way sift through the refuse for anything that can be salvaged or sold. The men, women and children are uniform in the murky light, with their grey, patched clothing and sunken cheeks. They search for scraps with the same dogged determination of hopefuls who pan for gold. It's a different world from my home in Mayfair on the pristine, quiet South Street. I grin at Taff. "What? Have you forgotten Toxteth Docks, Taff?"

"It's a long time since we'm been there, Miss Heloise," he grumbles.

"Yes, I suppose it has been," I murmur. And thank heavens for that. I step briskly up the path to Mme Silvestre's front door.

I tap on the door which is almost immediately drawn open by a huge, bald man. He blinks and says, "Well, if it's not Hell's Bell."

I laugh. "Mr Critchley! You still here?"

"Of course. Where else would I be?" He moves back against the corridor wall, but what with his large stomach and my voluminous gown the space is somewhat restricted. "You'd better go straight into the drawing room, Hell. Madame Silvestre will be pleased to see you again."

I admire his optimism. I'll be very surprised if I'm welcomed warmly, especially as I'd robbed Silvestre of some very lucrative business when I had left her protection. I push the door open to my right, and a surge of warmth, musky body odour and perfume assail me. Two large chandeliers light the long room, and numerous candles twinkle from the picture rails and tables. Luxurious rugs the colour of golden straw line the floor and the room is strewn with women in various stages of undress draped over velvet damask sofas and settees. Despite it being early in the evening, several men, dressed neatly in silk top hats and long coats, already hover over their favourites. As I pick my way slowly through the room, I notice that the bar is manned by a rather robust looking woman with lavish amounts of rouge rubbed into her cheeks and that an old acquaintance of mine, Tilly, is thumping out a tune on the piano which she accompanies in an unmelodious, yet enthusiastic, manner.

At the end of the room on a raised platform, seated in what could only be described as a throne, is Mme Silvestre. She is a very wide woman, and the billowing folds of blue and yellow satin that engulf her only make her appear broader. Her vast bosom wobbles close to where her chins finish, and she wears a Chantilly lace cap over her brown hair. In her lap is a white, long-haired cat, also of large proportions. Directly behind her, above the fireplace, is a painting of a sweet, simpering girl clutching a posy of peonies, her chestnut curls cupping her divinely pretty face. This is a portrait of Mme Silvestre in her younger, more innocent, days, before wine, fine food and lovers had spoilt her figure, but strengthened her business acumen.

Mme Silvestre's heavy jowls lift into a smirk when she spies me. "Ah. A compliment, to be sure, Martine," she drawls in the cat's ear. "Miss 'Eloise, come to pay us a call, 'ave you? Or must we refer to you as *Mrs* Chancey now?"

Mr Critchley places a spindle back chair next to the throne for my use. "Of course you can always call me Heloise, madam," I say politely, as I sit down, arrange my gown and gaze around the room.

Mme Silvestre is actually from Hackney, and has obscured a rather sordid past with a French background, just as I had done really. Her voice is deep, and with many years' practice, she has perfected an accent that rounds her speech as if she is sucking on a small plum, the French intonation facilitated by the cockney dropping of aitches, although once in a while a deep-rooted turn of phrase or word is surprised from her painted lips.

I have to speak loudly over the sound of music, women squealing and men laughing. "I see business is still good."

"This business will never go out of fashion, my dear," she says. "But 'ow is the acting going?"

There is a quizzical cast in the fat woman's eye. We both know my acting is just a pleasant pastime that takes no real place over my career as a courtesan. "I adore it. Did you see me as Peaseblossom? Not a large role, I must admit, but the costume was divine – Aspreys lent the diamonds for the gossamer wings, and the fairy dress was so transparent all I could see when I looked to the audience were opera-glasses trained upon me." I grin at the memory. "But I am taking a rest from stage-acting at the moment."

A look of surprise lengthens Mme Silvestre's face. "You 'aven't come 'ere to ask for your position back, 'ave you?"

My back stiffens. That's exactly what I'm here to do, but I can't bring myself to utter the words. I watch the women working the room. They appear to be enjoying themselves, carousing and playing with the gentlemen, and I realise that, apart from Tilly, I don't recognise any of them. Unlike me, most of the other 'older' women would have had to move on to a less exclusive establishment or maybe even the streets. I'm not sure that I can face the uncertainty of an evening's quest, the uncertainty of who will share my bed. And how will I have time to carry out my investigations if, like in the past, my whole time is monopolised by Charlies? It's too haphazard to consider. Damn that Priestly. I'm a good investigator. I don't need to be flat on my back or flashing my breasts to find this Eleanor girl. And I don't relish lying in wait, a sparkling lure on the hook, in order to catch the man mutilating doxies.

I decide upon a new tack.

"No," I answer, finally.

"No. You've been gettin' along grand without us," Mme Silvestre says tartly.

I ignore the sour tone in the older woman's voice. "I'm actually here to ask after a friend of mine. Her name is Eleanor Carter and I believe the last time she was seen it was here, with you."

"Ho! A friend of yours, was she?" Mme Silvestre sneers. "A nice, refined girl like that? Although..." her eyes narrow. "Although, maybe it was you 'oo steered her wrong in life, was it?"

"Listen, Mildred," I have the satisfaction of seeing Mme Silvestre blink at the sound of her real name. "It doesn't matter how I know Miss Carter. All I want to know is if you know where she is now?"

"No, I don't. She was 'ere for barely a day, so why you all thinks I know where she is, is a mystery to me," she says crossly, stroking the white cat rather forcefully.

"Why was she here?"

"That stupid Tilly brought her, didn't she? I give the girls a tip when they bring me a nice piece of muslin. But the squawking your Miss Carter set up when old Mr Bench put 'is 'and on 'er knee was enough to make yer teeth chatter out of yer 'ed, so she 'ad to go."

"Where?"

Mme Silvestre's head rears back a little. "Well, I'm sure I don't know. That's not my concern now, is it? I run a business 'ere, in case you've forgotten, *Mrs* Chancey, not a bloody orphanage."

I have to clamp my mouth shut in vexation. I'm getting no further than Sir Thomas' stolid male detectives. I look around again at the other women in the room. There are seven of them, all differing in height, build and colouring. A petite blonde leads a tall man down the hall, while a girl with pale orange hair lies back on a couch nearby, offering her pert nipple to a man so young he still has acne rash on his cheeks. I wonder if Sir Thomas' other detectives had interviewed Mme Silvestre at this productive time of evening and enjoyed the sights.

"Would any of your girls know where she went?" I ask.

"You'll have to ask them yerself," she says. "All I saw of 'er was 'er blotchy face from crying. She 'ad a 'ard bump on her belly, so's one of the girls told me, so's I expect she was knocked up. And as you know, 'Eloise, pregnant ladybirds are an absolute nuisance. They're of no use to me."

I stare at Mme Silvestre for a few moments. I remember all too well how she manages the sad business of an unwanted pregnancy. "In that case, I am sure you gave her advice on how to take care of her unfortunate situation."

"Don't be ridiculous, 'Eloise," she snaps at me, placing the cat on the floor with a grunt, fluffing the cat hair from her skirt. "I didn't know 'er long enough to spend that sort of capital on 'er."

I cast my eyes to the ceiling. "And you don't know where she went?"

"No. Although if I'd known so many people would be looking for 'er, I might 'ave taken some notice," she says crossly.

Slumping back into my chair, I let out a frustrated sigh. I think for a minute. She couldn't have gone far, could she? Surely someone around here must know what became of her. I really hope that Miss Carter isn't one of the victims to be found in the hospital morgue. I know that investigating the murdered women must be my next step, but I want to find the girl alive and well before it comes to that. I lean in close to Mme Silvestre and say in a soft tone, "Madam, have you heard about any suspicious deaths of prostitutes lately?"

Mme Silvestre looks startled for a moment, and then lets out a bellow of laughter that drowns out the girls' high pitched squealing and talking. "What do you mean by suspicious? 'Eloise, you know that prostitutes die off as often as 'orses in these parts. The only suspicious thing is that so many of them 'old on for as long as they do." She shakes her head and chortles, although her laughter seems a little forced.

"You haven't heard anything at all?" I push further.

She rolls her eyes. "If I 'ear anything, I will let you know," she says. "Where can I find you?"

I'm wistful for a moment. As much as I want to return home, I know I need to stay nearby for the duration of this investigation. And I'm also reluctant to reveal my new address to the madam.

"I'm not sure. Can you recommend an inn or hotel close by?"

Mme Silvestre's mouth widens into a smug smile. "You are very lucky, as my 'ouse on Frazier Street is vacant." She nods towards her girls, and her mouth tightens with scorn. "I 'aven't 'ad a piece of skirt able to fill that 'ouse for a long while." She peers at me. "Not all girls are as talented as you were, my dear."

She's talking of the house she keeps for any of the girls who manage to become the mistress of a wealthy man. When a gentleman decides he would like the exclusive use of a certain woman, Mme Silvestre hires out the house to them at a very nice rent. In my short time with Mme Silvestre, I'd stayed in that house before moving onto much better things.

"Sounds perfect," I say, briskly. "What exorbitant rent will you require this time?"

She names her price. I know I'm expected to object – that Mme Silvestre has said a price so much above the house's worth – but I only agree graciously, as the rent is miniscule compared to that paid in the better parts of London and I'm being reimbursed by Sir Thomas in any case.

An annoyed frown forms on Mme Silvestre's brow and I hope it's because she has realised she could have named an even higher price.

"You don't still have that yellow chink working for you, do you?" she asks, irritably. "People around 'ere don't swallow that sort of thing, you know. That's something for the tastes of those who frequent the dock areas."

My lips purse and she scoffs, "Ho! 'Ere we go. 'Ell's Bell about to let her steam whistle go."

"Who I employ is none of your business, Mildred," I say as I stand up. "I think I will find a local inn after all."

"Don't be ridiculous," she says, as she tries to struggle to her feet. She is unsuccessful and plops back into the throne. "Don't get so wrought up over a chink, fer God's sake. See Mr Critchley on your way out. 'E will give you the keys to the 'ouse."

The air's chilly and stale when Taff and I enter the small house at the end of the terrace. I light the tallow candles I find on the hall table and direct Taff to the one bedroom up the narrow staircase with my numerous cloak bags and trunk. Taking a candle with me I have a quick glance at the small kitchen, dusty and barren, at the back of the house and then I stand in the middle of the sitting room.

Nothing has changed much, but everything seems shabbier, smaller, than I remember. When I had first come to this house as a very young woman – hell, I was a girl really – I felt so bloody happy. I no longer had to share a filthy room in Liverpool, the pong of the docks seeping in through the window with the icy draught. And I no longer had to snatch sleep in the musty boudoir of Mme Silvestre's brothel, with its frilly curtains and festoons of red velvet, in which there was a rotation of 'pleasure' time with another girl and her clients. No amount of lavender or camomile oil had rid the lumpy mattress of its sweet, fetid stench of sweat and semen. I close my eyes and lift my scented wrist to my nose to rid myself of the memories.

That had been the first time in my short life that I'd had a space to call my own, even if it was only for an unforeseeable period, and I can't help but smile as I think of the young man who'd made it possible for me to move into this house. He was a banker's son, and handsome, and for many months he imagined himself in love with me. Very lately, at the opera, I saw him again. His handsome face, now meatier and flushed, was covered in a stiff beard and moustache and his chest and stomach protruded with self-importance as he ushered his equally rotund wife before him. When he saw me, he froze for a second, and then, to my surprise, he smiled and nodded. I almost had the idea that he would have liked to hail me, to exchange friendly words, but of course he couldn't.

Taff stands in the doorway. "All your baggage is above, Miss Heloise."

"Thank you, Taff." I look at the dry, blackened fireplace. "Do you think you could start the fire for me? Here and in the bedroom? It's not a very cold evening, but I feel some firelight might make the place more homely."

I slowly tread up the stairs to the bedroom. I light a few more of the smelly, tallow candles on the dressing table, which only provide a shadowy flicker against the yellow walls and I'm thankful that in my home in Mayfair, bright, gas lighting has lately been installed. As I pull the heavy gowns from their cases and hang them in the closet, I find that the closet door cannot be closed against their fullness. Taff comes in to light the fire.

"I'm not happy about leaving you'm here, Miss Heloise," he mumbles from the fireplace.

I try to grin at him. "I know you're not. But I'll be fine." I place a few pairs of pretty shoes against the wall. "Although I wish I had brought Amah after all."

"Well, why didn't you'm?"

I cock my head to the side as Taff straightens up from the fireside. "It would not have worked out. You know how she is." She would interfere, creep behind me. And she'd stand out, which might make it difficult for me to be discreet.

Taff shrugs and I follow him down to the front door to let him out. After assuring him I'll call for him if I'm in need of aid, I return to the sitting room. All is very quiet, except for the crackle and spitting of the fire, and suddenly I'm a little forlorn. At this time of evening I'm used to company – frivolous, amusing and, sometimes, lascivious company. There's a rattle at the front door and my heart lifts. Maybe it's Taff returned, unable to leave me in this place alone. I'll have him go to the closest public tavern to fetch wine and food and we'll have a cosy chat. With luck he will clean the kitchen.

But when I reach the door, all I find is a folded note lying on the worn carpet that has been pushed through the letter slot. Opening it, I read: *Fornicator! As bitter as poison! Be gone from here.*

Chapter Three

It was well after midnight by the time I fell asleep last night. On re-reading the note's contents for the umpteenth time, I'd pressed my ear to the door, and hearing silence, pulled it open. Nobody hovered in the tiny courtyard, and on the street itself I could only see two drunkards, arm in arm, weaving their way home and a young boy scraping up the muck from the pavement. I'd bolted the door and then checked the kitchen door and windows, ensuring they were as tightly locked as possible. For many hours I lay in bed, wondering who had left the note. Was it for a former tenant of the house, or was it directed specifically at me? It made my skin crawl to think that someone on the other side of the front door might feel such malice for me. I'd slept very lightly, each creak of tired timber or the tapping of a moth's wings waking me with a start.

It's while I lie there in the grey dawn, wondering what my next move is to be in finding Miss Carter, when someone knocks lightly at the front door. I pull on a silk robe and, make my way to the front of the house. "Who's there?" I call through the closed door.

A girlish voice answers. "My name is Agnes. Mme Silvestre sent me over with some food and such for you."

My visitor is a sturdy looking girl, maybe twelve or thirteen years of age. Her hair, not quite blonde and yet not quite brown, snakes down her back in a long plait and she wears a white pinafore over her blue-stuff dress. She carries a wicker basket, laden with fruit and bread, which she balances on one bent knee.

I lead her to the kitchen, where we deposit the basket on the wooden table.

"Don't unpack it yet," I say, grimacing at the dust in the kitchen. "I'll need to neaten this place up before we can set food in here."

With Agnes' help, I find some rags and water and wipe the kitchen surfaces down. Between boiling the water for tea, and cleaning the ice box for the milk, I discover that Agnes is a distant cousin of Mme Silvestre's and has worked in her kitchen for nearly a year. We finish up and I lead the girl to the front door.

"When I visited Mme Silvestre last night, I noticed that my friend Tilly still works there. I need to have a word with her so I will come by again later. Please let Mme Silvestre know."

Agnes sniggers. "Well, you'd better come by much later. The dolls are all still asleep. Last night was a busy night."

I watch her march down the front path and wonder if she too is destined to be one of Mme Silvestre's dolls in the near future.

Having spent most of the day in a cab, pitching between brothels and inns in the near vicinity asking after Eleanor Carter, I realise I'm getting no further along than the others who searched for her. But there is one place they haven't yet looked – I must face up to visiting the hospital mortuary where the last prostitute's savaged body was left. Sir Thomas and Priestly are right. Maybe she has become the victim of whoever is murdering local women. She is with child, after all. She might have inadvertently fallen under the butcher's sway. But I won't report my visit to the morgue to Sir Thomas, because then he'll make me surrender the job up to one of his male detectives and I'm now determined to plough on by myself.

I'm as wary of hospitals as most people, so I watch the squat, rectangular building for some time before asking a woman who is emptying a bucket into the gutter if she could point me in the direction of the mortuary.

She nods towards a side door, wisps of her iron grey curls falling untidily from her cap. "I work in there on occasion, cleaning and sorting out the mess. Are you here for someone in particular?"

"I'm not sure," I say. I repeat the story I'd been offering all that day. "A cousin of mine has gone missing. We are afraid something has happened to her. I have had the dreadful thought that I might need to check here..."

"Well, Mr Pike and Mr Wilston have already gone home for the day," says the cleaner.

"Oh dear." I bite my bottom lip. I hold out my hand to the other woman. "My name is Mrs Chancey. And you are?"

"Mrs Dawkins," she announces, squeezing my middle finger briefly.

I try to look as beseeching as possible. "Could you show me around?"

But she shakes her head. "No point anyway. We haven't got any new bodies in there at the moment."

I've reached a dead end again but the brief moment of relief I feel at realising Eleanor's body is not in the mortuary is fleeting.

"Haven't had a body since they brought in that poor prossy a few days back."

"A few days ago? How do you know it was a prostitute and not my cousin?"

Mrs Dawkins shakes her head again. "Can't say to the likes of you, missus. Too delicate."

I place my hand on the cleaner's arm. "No, please. Tell me, so I can be sure it's not her."

"Well, if you must know, she had bits cut out of her. Lots of prossies lately have been turning up with bits cut out of 'em."

Even though I already know this piece of information, I still feel that curl of horror. "That's awful. I hope nothing terrible has happened to her." I search in my bag and bring out the picture of Miss Carter. "Could this be her?"

She squints and holds the small photograph at arm's length. "I really couldn't say, Mrs Chancey. Me eyesight's not what it was."

"Oh, I hope it isn't Eleanor."

"Eleanor. Is that 'er name?" she asks me. "Funny. All we knew about the last girl was that she was called Nell. That's short for Eleanor sometimes, isn't it?"

Genuine dismay flushes my cheeks this time. "I must see this body. It might be her."

"They're not going to show a missy like you," Mrs Dawkins says. "Have you got a man you can bring along to look?"

I shake my head.

"And I'm not even sure if the body is still there, anyhow," says the cleaner.

I tell Mrs Dawkins my current address and beg her to send word if there is any new information. I actually wring my hands together and endeavour to look as anxious and care-worn as possible. It's not for nothing that I receive acting roles at The Grecian and The Gaiety. Mrs Dawkins' features soften.

"Lookee. Come back tomorrow. Not too early mind! After Mr Pike and Mr Wilston have left for the day. I'll let you have a peep."

I stare up at Mme Silvestre's bagnio and again wish that Amah was with me to dress and curl my hair. The best I can do with it is a braid and then coil it into a low bun. The gown I've chosen to wear is of a plain hue, for all the gowns I've brought with me are of a modest appearance so as to be easily maintained without my maid. My bonnet has pretty blue ribbons though, and around my neck I wear a jade and onyx locket which is suspended from a pearl choker. Pressing my fingertips against the locket's grooves, I'm thankful I'm wearing such a precious piece of frippery, but I still feel frumpy on hearing the squeals and music emanating from Mme Silvestre's.

Although the evening is already quite dark as Mr Critchley leads me into the establishment, it's early hours for entertaining gentlemen. The long parlour is as warm and bright as the night before, but custom is slow, with only three men canoodling on the sofas with the half-dressed women. As yet, Mme Silvestre isn't seated on her throne, so I move to the bar and ask the tall attendant I'd seen the night before for a drink.

"What do you want, love?" he asks in a gruff voice.

I stare at his face and clock the slight shadow on the cheeks and the Adam's apple bobbing beneath the thickly made up face.

"What do you have?" I ask.

"Gum-tickler. Beer. Gin. We have some Veuve, if you have the blunt."

"Well, I have the blunt, so pour me one of those, please." I drop a few coins onto the sticky countertop and glance about. "Where's Tilly?"

"She's with a Charlie. You'll have to wait a while if you want to meet with her. Although she was with old Packer, so maybe she won't be too long." We smirk at each other. "My name's Henry. Are you that Heloise what visited Silvestre last night?" I nod. "Poor Silvestre thought all her luck was in when you walked through the door. Thought you were here to help her lift business." The ringlets of his wig sway as he shakes his head.

"Have things been slow?" I watch as a small group of merry middle-aged men enter the room. "I thought it looked as busy as ever here."

"Her heart's just not in it," he says, his ringlets bobbing again. He nods towards the doorway to the back of the house. "There's Tilly now."

I ask him to pour another champagne and carry the two glasses across the room to catch Tilly before she is commandeered by a determined looking young man with tow-coloured hair. We settle onto a Turkish divan at the back of the room. Tilly is wearing a pair of lace drawers and a silk chemise, and her fair hair has been tinted pink.

"I like the new look," I say, touching one of the pink curls.

"Do you?" Tilly cups her hand around her hair. "When I was in Paris I saw Cora Pearl. Her hair was pink like this, although I've since heard that she's coloured it yellow."

"When were you in Paris?"

"Oh, two years ago. A rich John took me," says Tilly. She pouts. "It's been a long time since I was treated that well. Now I'm just stuck here, all day, every day."

I take my silver, diamond-point cigarette case from my reticule and offer a cigarette to Tilly. "Where's Peg? And Floss?"

"Long gone. Peg died of the gasps, I heard. And I see Floss around sometimes, but she's set up in Piccadilly now, I think."

"Still working?"

"Nothing like this. I think she just hires out a room when she needs it." Tilly shrugs with nonchalance. "What about you though? Everything's rosy for you, so I've heard."

I smile. "I was lucky." I don't want to boast of my good fortune – how a wealthy older son had led to a rich man of business and then to a peer of the realm and ultimately to a state of financial stability – so instead I gossip about well-known Londoners with a fascinated Tilly.

"Ooh, listen to you with your dandy accent," says Tilly. "You've lost most of your dirty Liverpool lilt."

"Well, I had to learn to speak proper English if I was going to be on the stage, Till," I answer, with dignity. "Bu' shut yer forkin' yap, cos I can still tork out of me arse when I wanna."

Forkin'. Now there's a word I haven't managed to mould away from my past, no matter how many elocution lessons I take.

Henry re-fills our glasses, as Tilly points out a French girl and a Dutch girl working the room. We try out those accents with each other too. I'm good at the French one, having lived with a Frenchman for a year or so in Paris. We're talking so loud an older man with whiskers frowns at us and Tilly pokes her tongue out at him.

"What do you think of our Henry?" she asks.

"Where did he come from?" I glance over at the barman-lady. He puts an apron on over his green gown and touches up his wig. "He could teach me a thing or two regarding hair styles, at any rate," I grin.

"He just turned up one day," says Tilly. "He's Silvestre's man."

"No!"

"Yes, he is."

"How on earth would they both fit in the same bed?" I squint a little as I try to imagine it. "One so stout and one so long."

"I'd wager he is long too," snickers Tilly.

We smoke in silence for a few moments. "But you didn't come here just for a cosy chat with me, Hell," says Tilly. "Ol' Silvestre says you've been asking about that washy little girl I brought home to her last week."

I nod as I pick tobacco from my tongue. "Yes. Some people I know have asked me to find her. But I'm struggling. Have you any idea where she could be?"

"No idea, Hell. She could be anywhere," says Tilly.

"Where did you find her in the first place?"

"She was sitting in the park, crying over a cup of coffee. It was Katie Sullivan – you remember her? From the coffee stand down the street? – who pointed her out to me."

"Do you know where she was staying before she came here?"

"No. She had her case with her. Been pushed out of her last doss-house for not having enough money, I think. It was difficult to understand her under all the blubbering." Tilly lights a fresh cigarette from the last one. "Mind you, one of the girls thought she was pregnant so she might've told her where she could be fixed up."

"Do you know where?"

"The only scraper we use is that Dr Mordaunt."

I can't stop myself from grimacing. "I can't believe you still use him."

Hearing his name makes my stomach clench in remembered fear and pain, and I can almost smell the pungent smoke from the cigar that he puffed upon throughout the procedure.

"Just used to him, I suppose," says Tilly. "But there's a new doc in the area, so I've heard. I don't know if he's a scraper though. That Dutch girl over there had to see him about the pox, and she said he's ever so handsome and young and very sympathetic."

"Really? I might have to meet him."

Tilly laughs. "He'll be too poor for the likes of you, Hell." She throws the remainder of her cigarette into the fireplace.

I smile but I'm already thinking of other things. "Till, I stayed at Silvestre's house on Frazier last night and someone slipped a nasty note under my front door. Have you heard of anything like that happening lately?"

Tilly's mouth pulls down on each side as she shakes her head. "I mean, you know how sometimes we get spat upon or growled at, but I haven't heard of notes being sent."

"It's just that I don't know if the note is for me or for a previous tenant of Silvestre's house." I look at Tilly. "And I'm a bit worried because apparently horrible things have been happening to the girls around here."

"What things?"

"Girls being... I don't know... cut up and suchlike."

Tilly laughs again. "You're starting to sound like stupid old Mrs Hawes, rabbiting on about girls dying in pools of blood."

"Who's Mrs Hawes?"

"She's this old cow who runs a few girls in the hovels behind the bridge." She stares at me, in disbelief. "You're not going to take her seriously, are you?"

A very high-pitched whistle sounds. Mr Critchley throws open the door and clangs a bell. "It's a raid, it's a raid. The Brown boys have let off the signal."

"'Ow far?" shouts the French girl.

"Coming down the street right now," he bellows back as he helps Henry slide open the false backs of the drinks' cabinets to push the liquor through to their hiding spot. Glass tinkles as the girls shove glasses into pot-plants and china rattles as tables are set with tea things. The gentlemen stand around in the bustle, cheerfully calling out encouragements to the girls, who are pulling robes over their scanty underwear. They are all seated in companionable silence, decorously drinking tea when the first of the policemen enters the room.

"I thought alcohol could be served until midnight," I whisper to Tilly.

"But it's Sunday. No grog on Sundays. The buggers thought they would catch us with our pants down," Tilly answers with a smirk. She takes another one of my cigarettes and lights it, blowing smoke defiantly in the direction of the first policeman to reach the back of the room. He is a gaunt, fair young man with pale blue eyes. He glances at Tilly, and then stares a little harder at me, seeming to notice my full, sober attire compared to Tilly's frills. I gaze back at him.

Mme Silvestre stomps into the room at that moment and claps her hands. "What is all this ruckus about?" she asks. "You, police officer." She points at the oldest constable in the room. "Are you in charge? As you can see, we are 'aving a quiet, informal evening, with nothing more 'armful than tea and sandwiches. Why do you 'ave to burst in like this? It is quite an embarrassment." She smiles graciously at some of the gentlemen who are seated quietly around the tea tables.

She watches as the policemen continue to take a cursory glance around the room for alcohol, not moving her bulk when they need to pass. She then escorts them to the door, and discreetly presses a wad of notes into the hand of the leading police officer.

Li Leen

She has been gone two days. I do not understand why she will not take me when she is doing these investigations for Sir Thomas. I do not like it. I am stuck in this large, empty house and the only distractions are the number of gentlemen who knock at the door, asking for the ravishing Mrs Chancey. Bundle turns them away, and from the window I watch them leave slowly, trudging down the front steps, their hopes ruined for the evening. She thinks she has power over these men, that her skills in pleasure and the charms of her body are enough to keep her safe, but when will she realise she has no real power? They hold all the power, over her money, over her body, over her beauty.

And what do they know of beauty? Her beauty is nothing compared to that of my mother's beauty. What are her curled tresses compared to Mother's black, silken hair? And her face, pretty as it is, with the brazen dimple in the cheek, what is it compared to the perfection of my mother's oval face, with her dewy, porcelain skin? Grandfather told me that my mother could have had any man she chose. Any man. The rich Chinese of Makassar, the Dutch, the Malays. They all desired her. But she chose my father. A British man. A gweilo.

Chapter Four

The alleys near the bridge are even more inhospitable than the slum area of Liverpool where I'd spent some of my early years. No rambunctious children, playing and weaving through the crowd; no spruce vendors selling coffee or pickled oysters and whelks. It's early in the morning and the narrow lanes, crusty with dry mud and manure, are inhabited by only a few emaciated women. I draw my cream, merino shawl close and smile in a friendly manner at the women, who stare past me, the languor of boredom heavy upon their limbs. Spying a girl of perhaps thirteen or fourteen years sitting in a doorway, a little away from the other women, I ask, "Do you know where I can find Mrs Hawes?"

The girl stands up. She is very thin and pale. Her wavy, brown hair is loose and as she speaks, her thin top lip can barely reach over her bucked front teeth. "I'll take you there," she replies.

As we walk the girl gazes upon me, and even touches the silk of my gown and the soft wool of the shawl. At the end of the road we enter a building and climb a set of rickety steps. The stench of cat piss, boiled vegetables and sewerage is overpowering. As we approach the first landing, the girl points to a door and then turns around to walk back down the stairs leaving me alone. I knock on the door several times, but receiving no answer, pull a special blade from my bag and jiggle it in the key lock until I hear it click open – I've had a vast and varied education over the years. Turning the handle carefully, I peer into the room. The landing is shadowy, but the windowless room is in almost total darkness.

"Mrs Hawes?" I call lightly, moving towards where I can hear rasped breathing. The room is not overly large and is crammed with furniture. I bump into various tables and cabinets before I grope my way around a bed to the slumbering figure upon it. Although my eyes are becoming accustomed to the bleakness of the room, I light the candle on the bedside table and look down at Mrs Hawes by its ghostly light. The old woman is on her back, her mouth wide open, showcasing a mouth missing most of its teeth. Her skin is a sickly, greyish hue, and her hair is tucked into a filthy cap which has slipped to the side in her sleep.

I prod her on the arm a couple of times and call her name again until slowly, grunting and wiping dribble from her chin, the old woman comes around. The stench of stale gin is heavy on her breath as she grumbles, "What the 'ell you wakin' me fer? And 'ow the feck did you get in 'ere?"

"Mrs Hawes, my name is Heloise Chancey. I've come to ask you about the women who have been dying around here lately. I heard you were concerned that someone was harming the girls on purpose."

The old woman tries to sit up. She places her feet on the floor, but holds her head in her hands and groans. She takes hold of a green bottle on the bedside table and swigs from it, sighs, then breaks into a gagging cough. I step back in case she vomits.

She then stares up me, her eyes bleary and confused. "'Oo are you?"

"I'm Heloise Chancey. I've come to ask about the prostitutes who have been dying."

"Murdered they be," she says, sucking her cheeks in and nodding slowly. "Murdered." She looks around on the floor. "Where's me pot?"

Reluctantly I glance under the bed, and seeing where the chamber pot is, slowly nudge it towards the old woman with my foot. Mrs Hawes places her feet on either side of it, slides her bottom off the bed, lifts her skirts a fraction and squats over the pot, still leaning against the bed as she relieves herself. I turn away and see that the tables are covered with an assortment of goods, from snuff tins to cheap jewellery to silver utensils. Probably stolen, ready to be fenced. Mrs Hawes flops back onto the bed and her foot knocks the chamber pot so that its contents slop over the sides.

"What are you doin' 'ere?" Mrs Hawes asks irritably as she lies back onto the bed.

"I'm here to ask you about the girls."

"What girls?"

"The girls who are dying," I repeat, exasperated. "You just said they were murdered."

The other woman looks frightened for a moment and clutches a blanket to her. "So much blood."

"Whose blood?"

"Countless of 'em," she says. "The last one was poor Nell. Poor little Nell." Her face crumples as if she is going to cry, but then she closes her eyes and falls asleep.

I grab hold of her scrawny arm again, and shake her awake. "Who was Nell?"

Mrs Hawes opens her eyes a fraction. "Nell? She's dead."

"Yes, but who was she?"

"Just a poor young thing. They're all poor young things. Lucky they 'ave me to watch over 'em." The old woman rolls onto her side again and before long she's snoring.

The young girl who had given me directions giggles from behind. She must have come back up the stairs to follow me in.

"She just watches over us to make sure she gets her share of the ready, the old cow."

"But she said that some of the women around here are being murdered," I say, leaving the room and closing its filth and stench behind me. I accompany the girl down the stairs. "Is that true?"

The girl shrugs. "I only saw the last girl, that Nell. Mrs Hawes was right, though. There was a lot of blood."

"Did you know Nell?"

"Nah. But I don't know many of the other renters. I've only been here a short while."

"Where are you from?"

"Basingstoke," she answers. A slow blush creeps up her face from her neck.

I feel a pang of compassion, which surprises me, for I've seen all this before. I look around at the other women propped up against the wall, gossiping and smoking or drinking from bottles of gin. All of them would have their own unfortunate, particular yet similar, stories to tell. I have one myself.

"So you don't know of any other women who've died like Nell?" I ask.

"No, although some of the others have started talking about it, especially late at night when the streets are empty. They say there's a devil after us." She's thoughtful for a moment. "I sometimes wonder about a woman I met when I first came 'ere. She was nice to me, let me share 'er bed if I pulled enough Charlies for the night. But she's gone. Just gone. I don't know where."

I take some coins and press them into the girl's hand. "Thank you for your help." I want to say something encouraging, something to keep the young girl safe, but it's pointless.

It's late into the afternoon before I return to the hospital mortuary. I linger by a coffee stall and eat a piece of currant cake, watching for Mrs Dawkins. Finally, not having seen the older woman, I approach the side door of the mortuary and knock. Before long, Mrs Dawkins' grey head pops around the doorway. Her eyes glance around the lane quickly before she pulls me into the building.

"Mr Pike has just gone home. I was afraid he might have returned," she whispers loudly. She picks up her bucket and sponge and guides me down the corridor, pausing in front of a large room. The floor is covered with large white floor tiles, which are slightly discoloured, while smaller tiles, the grout worn and dark, cover the walls. Lining one side of the room is a long sink, its work bench laden with dark bottles and in the middle of the room is a large, rectangular slab of porcelain the height and width of a standard dining table, which has a sink hole at one end. The room smells strange, a mixture of astringent carbolic and the sweetness of a butcher's shop. The cake shifts and swells in my stomach.

"That's the room where the gentlemen cut up some of the more interesting bodies. They cut them open to find out how they died," Mrs Dawkins says, with a knowledgeable nod. She eyes a small smudge on the surface of the porcelain table and darts forward, scrubbing it with her sponge. She wipes her hands on her damp, grubby apron as she leads me to the next room.

"This is where we keep the bodies," she says.

The narrow room is plain and untiled. Four benches line the middle of the space, with only two of them occupied. One bench is taken by a large man, with dark hair and a moustache, dressed in a dirty white shirt and dark breeches. His arms are stiff and awkward by his chest, his head at an uncomfortable angle. Next to him is an old man, who, besides the blue tinge around his lips, appears to be asleep.

"There's no female body here," I say.

Mrs Dawkins shakes her head. "No. Mr Pike and Mr Wilston got rid of her yesterday. She had started to go off."

"Where did they take her?"

"She'd be under the ground now, dearie." She takes me by the elbow and leads me to a table. "Here's one of them photographs of your Nell. There's none of the other women who had bits cut out of them, but by the time this poor girl came along, the police started to take some notice. Her body is covered with a sheet. Mr Pike keeps the grisly photographs in his desk."

I gaze down at the dark photograph the older woman places in front of me. There's a mania for images of loved ones who are recently deceased. I've actually seen examples of these in which the departed are dressed in his or her finest raiment. They're positioned in what appears to be a natural pose, sometimes next to a troubled looking sibling or held in the arms of a mournful parent. It's amazing how life-like the deceased appear to be. But this young woman looks more like a badly composed wax figure, lifeless and featureless. Nonetheless, I can see that this photograph of Nell is not of young Eleanor – this poor soul had a longer face, darker hair.

I let out a loud sigh, not realising I'd been holding my breath. "No, that is not my Eleanor."

Mrs Dawkins rubs me on the back. "That must be such a relief to you, Mrs Chancey, I must say."

There's footfall behind us, and we both turn just as a young man stops in the doorway.

Mrs Dawkins clutches her hand to her chest. "Ooh, you did give me a turn, Mr Chapman. I thought it was Mr Pike or Mr Wilston returned."

"No, just me, Mrs Dawkins," he replies to her, although his eyes are on me.

It only takes me a moment to realise that this is the policeman who had stared at me in the raid at Mme Silvestre's brothel. He's no longer in uniform, but I well remember those pale eyes. He's not a handsome man, but there is something arresting about the uneven plains of his face, and although his voice is deep and gravelly, he's well-spoken. A bowler hat tops his fair curls and he's attired in a sober, brown waistcoat and suit.

His eyes flick around the room. "Have they taken away her body, Mrs Dawkins?"

"Yes, sir, they have. And not a moment too soon, I might add," she says. "And this lady here is just glancing at the photograph to make sure her dearly loved cousin is not one of the unknown souls brought along to our hospital."

"Is that so?" He watches as I place the photograph of Nell back onto the table. "And there's nothing new to report, Mrs Dawkins?"

The cleaner shakes her head. "No, Mr Chapman. We must thank the Lord that there is nothing new here for you to investigate."

"The Inspector will be pleased to hear that."

"Well," I say, clasping my hands together. "I must leave you to your work, Mrs Dawkins. I am so relieved to find it's not my dear Eleanor. Thank you so much for your assistance."

She goes to escort me from the building, but Mr Chapman stops her. "No need, Mrs Dawkins. I will accompany the young lady out onto the street. I rather think there might be some questions I'd like to put to her." With that he takes my elbow, quite firmly to my annoyance, and leads me back out into the dreary sunlight.

"You're searching for a cousin, miss?"

I nod. What business is it of his anyway? I try to pass, but he keeps speaking to me.

"I believe we have met before."

I pull my gloves more firmly over my wrists. "No, sir, I am sure we have not yet been introduced."

"Ah. But I am sure I have seen you before. Did I not see you at a certain establishment on Pearman Street?"

"I don't think so."

"At a certain Madame Silvestre's establishment?"

I pretend a look of mild offence. "Do I look like the kind of lady to be found at a Mme Silvestre's establishment?"

His eyes take in my frilled bonnet and the blue silk dress and fur tippet. "No, you don't," he says, dryly. "Which is exactly what I thought when I saw you there yesterday."

I allow my dimple to show. "Well, that's very generous of you, sir." I tread along the side-street towards the main thoroughfare. "To tell you the truth, I have been searching and searching for my cousin, Eleanor Carter. She has gone missing in this area, so I have approached all the inns and boarding houses, and even some... bagnios, as they're called. That is how you found me in Mme Silvestre's house. We are but a small family, so it fell upon me to discover her whereabouts." My eyes search the road for a cab.

"But surely the police could be of assistance, then," he says. "Why don't you come to the station with me and report her missing?"

I wave my hand. "We have done that, of course," I lie. "But nothing has come of it. And then when I heard of the body of that poor girl in the hospital mortuary I became so afraid that it might have been my Eleanor, I just had to check."

He regards me for a few moments. "Look, over there is an eating house. I've frequented it numerous times. It's not the most genteel of places, but the tea is drinkable and the bread is sound. Why don't you join me in a meal and tell me about your cousin and her plight?"

I consider him for a few moments. I don't like the way he's watching me but it could be quite useful having a policeman on side. I demur though. "I don't know who you are, apart from your name being Mr Chapman."

"It's actually Sergeant Chapman," he replies. "I'm trying to become a Detective Sergeant, so I'm doing some of the investigations in my own time. Try to impress the boss, and all."

I put out my hand, which he takes in his briefly. His hand is calloused, scratches my palm slightly. "Mrs Chancey."

"But where is your husband? Why is he not by your side while you search for your cousin?"

I drop my chin and stare at the ground. This is my sorrowful look. "He died three years ago." I lift my face again. "It is very sad, but I have learnt to be strong in the meanwhile."

"No maid?"

"My circumstances don't extend to that sort of extravagance," I say, haughtily, trying to halt his questioning.

He appraises my attire again. He's not convinced, I can tell. But what can he say?

We weave our way across the busy road, dodging carriages, dogs and street children until we are safely ensconced at a small, round table in Wheel's Eating House.

Over a plate of fish paste sandwiches and watery tea, I tell Sergeant Chapman my by now well-rehearsed story of Eleanor Carter. He looks grave when I finish talking.

"So, this French fellow threw her over when he realised she was with child?"

"I'm afraid so. And now she is all alone. I don't know what she is to do."

"Are you absolutely sure she is even still in Waterloo?"

"I'm not sure of anything at the moment," I answer, truthfully. "I will stay on a few more days but then I am afraid I will have to give up the search."

Tea being finished, I gather up my reticule and tippet. Sgt Chapman accompanies me back out onto the pavement.

"Where do you plan to search next?"

"I might ask some doctors in the area if they have attended Eleanor," I say, frowning. "There is one in particular I would be interested in speaking to."

Sgt Chapman smiles. I like his smile. It's crooked from where his upper lip is swollen over scar tissue. "I can see you're quite the sleuth, Mrs Chancey. It's a pity we don't have a place for female detectives at the station."

Chapter Five

This time I find the note on the front doormat as I let Agnes into the house with a basket of food.

"What's that then?" she asks, as I open it to read.

Disease consumes your body! It will be cut from thee by force. Let this be a warning.

I crumple it up and shove it into my skirt pocket. "It's nothing. Just a note from the neighbours. Their cat is missing."

Leaving Agnes to empty the basket and neaten the kitchen, I return to the bedroom to finish dressing. I take out the note again to re-read. My heart drums so forcefully against my rib cage I can feel it when I press my hand to my chest. What kind of threat is this? Is somebody actually threatening to stab me? There's something almost churchlike about the language of the note which actually makes me feel worse; the zealots I've met who think they're acting on behalf of God, they're scarier than anyone. I place the note down next to its predecessor. Someone's clearly watching me. But I won't be an easy quarry.

I rummage around in my purse until I find a small handgun. It has an ivory handle, cool to the touch, and a pretty filigree pattern is carved into the silver shaft. It's served me well in the past. I check that it's armed and then tuck it safely away.

I walk briskly to a certain lane in Waterloo that I never thought I would have to visit again. The house I'm after is not far from Silvestre's, enclosed behind a black, wrought iron fence, second from the end of the cramped cul-de-sac. Two women sit on the doorstep of a neighbouring house, watching a near-naked baby play in a puddle and from another doorway a woman throws a bucket of slops into the street. I walk across the cobblestones as I've done several times in the past, both by myself or leading another dabber, until I reach its pine-green door. A small sign in the window declares that Dr E. Mordaunt, Healer of General Diseases and Fractures, practices within.

A small bell tinkles above the door as I enter.

A young man finishes writing in a ledger before looking up at me, his face a picture of indifference. His oily, wavy hair is parted in the middle and his suit is made of showy but cheap tan fabric.

"Yes?" he asks.

"Is it possible to see Dr Mordaunt?"

"No," says the man, in a carefully-practiced, prim voice. "No, the doctor is out at the moment. He won't be seeing any patients again until tomorrow. Would you like to make an appointment for then?"

I shake my head. "No, I think I will just return another time and hope for the best."

I leave Dr Mordaunt's rooms and return to the street, but instead of summoning a cab to take me home, I wait around the corner and nibble on a hot potato I buy from a vendor's cart. Several people come and go from Mordaunt's premises, but one man in particular, dark and clean-shaven, catches my eye. There's something familiar about his frame, his gait, but for the life of me I cannot place where I've seen him before. He's attired in a plaid, brown suit with sturdy black boots on his feet and a derby hat rammed low on his head. He hops onto an omnibus, and I lose sight of him before I can work out who he is.

I don't have to wait much longer before I see Dr Mordaunt's prissy assistant walk out onto the main road. Tossing the potato skin into the gutter I step forward and watch as he trots briskly down the road, before taking a sharp left-hand turn. I retrace my steps to Dr Mordaunt's rooms. I rap on the door and hearing nothing, take out my trusty pin and effect a tidy, swift entrance into the reception room. The bell tinkles as it had before, and I stand very still, listening for any sound of life.

Tip-toeing softly down the side corridor, I pause. I want to have a look around Dr Mordaunt's office, which is to my left, but at the end of the corridor is a closed door, and I know well what's behind it. The faint, sweet scent of ether assails my sensitive nostrils and I gag. I'm glad the door's shut. Taking a deep breath I admonish myself to get on with things, and enter the office.

Besides a large, mahogany desk by the window, and two hard-backed chairs, there's an oak filing cabinet against the wall. I start there, but not really knowing what I'm searching for, besides maybe a file on Miss Carter, I give it up. From what I can see it appears that Dr Mordaunt keeps records of his more usual medical cases, but not of the operations he performs in the dead of night. I discover the key to his desk drawers on a hook at the back of the desk, and rummaging amongst the paperwork, writing utensils and empty bottles of whisky, I finally come across a notebook bound in black leather with a marker of red ribbon. Flicking through its pages, one line catches my eye: *Therefore I followed her by foot...* when I'm distracted by a rattle from the front door and then the tinkle of the bell above it. I can't hide as my dratted gown makes it impossible to conceal myself behind anything smaller than an elephant so, shoving the notebook in my pocket, I sit down in a demure fashion on one of the chairs.

I turn innocent eyes upon Dr Mordaunt when he enters the room and reels in shock when he sees me.

"I am extremely sorry, sir, to give you such a fright," I say. "I have been waiting here for quite a while, for I really need to speak to you upon a very important subject."

Dr Mordaunt is a tall man with broad shoulders. His face is clean of any whiskers and a pair of thick spectacles magnify his hard eyes. He wears his hair unfashionably short and his jaw is almost always clenched. In other attire he could be mistaken for a paid street brawler. He frowns angrily. "But how did you get in here, madam?"

"I came in earlier while you were out. It seems your assistant forgot I was waiting here," I answer.

He stares at me over his glasses for a moment and takes the seat opposite. "What is this important business you need to discuss with me?"

"It's my cousin. She's simply disappeared from this area. She was not well, so I was wondering if she came to see you."

"What's her name?"

"Eleanor Carter," I say, taking her photograph out. "Have you seen her?"

Dr Mordaunt hesitates a moment over the likeness of Miss Carter, before turning his frown back to me. "What was she unwell with?"

I allow my eyelids to droop as I peer at him. "Let's say she was... unfortunate."

"How do you think I could help her then?" he asks, his voice terse.

I shrug. "I have heard that you can help a woman who is in... distress."

His face reddens. He leans back in his chair and folds his arms. "I haven't seen her. Ever."

I know I'm not going to draw any more information from him so I stand up to take my leave.

"But you look very familiar," he says, as I reach the doorway.

I stand stock-still, but don't turn around. "I doubt you know me, sir." I return to the street, the bell above the door tinkling behind me.

"Of course he didn't recognise you," laughs Tilly. "He was concentrating on your back end the last time he saw you."

I smile too, but shudder at the same time. "My breakfast nearly crept up my insides to be back in that place."

I take a sip from the tumbler of gin and pull a face. I'll never like gin, but it's better than the cheap, fierce brandy the men are knocking back. We're seated at a tall table in The Old Trout, a tavern not far from Mme Silvestre's establishment, smoking my elegant French cigarettes. We're on high stools and our feet dangle below our frilly petticoats, displaying pretty ankles to the appreciative male clientele.

"You're no closer to finding her then?" asks Tilly.

"No. It's so frustrating. I'm not sure where to look next."

"Ready for a bit of carousing, are you? You best come back to Silvestre's with me, make a bit of pin money. That'll take your mind off things." She throws back the last of her gin and hops off her chair. "That said, I'd better get back or she'll be as mad as a wet hen."

As we leave the tavern, two men in cloth caps and grubby breeches nudge each other and follow. They're rollicking drunk, and once outside, they call out to us, between whistles and burps.

"Come an' gimme a suck, ye tasty tart."

"Come an' pull me pipe."

Tilly turns to fling some choice insults back at them, but I tug her forward and walk her briskly to Mme Silvestre's. When Mr Critchley opens the door to our strident knocking, he appears half asleep with his collar askew, his trousers loose at the waist.

"Can't a man have a rest before work?" he moans. "Good evening, Hell."

"Good evening to you too, love," I say. "We're in a bit of a hurry to come in because we have two loose buffoons on our trail." I nod towards the men, who hesitate by the front gate.

"Oh, no," says Tilly. "They're not coming in, are they? That'd be just my luck to have to entertain them."

One of the men clamps his hand on his crotch and yells, "Come on, I'll fuck your tight cunny," while the other doubles over.

"He's heaving his guts up in Silvestre's rose bushes," says Mr Critchley, sternly. "She won't like that." He storms down the path, growling. The first man turns tail and staggers off but Mr Critchley just reaches them in time to kick the vomiter in the pants.

He returns, satisfied. "We don't entertain that sort at Mme Silvestre's. You know that," he says as he ushers us into the hallway.

I follow them to the back of the house, where we find the other girls in the kitchen. I take a chair next to Tilly and join her in a supper of mutton soup washed down with watery gin. Mostly the women banter with us, although the French woman with the rich, brown curls and the Dutch girl, as pretty as a china doll, keep to themselves, rarely even speaking to each other. It's not long before I fall into swearing and cheap talk, all my elocution lessons cast away for the moment. And although I would murder someone before I'd be trapped back in a place like this – it makes my blood quicken to realise the truth of this statement – I'd forgotten the fun, the closeness, of working within a group of dabbers. But finally, despite lewd pleas to stay the course of the evening, I leave, remembering that I have Dr Mordaunt's notebook to inspect.

It's quite dark when I reach the street. I'm a little muddled from the gin, so I look around for a cab. A woman's selling hot milk from a make-shift stall, while a small crowd of workers on their way home swarm around a man selling meat-puddings. In the distance is Katie Sullivan's coffee stand and directly across the way from me is a glossy, black carriage drawn by sleek, chestnut horses. But there's no cab.

Walking in the direction of my temporary home, I step deftly over food scraps and manure. A short distance on I get that creepy feeling that someone is watching me, but looking over my shoulder cannot spot anyone who displays the slightest interest in my movements. I walk a little more briskly, keeping pace with those who are rushing home. I hug my shawl around my upper body so that my pendant is covered.

A grubby girl begs me to buy some onions. Normally I'm pretty nifty at avoiding street vendors but I'm distracted, and when I pause to consider her wares, I notice the black carriage has moved along the street too. The coachman, his top hat shiny in the lamp light, pulls his horses to a halt. I resume walking, and the carriage's wheels roll again, rumbling along the road behind me. I can't be sure if I'm imagining that the carriage is following me, so I stop in front of an old lady who crouches on the ground, selling posies of flowers which are spread out on a blanket. I buy a small bunch of impatiens and straightening up, notice that the carriage has stopped again. A tremor of apprehension tickles up my spine as I stare at the red curtains across the windows of the black carriage. Who's inside? I can almost feel their gaze crawling over my skin.

I reach my street and the road is quite deserted. No vendors, no coaches, no stragglers. I can just about see the tiny house I need to reach on the next corner, but dread walking the gloomy distance with the carriage in attendance. How stupid to be so careless in this area. I've become too complacent living in Mayfair, too complacent with my personal safety. I glance back at the carriage. Maybe it contains the person who's been leaving me the threatening notes. And what of the person who's cutting up prostitutes? Am I to be next? But almost worst of all – what if the carriage contains men waiting to yank me off the pavement, ready to force from me what I'm not willing to give? My stomach twists with sick fear. I remember an evening, a very long evening, from years before. The memory of that black night ebbs and flows with every action and thought I ever have. The ripping pain. The smell of blood, their musk and their brutal body odour, the smell of the leather seat my face was rammed into. Most of all I remember the humiliation. I pick up the skirts of my gown and run as fast as my cumbersome petticoats allow.

I'm halfway down the short street when the carriage clumsily turns the corner, and a voice calls out to me from the left. I shy away from it, but a small yet strong hand darts from some bushes and pulls me in. Tripping on the hem of my skirt, I fall onto the hard ground behind a wrought iron fence.

"Lie still."

I lie as flat as I can but my crinoline hoops pop up above my lower body like a shopfront awning. Possibly because it's so dark, possibly because my dress blends in with the shadows of the bush, the carriage passes slowly by and disappears around the next corner.

"Cor. You could fecking 'ide under that thing."

I'm lying next to the young boy I've often seen scraping up litter on Frazier Street outside my temporary house. He's staring with wonder at my billowing skirt.

I stagger to my feet, grasping onto branches of the bush to steady myself. "Thank you for that," I say, wiping the dirt from my gown.

I scoop up some coins which have slipped from my reticule and offer them to the boy. The fragile, pink petals of the impatiens are quite squashed into the ground. I'd forgotten about my handgun and feel for its reassuring bulk. I should've drawn it on the carriage, but really, I would've felt foolish brandishing a gun like I was a cavalryman or something.

"You lives in the ladybird's house on the corner, doncha?" the boy asks.

"What makes you think it's a ladybird's house?"

He snorts. "It's always been a ladybird's house. Mind yous, you don't look like a renter, I'll vouch fer that."

I drop him a small curtsey. "Thank you, kind sir."

The boy accompanies me as I walk the rest of the way to the house. My legs are a little wobbly from the run and fright.

"What's your name?" I ask him.

"Me da' calls me Chat."

I open my front door, glancing over the street one last time for the carriage.

"Thank you for your help, Chat," I say, slipping into the house and closing the door against the darkness.

Li Leen

It is always cold here, and it is not yet winter. Even though I have gweilo blood running through my body I have never, ever grown accustomed to the constant chill in the air. While she is away I sit by the fireside and the dry air and the heat that crackles from the flames withers me away. The skin on my arms and on my shins is becoming like a snake's, but without the shine. It is never this cold from where I come, not even in the early morning when the malkohas first cuckoo and the geckos tut. Here I never feel moist perspiration settle like dew at my hairline or the refreshing trickle of sweat between my bosoms.

My father left Makassar when the Dutch returned and expelled the British for good. He took my uncle with him on the ship, but left my mother and me behind. I was only an infant, so I do not remember him, but Mother told me that he was a very pale man, and that he had tiny, gingery freckles all over his body. I too have these spots scattered across my nose and cheeks and no amount of pork lard or menthol rub made them disappear.

Not long after my father left us, Grandfather insisted my mother marry a local merchant. Grandfather said it was because he was of Chinese blood like we were, but I now wonder if we were sold off to pay his mahjong debt. Tiri, as I called him, was the wealthiest of the Chinese merchants in Makassar and he controlled all the illegal gaming houses and brothels. Everyone was wary of my stepfather. Even the Dutch governor and his staff did not interfere with Tiri.

Being Tiri's stepdaughter meant I had servants of my own — one to chaperone me to the temple and one to sweep my room and wash my clothes and even one to fan me whilst I slept. But that all changed when I was made to leave Makassar and voyage across the world so that I could work in my uncle's noodle shop in Liverpool. No more the balmy warmth of home, just the unpleasant heat of the kitchen as I toiled over the boiling stock made from water and my sweat. And now this chill. Always this chill.

Chapter Six

"Mrs Chancey, there be a gentleman at the door for you," Agnes calls from the hallway.

When I pop my head around the bedroom doorway I'm surprised to see that it's Sergeant Chapman.

"Good morning. I'm just at my dressing table, I'll be down in a moment. Please wait in the sitting room."

What on earth is the sergeant doing in my house? I drop Mordaunt's notebook on the bed. The evening before I'd only glanced over it. Being shaken by the encounter with the carriage, I'd gulped down several small glasses of wine until my emotions had blurred enough to fall asleep. I'd woken four times during the night, heart racing, night dress drenched in sweat, but apart from flashes of memory – a bloom of poppy red, frayed white linen, dark words I couldn't decipher – I don't remember the nightmares.

I feel a bit seedy and two of my fingernails are torn from when I fell over the night before. I'd gingerly bathed away the blood from my knees but my petticoats brush against the scrapes uncomfortably. I can't help but frown at my reflection in the mirror. My shiny, charcoal grey dress is so boring. It's really such a drab colour and my white petticoats could do with a wash. I have a sudden, pleasing thought and rifling through all my hatboxes I come across the headpiece for which I'm searching. It's a black, velvet pork-pie hat of the very latest fashion with a pert plume of purple feathers, and it has yet to be worn. I attach it rakishly at an angle to my head and spray my décolletage and wrists liberally with Eau de Cologne Impériale.

Sgt Chapman springs up from the sofa as soon as I enter the room. I urge him to sit.

"But how did you find me?" I ask.

A small smile hovers under his moustache. "I have my ways. I'm a detective, after all."

I grin back at him, but I still want to know how he's tracked me down. "I don't think that answer is good enough, sir."

"Actually, you left your directions with Mrs Dawkins. She supplied me with this address."

"Ah. And why did you feel the need to seek me out?"

His face becomes serious. "Unfortunately I had cause to be at the mortuary again this morning, and happened across Mrs Dawkins there."

I can only gape at him for a moment, and my voice is deep with dread when it finally surfaces. "Tell me, what was it that made you return to the mortuary?"

"Another body has turned up. Another woman."

"No," I breathe. "No. That is terrible."

"Yes, yes it is." Sgt Chapman watches me, grim. "I'm afraid it might be your cousin this time, Mrs Chancey."

I press my fingers against my mouth, mashing my lips until they sting. "How ghastly. Was she... Was she...?" I cannot form the words. "Like that poor woman at the morgue?"

"I'm afraid so." Sgt Chapman pauses to let the words sink in. "She has come to the same end as the other victims."

"Terrible." I wring the tip of each finger on my right hand. They're icy. "I suppose you need me to identify her?"

"If you feel up to it, that would be helpful, Mrs Chancey," he answers. "Her body has been removed to the police station. If you would accompany me there, the Inspector would be very thankful."

He allows me a little time to collect my reticule and a parasol for a light rain has set in, and he helps me climb into a police buggy which awaits us. It's not too far to the police station, a Georgian three storey building which is situated directly next to the more ornate magistrates' court. I follow him through the station's arched doorway into its cool interior.

The whitewashed walls of the entrance hall are a pale yellow. A tired looking woman clutching a toddler to her side is seated on a wooden bench next to a sleeping man who smells strongly of spirits. Behind a desk stands a policeman, tall and official in his dark blue tunic with its brass buttons and high neck. He greets Chapman with a nod, then turns back to his paperwork.

A portly man in a black frock coat comes forward to meet us. "Is this the lady's cousin, Sgt Chapman?" he asks, as he clasps my hand.

"I am," I answer, introducing myself. "Mrs Chancey."

"Inspector Kelley." He ushers us through the station to the back, until we stand in its cobblestoned yard. "Horrible business to put a lady through, but it would be very useful if we could finally identify one of these women." He places his plump hand on the door handle of what looks like a large outhouse. "Are you ready, my dear?"

I find I can't speak, but feeling Sgt Chapman's hand on my elbow give a supportive squeeze, I nod my head.

"Right," says the inspector, as he flings open the door.

The room is chilly and very bare, except for the shrouded figure which is laid out along a cot-bed. A constable carrying a lantern precedes us into the room to shed light on the body. I can see a stain on the lower half of the sheet, a blotch of rusty red. I doggedly keep my gaze on the inspector's face. He's standing opposite me on the other side of the body and I wonder at the daintiness of his fleshy fingers as he picks up the corners of the sheet and looks at me expectantly.

"Ready?"

I nod again, mouth dry, and force myself to gaze down upon the face of the latest victim. In death, the young woman's skin is the colour of aged ivory and has lost its youthful rosiness. Her pink lips are swollen and bruised, and tinged with a deathly blue. The pretty, china doll-face shattered. From the corner of the woman's eye, snaking its way down to her temple and through to her hair, is the dry trail of a tear.

I've never fainted, not when my corset's so tight I can barely breathe, nor when the stage becomes so hot with candlelight I feel I could suffocate. Not even back in those days when I couldn't find food for days, and I wandered the lanes delirious with hunger. But I find the room whirls around my ears in a warm, nauseous rush as sweat pricks at my skin.

"Is this your Miss Carter?" asks the inspector.

I shake my head slowly. "No. It isn't. But I know who she is."

Chapter Seven

"It was definitely that Dutch girl, Till," I say, taking a sip of the sherry cobbler we're sharing. We're seated together again at the tall table in The Old Trout and the alcohol warms my chest and loosens the tension in my shoulders.

"Bloody hell," whispers Tilly. She takes a long pull of the sherry through her straw. "Bloody hell."

We smoke and drink in silence for a few moments. I shiver, and pull my shawl more securely about my shoulders, and wish that we could be seated nearer to the fireside, but women are banished to the far end of the room for fear that their layers of skirt and petticoat catch alight. I've seen several cases of women rolled upon the floor, while the smoke and flames are smacked from their gowns. An uneasy giggle rises in my throat, 'cause it looks funny, but also 'cause it's so awful. The stench of singed hair, scorched skin mingled with burning fabric. Awful.

"Poor Anneke," says Tilly.

"Was that her name? I didn't know."

"The Charlies called her Annie. She used to always boast she was good with her quail pipe, which was lucky 'cause half the time she had shocking shankers." Her mouth lifts in a wry smile and she takes another sip of the sherry cobbler.

"Did she see a doctor?"

Tilly shrugs. "She saw that nice young doctor last year when she was poorly, but usually Henry helped her out."

"Henry?" I think of the barman at Silvestre's. "Why Henry?"

"He used to be a dispenser in a pharmacy or something," Tilly answers. "He's always giving us evil tasting draughts when we're sick." She pushes a pink strand of hair back from her forehead. "Where'd they find her?"

"Down by the river next to Rooper's fishmonger. Apparently she lay in the mud for quite a while because passers-by thought she was just another tail lushy from too much gin. A fruit vendor finally noticed the blood and summoned the police."

"Terrible," she says. She looks at me, puzzled. "How do you know all this? Why did they send for you?"

I explain how I'd met the sergeant at the mortuary, and that they had collected me in the hope of having the body identified. "They thought it might be Eleanor Carter."

"And you reckon Anneke died like the other girls?"

"I do. Till, have you heard of women having their insides taken out – their wombs?"

"Of course. When I lived with my aunt in Clerkenwell, the churchwarden's wife had terrible pains in her middles and had her womb removed. She was so sickly and sad afterwards because she could never have children."

"Well, that's what's happening to these women. Other renters like us, Till. They're not just getting a scrape. Their whole wombs are being sliced out too. And their other bits. Their quims."

She freezes over the straw. "So it's true. The girls by the bridge are calling it the devil's scrape, but I thought it was all talk. Just their pimps trying to scare them silly."

"Yeah, it's happening. They bleed to death." Something occurs to me. "Do you think Anneke was pregnant?"

"I wouldn't know. We weren't that close," she says. "But I did see her puking the other day. I've only been in the pudding club once but I was as bleak as a periwinkle's arsehole. Dr Mordaunt took care of me." She gives me a sharp look. "Dr Mordaunt wouldn't do this, Hell."

I'm unconvinced. "But didn't you say she was seeing another doctor?"

"That's right. Dr Blain. Sabine, that French girl, pointed him out to me one night when he was eating his supper at the Lion's Inn."

"Is that so?"

"The girls adore him, from what I heard. Luckily, I haven't had any call to see a doctor for years so I haven't been to him. You don't think he could have hurt her, do you?"

"I don't know. But, just tell the girls to be careful."

"What? Keep their legs crossed?" Tilly guffaws. "Jesus, I never thought the day would come when it'd be preferable to have a bairn than have a scrape." She rolls her eyes, smiling.

"I agree. Who wants a bairn?" I say, the last of the sherry cobbler bubbling up the straw. I make sure she can't see my eyes. "How do you avoid it?"

"I have these French regulating pills." She takes a brass trimmed pill box, hidden under the folds of her skirt, to show me. "Oh, they cramps up your middles something awful. Sometimes I have to take time off from the Charlies. What do you do?"

"Not a thing," I say, hopping down from my stool. "Just good luck I suppose."

As we round the corner onto Pearman Street, Henry brushes past us, smoking a cigar. He's dressed in a green and white gingham gown, and his wig is a little askew.

Tilly looks over her shoulder at his receding figure. "I wonder where he's off to in such a hurry."

Just then Sergeant Chapman comes out through Silvestre's gate. He lifts his hat to Tilly as she slips past him, and then bows in my direction. "Mrs Chancey."

"Sgt Chapman. Are you here to ask about the Dutch girl?"

"That's right. Inspector Kelley wanted me to find out what I can about her."

"And did you find out what you needed?"

He smiles his crooked smile. "Unfortunately, Mme Silvestre and her girls were not disposed to talking to me. However, you seem quite friendly with that woman with the pink hair. Did she tell you anything of interest?"

"I think she might have."

Sergeant Chapman offers me his elbow. "Well, I am famished. How would you like to join me for lunch and tell me all you have discovered?"

Tucking my hand into the crook of his arm I allow him to lead the way. If he is to pump me for information, I can draw some from him too, after all. We come to The Pond and Swan hotel not quite two streets away. The large room is cosy and well-lit, and we're seated at a small round table with a fresh, linen cloth. We each order the roast meat and vegetables.

"And to drink?" asks the waiter.

"I'll have a glass of claret," says Sgt Chapman.

"And for madam?" asks the waiter, still addressing the sergeant.

Sgt Chapman raises his eyebrow at me.

"A glass of claret would be lovely," I reply.

The waiter bows slightly and withdraws.

"He must think you're my little wife," says Chapman.

"Or he's pretending I am, at any rate."

"In that case, why don't you call me Bill from now on. After all, we seem to be becoming quite well acquainted."

He busies himself with the serviette, avoiding my eye. He's becoming jolly friendly all of a sudden.

The waiter places our glasses of wine before us.

"Then you must call me Heloise."

"Your name is French?"

I smile. "Almost certainly. I'm afraid all my maternal relatives are from the continent." Another lie. He probably wouldn't be able to pronounce my real name. And he certainly wouldn't be sitting there, looking chuffed with himself, if he knew all about me. I know it's wrong, but I always feel a thrill of mischief as the well-practiced lie slips easily from my mouth.

Our meals arrive and, as I fight to keep the blanched, watery vegetables on my fork, I tell the sergeant what I learnt from Tilly.

"So she may have been with child?" he asks.

"Maybe. Tilly was not quite sure. And I'm afraid Anneke's best friend in the house was the French girl, and I doubt very much if she'll talk even to me."

"And she once went to see this Dr Blain?" He reaches into his waistcoat pocket, withdraws a small notebook and pencil and starts to take notes. "But sometimes the girls were treated by Henry..." he murmurs as he writes. He looks up. "Do you know his surname?"

"No. I just know him as the barman at Silvestre's."

He folds the notebook and places it back into his pocket.

"These women... they're bleeding to death?"

Bill nods. "Yes, it seems that way."

"They must have been in agony." I shake my head and place my fork on the plate. "I don't understand. Why try to help these women but then leave them to bleed out and die?" I want to know more of the wounds the poor girls are receiving, but shy away from discussing their sexual organs with him. The botched abortions are bad enough, but why does this creature also find it necessary to remove their buds too? Is it to inflict pain or to simply deprive them of pleasure? I suddenly remember a discussion at my last soiree in Mayfair – wasn't there talk of a doctor who was secretly slicing the buds from women to keep them sane? It seemed so ludicrous and cruel. I will never understand it. But I'd drunk a little too much champagne by then, I don't remember the conversation clearly... What was that doctor's name again? He had two names. B, B? It always comes back to some bastard of a doctor.

"I'm not sure. Maybe he or she is not well-trained?" Bill answers.

"She?"

He places the last bit of meat in his mouth and chews. "Well, yes. Often these back street abortions – these 'regulating' operations – are done by women. Mind you, usually the abortion is carried out in a much simpler fashion than the surgical removal of the whole... area."

He's right. Many madams have a rummage around their girls' insides with a piece of wire or an injection of some sort. Maybe it is a woman mutilating the girls. Silvestre? She did look a bit put out the other night when I questioned her.

I glance up from my plate and catch Bill watching me closely. "What do you think?" he asks me.

And I wonder, with a cold rush of dismay, if he considers me a suspect. It would be all too laughable if I didn't know from hard experience how devious, or even plain inept, our esteemed police force can be. I take too long to answer. I flounder between offering up Silvestre as a suspect and wondering how guilty I'd appear if I protest my innocence.

Bill continues, as he gestures for the waiter to take the empty plates. "Surely it can't be carelessness? It really is hard to say, at this stage. I think we need to know more about this Dr Blain, don't you?"

"I think you need to know more about him, not we. My only concern is to find my cousin, Eleanor."

"But surely you are curious to know if Blain could be our man?" he says.

I cannot deny a slight twinge of interest, but shake my head. My only mission here is to find Eleanor, and in that I'm doing an abysmal job.

"But what if he has your cousin right now? What if he is trying to regulate her right now?"

Mutilate her, he means. "Don't say that."

"I will need to follow him," says Bill, tapping the table. "It will be tedious work, but he is our only lead at the moment."

"That might take you an age until you find anything incriminating," I say. "It may not even be him."

Bill studies my face for a few moments, and I stare back.

"Lion's Inn, did you say?"

"Yes. Apparently he sups there."

"Let us summon a cab. We will have a look at this Dr Blain," he says, standing abruptly from the table. "Come along?" He holds his hand out to me.

If I object would that seem as though I have something to hide? I've nothing to go on with the Eleanor Carter case, and I'm interested to see this Dr Blain, after all. "All right. I will accompany you for a short while."

Li Leen

It is wretched this waiting to be of use. I might as well return to Limehouse and scrub floors or prepare dumplings until my fingers cramp and become deformed. Even that would be better than being cooped up in this house like a rooster in a straw cage. It is in these idle moments, when there is nothing to busy my hands or tasks to fret my mind, that I remember. I remember the jasmine scent of the coffea flowers. I remember my favourite dish, konro, and the tang of the lemongrass as the soft beef falls from the bone leaving a slick of gravy on my lips. I remember sitting in the shade beneath the guava tree, slicing pieces of the fruit's pink flesh to pop in my thirsty mouth. Most of all I remember my mother. I remember the smell of her, when she laid her head against my chest to hug me close. I remember how the palms of her small, delicate hands were always rosy and how her breath smelt of cacao seeds. And I will never forget the last words I ever heard her say: You must stop looking at my daughter.

Chapter Eight

The Lion's Inn, with its striking, slate-grey façade and ox-blood trim around the doorway and bay windows, is located on a busy crossroads. It's sandwiched between a bakehouse and a stable yard and is diagonally across from an upholsterer's workshop. It's only mid-afternoon, long before the steady stream of workers begin their trudge home, although the costers are already fervently pushing their products on those who do pass. Bill leaves me by a fruit stall and has a quick look around the interior of the Lion's Inn. On his return he shakes his head. "He doesn't seem to be there. The barman said he usually arrives around tea time and sits in that bay window there." He points across to the window closest to the stable yard.

He suggests we have a stroll around the immediate area to pass the time. One street over we find a crescent of newly built homes which overlooks a charming park. Bill leads me to a bench and wipes it clean with his kerchief before we sit.

"Are you quite comfortable?"

"Yes, quite, Bill, thank you." I stare straight ahead, watching a sparrow hop on the grass. If I'm silent he will feel compelled to speak. In my long career of tending to men, I've found that they enjoy talking about themselves. And although I'm a master of entertaining chatter, as careful as I am, small truths sometimes slip out.

However, he remains quiet too. Glancing up at him I see that amusement crinkles the sides of his eyes. "You think if you're quiet enough I'll do all the talking," he says. "You really are a loss to the police force."

I lift my shoulder. "I wouldn't enjoy wearing that itchy, woollen uniform in any case." I look at his suit and ask, "And why do you not wear your uniform anymore?"

"I'm still on leave from my normal duties to carry out these investigations. Inspector Kelley thinks it is best if I am in informal dress."

I turn to face him. "Tell me, how did you come to be a policeman?"

He takes the hat from his head for a moment and runs his hand through his fair curls. A hardness shifts across his face before it relaxes into its usual complacency. "I was up at St Andrews until a few years ago, but my poor old father could not afford to keep me there. He's a scientist, you know, up at the Royal Institution, but his last experiment failed, left a hole in the family finances. I was reading law, so rather than become a clerk in the dusty law firm my father had in mind, I joined the police force. Much more exciting." He taps the skirt of my gown with his hat. "It's now your turn. You must tell me what you do when you are not searching for your cousin."

I watch his hands for a moment. There are scrapes across his knuckles, alongside the inside of his right forefinger. His hands are strong, a worker's hands. I like men's hands. I like holding them, moulding them to mine, feeling for the grooves and creases of their lives. I like that a man's palm is larger than my palm, that his fingers can engulf mine. I've found that often, before I discover the intimate details, I can learn much from a man's hands. His pastimes, his passions... maybe even some proportions. As Bill twists his hat, I can see that his fingers are long. I press my lips together, suppressing a grin, and quickly glance up into the shadows of the oak tree above.

"The usual things. A little sewing, a little playing of the pianoforte and sometimes, when I become very low and bored, a light supper, a card game maybe, with family." Nothing more innocuous than a widow on a modest independence, after all.

I look into his pale blue eyes. If only I could know if he considered me a suspect or an accomplice.

Placing the looped ribbon of my reticule over my wrist I stand up. "I think we should pass the Lion's Inn again and see if Dr Blain has arrived yet."

We make our way back to the busy crossroad, and standing by the fruit stall again, see that a good-looking man is seated in the bay window.

"That must be him," I say. "He doesn't look that evil from this distance."

Bill smiles down at me. "You would be surprised."

I nod, keeping my face blank. If only he knew what I'd seen. But I've left that all behind. I smile up at the policeman and say, "You are right. I am being silly."

He rubs his chin in thought. "I must keep an eye on him now. I will send you home in a cab. You won't be offended if I do not escort you?"

I peer at Dr Blain through the window. "Surely your plan to follow him will yield no results. And if they did, it might take a long time." I turn back to Bill. "Allow me to interview him. I might be able to make his acquaintance – see if we are following the right clues."

"But in that case I could just march in there, make his acquaintance myself."

"Of course you could," I agree. "But he'd be more likely to let his guard down with me, after all."

A troubled frown forms on his face. "I don't think I can allow you to do that. It might be dangerous."

"How dangerous can it be? We will be in the crowded dining area of a public house and you will be right here keeping an eye on things."

He rubs his chin again. "You may be right. But what will you discuss with him? How will you meet him?"

I re-tie the bow of my bonnet at a coquettish angle and arrange the fur tippet around my shoulders. "Leave that part to me."

Luckily the dining room of the Lion's Inn is crowded with folk having a drink after work, early supper or tea. There are no vacant tables so I make my way to Dr Blain's table, and hesitate. When he finally notices me, I give him my most winning smile and ask, entreatingly, "Do you mind if I sit at your table, sir? There does not seem to be any other room in here to have a nice cup of tea. I'll be as quiet as a mouse."

He folds his newspaper neatly into quarters and places it next to his teacup. He blushes a little as he stands up and lifts his hat from his head. "Not at all, madam. Please take a seat."

He's a tall, angular man with a very upright posture. He's handsome, but his suit is a little too neat, his brown hair and beard trimmed a little too fastidiously. The intensity of his stare under the straight, dark eyebrows is quite disconcerting.

"Would you care to share my tea?" he asks.

I glance at the dark tea in his mug and the assortment of cakes on a saucer. "Thank you. That would be delightful."

Dr Blain attracts the attention of the waiter and orders another cup and once this is done he opens out his newspaper and continues to read.

My quarry hides behind his newspaper and, glancing out the bay window, I can see Bill at a safe distance. I pour myself tea into the cup the waiter has placed before me.

"I see that the news is not so dreadful anymore coming from the Americas," I say, loudly, peeping around the side of the newspaper to catch Dr Blain's attention. "War is so distressing."

He looks at me in surprise, then shakes out the newspaper and turns over the front page to read. "Ah, yes. Terrible business. I have relatives living in Tennessee. It was a very worrying time for them." He places the newspaper on the table between us. "I'm afraid the paper is often full of terrible news."

I allow for a concerned expression to wash over my face. "It's not a very happy day, is it? The only reason I am here is because I am waiting for a letter from my sweet, young cousin to be delivered, but every day I return and each day I am disappointed."

"That's no good. Is she not in London?"

I shake my head, sadly. "I am not sure. She has run away from her family and we are very worried for her safety. She left word that if she desired to contact us she would leave a message here at the Lion's Inn." I take a sip of tea. "I've taken a house nearby for the duration. My home is actually in Watford. So far away."

Dr Blain reaches for his newspaper again. "I am very sorry for your difficulties, madam."

"Not at all. It is very kind of you to listen to a stranger's woes. You must be a very charitable gentleman." I put my hand out so that he can't pick up the paper. "Please let me introduce myself. Mrs Heloise Chancey."

He accepts my hand in his. "Dr Nicholas Blain," he stammers.

I pretend to be struck by a thought. "Maybe you have seen her. Yes, maybe she has been here and you have seen her, sir." Rummaging around in my purse I bring out the photograph of Eleanor. "Have you seen my cousin?"

I watch him closely as he gazes at the photograph. He looks at it for a few moments, and rubs his thumb down its surface. "I may have," he says. "I have a practice near here, I am a surgeon, and she may have been in to see me, but I really cannot remember." He shakes his head as he passes the photograph back to me. "Maybe I should keep this likeness for a few days? Show it around to my neighbours and patients? Someone else may have seen her."

It's a little difficult to tug the photograph from his grip. "That is so generous of you, sir, but I'm afraid this is the only copy I have and naturally it is something I treasure too much to part with." I sigh. "I will just have to return here every evening until I hear more."

"What a chore for you, Mrs Chancey," he says. "But I am here most evenings. I will keep you company. Unless, of course, Mr Chancey objects."

I look away, just as I always do when I talk of my husband. It's then that I glance down at the open newspaper and a certain article catches my eye. I pull it to me and read the title out loud. "Ghastly murders of prostitutes in Waterloo. Police baffled." I don't need to pretend shock because I didn't realise the press had notice of the deaths, but I'm quick-witted enough to glance at Dr Blain to gauge his reaction. He frowns and tilts his head to scan the article upside down. His mouth tightens in anger as he reads.

By the time our cab rumbles up to the house on Frazier Street the rain's falling heavily. Bill shrugs out of his jacket and stepping down from the coach he holds it high so that I can shelter beneath it as we run to the front door. Once under cover I brush raindrops from my hair and peer quickly onto the dark street. There's no dark carriage lurking in the shadows.

Bill smiles at me crookedly, and the steady gleam of admiration in his eye gives me a thrill of pleasure. I thank the sergeant for his assistance and sweep through the doorway. I press my back to the closed door and grin. No nasty note has been put through the letter slot and I'm pretty sure the sergeant has taken a liking to me despite himself. It's been a good day.

Chapter Nine

The next morning dawns glorious and warm, but I wake with a headache, the tail-end of a dream weighing upon me. I remember trying to run, run away, but my feet couldn't make purchase on the ground, my legs swimming through the air. It's left me feeling unsettled, so I enjoy a leisurely lie-in followed by a light breakfast of tea and raspberries while Agnes dusts the living areas. The girl lingers most mornings, finding inane tasks with which to fill the time. I reckon, from her chatter, she has a poor time of it in Silvestre's house, between the bossiness of the cook and the disdain of the working girls. I half listen to the girl's complaints of the brothel's bed sheets as I write a quick letter to Sir Thomas outlining my progress in the investigation.

"Two days ago wus the wust," she says. "Look at me 'ands, from all that scrubbing. All chapped they is. Those sheets 'ad all kind of muck on 'em." She wrinkles her nose at the memory.

I place the sealed letter and some pennies into her outstretched hands. "That's terrible, Agnes. Why don't you post this note for me and have a short rest. Treat yourself to a bun or tart."

I leave the house not long after Agnes. Birds peck at the sparse patches of grass and quarrel over space in the tree branches. I let my shawl slip to my elbows and revel in the feel of the warm rays of sunlight caressing the back of my neck. I come across Chat who's sitting in the gutter, scraping at a splotch of stubborn mud. Despite the sunshine the roads and walkways are still damp and clogged with refuse.

"Ah. It's my saviour from the other evening." I smile down at the boy. His stubby fingers are smudged with filth but his bright, grey eyes beam clear from his dirt-streaked face. "What are you scraping up there?"

He holds up two rag bags. "I got some dog turds in 'ere, and this one I keeps for rubbish nobody wants no more but me da' can sell." The stench from the opening in the bag wafts up and my stomach squelches in revulsion. "Bu' whatever the tanners give me for the dog gems I get to keeps for me self."

"Is that how you make your money?"

The boy resumes scraping at the mud of the street and shrugs. "The renters sometimes give me a few coppers for cleaning up the road. It's enough for me da' an' me."

I bring out three halfpennies from my purse. "In that case, please take this," I say, offering the money to the boy, before moving off. "I appreciate you keeping the path outside my house so clean."

The curtains are drawn at Silvestre's house, and chaos ensues outside The Old Trout where the brewer's dray has become ensnared with a donkey cart. The man with the dray is being harangued by the tavern keeper while a costermonger pushing a barrow of radishes joins the affray on behalf of the donkey cart owner. I'm tempted to pause and watch the fun, as insults are exchanged between the men while two female vendors fling curses from across the way.

Turning onto a wide thoroughfare lined with majestic plane trees and a park to the side, I inspect some pastries displayed in the window of a bakehouse. I remember the days when a soft, sugary bun was the surest reward for a long day on the street. I can almost taste the cinnamon glaze, but it's so hard to squeeze into my corsets as it is, I resist the urge to buy myself one. A barker shouts to passing shoppers, extolling the virtues of his ginger beer and three horseback riders race noisily down the wide lane, so it's no surprise it's a few moments before I realise someone is calling out to me. Looking over my shoulder I notice a short woman with wiry brown hair beckoning to me from the other side of the street. I wave back and hitching up my skirts, weave through the horse and carriage traffic until I join the other woman.

"Katie, I haven't seen you for an age." I clasp the other woman's hands. "How is your coffee stall?"

Katie Sullivan puts her hand around my waist and steers me towards the stall. "Never better. People always want their coffee," she says, a vague Irish brogue accenting her speech. "My sisters help me out when they can leave their bairns, and so does my daughter now and then. That's her there now servin' the customers." She gestures to the young woman behind the counter who hands her a cup of steaming, black coffee which Katie passes on to me. "Syrupy sweet, just how you like it."

I take a tentative sip of the hot liquid. There's nothing like Katie's strong brew.

"Tilly told me you were looking for that young girl who was cryin' her eyes out in the park a while back," she says.

"Yes, but I haven't managed to find her."

"That is a pity. But I'm glad I saw you across the way," she says, pushing her black velveteen bonnet back from her forehead. She has marvellous, light brown eyes with uneven amber flecks around the iris. "I was goin' to ask Tilly where I could find you, but then I saw you standin' there, sighin' over old Mrs Rodd's pastries."

"And why were you looking for me?"

"There be a young woman, a girl really, askin' after you yesterday."

"Really? Do you know who she was?"

"She said she met you the other day, down by the bridge."

I think for a moment and realise she must mean the girl who'd led me to Mrs Hawes' home. "Did she have bucked teeth? Skin and bone?"

She nods. "Aye, that'd be her."

"But how did she know who I was?"

"I don't know. She knew you by name. Said she knew of something you might be interested in."

"Oh." I frown, wondering what the girl wants to tell me.

"What trouble you got yourself into this time, missy?" she asks me.

I offer a sly smile. "Must keep oneself busy, Katie."

The girl's sitting in the same doorway as on the previous occasion, but this time her face is buried against her bent knees and she doesn't notice my approach. I gently pat the girl's head and smile when the girl peers up at me with bleary eyes.

"Long night?" I ask.

The girl springs to her feet, but sways slightly and leans against the doorjamb. "I haven't had a full night's sleep for close on a sennight now," she mumbles.

I open the cotton neckerchief I'd borrowed from Katie to reveal an assortment of Mrs Rodd's pastries to the girl. I'm gratified to see colour come into the girl's cheeks as she takes a sticky bun with unsteady fingers.

"Thank you so much, miss," she says, covering her mouth with the back of her hand as she chews.

I urge the girl to sit again and press the kerchief and remaining pastries into the girl's lap. "Katie Sullivan from the coffee stall near the park said you were asking for me."

The girl nods her head vigorously as she licks the icing from her fingers. "Yes, I have something to tell you."

"But how did you know who I am?"

"One of the tails down the street saw you with me that day and told me that she recognised you from this penny opera thing she sneaked into a couple years back. She said you were on the stage, all done up in silks and powder and rouge and such." The girl pauses in her eating for a moment, her head lowered. "She also said you used to be a tail like the rest of us." The blush spreads to her ear tips.

I glance over my shoulder at the older prostitutes a few doors down. They're smoking and drinking like the last time I'd seen them, but this time they stare back at me. I look down at the girl again. "And you know my name?"

"Heloise something."

"That's right. But I don't know yours."

"It's Cecilia, miss."

"That's a pretty name. Cecilia. Why don't we take a short walk and you can tell me for what reason you came in search of me?"

Cecilia wraps her pastries up neatly in the kerchief. "We won't have to go far." Just as before, she can't help but run her fingers across the softness of my merino shawl as we walk.

"Is it something you want to show me?" I ask.

"Well, remember I was telling you about my friend who disappeared? The woman who was so kind to me when I first came here?"

"Yes, I do. Don't tell me she's back?"

The girl nods. "Yes, she is. And this time I have to look after her."

Why has Cecilia summoned me to tell me about her friend? Maybe she imagines that I can assist them in some way.

"And where is this friend of yours?"

Cecilia pulls me towards a building which is almost directly opposite Mrs Hawes' dreadful dwelling. The heavy door creaks as Cecilia pushes it open and beyond the sunlight that creeps through the doorway all is darkness. She drags a brick across to the door to prop it open and as we enter I gaze up at the steep stairway. The air is dank but not as foul-smelling as the entrance to Mrs Hawes' building.

"We don't need to climb those stairs," she says. "She's over here."

Cecilia leads me to the back of the room and points towards the alcove beneath the stairwell. There, huddled in the corner on makeshift bedding, lies a woman. She's slumped against the wall, her dark hair falling out of its clasps, her knees, covered in flimsy, brown stuff, drawn up to her chin. Her eyes are pressed shut but her mouth hangs open. It's hard to tell how old she is in the gloom.

"What is her name, Cecilia?"

"Her real name's Prue, but the others call her Loose-Pruce, I think on account of the curls around her face."

"Why did you bring me here? Is she ill?"

"She is ill. But that's not why I brought you here," the girl answers. She kneels down and softly shakes the woman by the shoulder. "Prue, Prue," she whispers. "I have that lady here I was telling you about."

A spasm of coughing consumes Prue and she keels forward, eyes still shut, and continues to cough and wheeze for many moments. When it passes, she leans back against the wall, exhausted. Cecilia wipes the perspiration and spittle from her face with her skirt and cooes tenderly to the older woman. She helps Prue take a sip from a bottle and offers her the pastries, which Prue pushes away feebly. Cecilia beckons for me to move closer.

I crouch on the floor and try to sit as close to the other woman as my crinoline will allow.

"She's been in the workhouse all this time. That's why I couldn't find her," says Cecilia. She holds Prue's hands and turns them, palms up, for me to see. The fingertips are raw, tiny fissures cracking her skin. "They made her pick oakum."

"I tried sewing before that," Prue croaks as she pulls her hand away. "But the hours were even crueller. I couldn't keep up, I was so poorly. That's how I ended up in the bloody work'ouse." The last word catches in her throat and she coughs up phlegm onto her sleeve.

"Tell her why you were poorly, Prue," urges Cecilia.

Without turning her head, which is resting against the wall, Prue's eyes peer around at me. "Cecilia tells me you've been asking around about the renters who have been cut up."

"That's right. The girls who are dying."

"Well, I was cut up too, but I didn't die."

I breathe in sharply and cover my mouth. "What do you mean?"

"I mean, I was cut up like all those other renters Cecilia here has been telling me about, but I didn't die."

I grasp the other woman's arm. "Who did this to you?"

Prue shakes her head slowly. "I don't know."

"But how could you not know?"

"How could I not know?" She tries to laugh but no sound escapes. "I was too far gone with gin and puff, wasn't I? All the punters are the same to me then. And if I please, I can pretend they are all one and the same."

The three of us are silent for a minute, listening to the rattling coming from Prue's chest.

"He took all of my lady laycock, the bastard," says Prue. A tear falls down her cheek. "I woke up in hospital, I did. Someone had found me, covered in blood and taken me there. They kept me for a while – long enough to clear up the clap and wait for the wounds to heal." She wipes the tear from her cheek. "They told me I could never have children." She smiles, even as another tear drops. "Strange, huh? It was a curse to be pregnant, but once the chance was taken away, I felt sad."

"Were you with child when you were attacked, Prue?" I ask, as gently as possible.

Prue nods. "I was just starting to show."

"And you don't remember anything of the person who did this to you?"

"I'm sure it was a man," she says, staring ahead as she concentrates. "He had a deep voice. He wouldn't stop talking, but I can't remember what he was saying. I was lying on my back, and my feet was in those stirrup-like things. And the smell... this sickly, sweet stench. It was nice, but wrong too, which made it worse. I was sick all over myself."

"Sounds like ether. And how long ago did this happen, Prue?"

"I'm not sure," she answers. "Long enough for me to be in hospital and for them to send me out to work. They found me a place at a dressmaker's, but the hours were so long I couldn't keep up or make enough money to buy food. And that's how I landed at the work'ouse again. But I couldn't do it no more. I'd rather be a doxy and feel no pleasure," she pauses for a moment, her face pinched, "than go back to that bastard of a place." She doubles over and coughs up some more, spitting into her skirt. This time, though, she leaves a smear of blood on the tattered cloth.

"I'm no more than twenty-five or twenty-six years old, if I remember right," she wheezes. "And look at me. Look what's become of me."

I look at her. Prue is much the same age as I am, and yet there are grey strands running through her hair and her thin face is haggard and lined.

"Thank you for talking to me, Prue," I say, standing up. I walk out into the sunlight and breathe in the air which, although it still holds the pong of the river, is fresher than that under the stairwell.

"What will you do?" asks Cecilia.

"I'll tell the police what Prue just told me."

"What shall I do, miss?"

There's nothing I can do for these women. Hand them over to the poor-house? I could never. Take them home? Bundle and the cook would probably leave, and Amah would skin me alive. I take the remaining money out of my purse and give it to Cecilia. But it's not enough. Not enough to dispel the guilt I feel for leaving them behind. So I take off the merino shawl and wrap it around the girl's shoulders. I have two more in my Mayfair home, in any case. "Take care of Prue."

Cecilia buries her nose into the soft wool and sighs. "It smells like my ma's Sunday best."

Chapter Ten

After a short rest I sit at the dressing table, wearing nothing more than silk drawers, pearl drop earrings and my necklace. Using a soft, sable-hair brush, I sweep scented powder across my neck and breasts. I place the brush back into my teak and brass toilette case next to the other beauty aids which are neatly lined up on the purple velvet inlay. I pull the crystal stopper from a bottle of perfume and dab the scent behind my ears and then pluck a few stray eyebrow hairs. Lifting the silver lid from a cut-glass jar, I apply pale, crushed pearl powder to my face. My hand freezes for a few moments as I gaze at my reflection in the mirror. How could one woman, such as Tilly, be so relieved to be childless, and yet another woman, Prue, be heartbroken at the loss. I place my hand over my lower belly and wonder.

But it's late in the day, I must hurry if I am to take tea with Blain again. I rub some rouge onto my cheekbones and smudge the tiniest amount of coal on my eyelids. I slip on a chemise and tie myself into a corset, crinoline and gown the best I can, cursing yet again for not bringing Amah. I've just pinned a rose into my chignon when there's a knock at the front door. As I trip down the stairs I tie the ribbon on my fanchon bonnet, then fling open the door. I'm pleased to see Bill standing on the threshold even if

I do wonder if he still considers me a suspect. Maybe he's keeping me close at hand to keep an eye on me.

I spin around and finish with a little curtsey. "I'm ready for Dr Blain."

"Yes, I can see that," he says, but he pulls a rueful face. "Unfortunately the Inspector thinks it is far too unsafe for you to interview Blain again."

"What? But I've set it up so." I was looking forward to probing the doctor for clues.

"It's just not a good idea. We can't allow a defenceless woman to interview Blain, especially if he turns out to be our culprit."

There's a finality to his tone. He's not going to let me go. Of course, I could still go ahead behind his back. I'm on Sir Thomas' clock, after all.

Bill's watching me, hasn't made a move to leave. Maybe I have it all wrong. Maybe it's not my feeble sex that prevents the police from using me. Maybe they really do suspect me of the mutilations.

I lead him into the sitting room and pour him a madeira. "It's all the chargirl has supplied me with, I'm afraid."

I pour myself a glass too and sit on a lounge chair across from his. All afternoon I've been wondering about how much I should tell Bill of what I have discovered. It's true that I stumbled across Cecilia and Prue in my search for Eleanor, but I've decided the best thing I can do is inform Bill of what they told me. It'll assist him in his investigations into the person butchering those poor women.

"I discovered something today," I say, taking a sip of wine. I tuck myself into the corner of the chair and curl my legs up under my petticoats and tell him of my meeting with Cecilia and Prue.

"That's remarkable," he says, placing his wine glass on the table. "Remarkable. I must interview her as soon as possible."

"I think you must make it as soon as possible, Bill. I don't think she can survive long now."

"It is a pity she cannot tell us who her attacker was."

"Yes, it's a great pity. But we now know for certain it is a man, and surely his use of ether and such must mean he sees these attacks as surgical operations?"

Bill nods slowly. "You might be right."

"And Dr Blain is familiar to these women too. So is Dr Mordaunt."

"And I assume they both have access to a surgery. But tell me, how did you come to meet these women?"

"Well, actually, I came across the younger one, Cecilia, when I was searching for Eleanor." It's now or never. At least if he knows the truth of my situation, he can stop wasting time on viewing me as a suspect, and maybe even help me find Eleanor in turn. "The thing is... The thing is that Eleanor is not my cousin."

He lets out a bark of a laugh. "I knew it. So who are you?"

"Well, my name is Heloise Chancey, and I am searching for Eleanor Carter, but not as a relative. I'm employed by Sir Thomas Avery." I look for recognition in his eyes but there is none. "He owns a private detective agency."

His eyebrows lift. So do his lips. "You're a detective?" There's amusement in his voice.

"Yes. I am." Amongst other things.

"What do you do, when you... detect?"

"Well, I don't know," I say. "Much the same as you, I suppose." I want to say that I spy on people, find out their secrets, but that's not very nice, is it? Not very lady-like.

"I don't think you do what I do, Heloise," he says. He's still smiling, but he shakes his head in disbelief. "It's rough work what I do, you know."

"Well, I search for people sometimes, like what I'm doing here now. Searching for Eleanor." And my work can be bloody rough too.

He considers me for a few moments, then leans forward, his hand extended. "Well, private detective Chancey, let me introduce myself again."

I take his hand, glad of the good spirit in which he's accepted my news.

"So, I will go ahead and meet up with Blain," I say to him. "I'm quite sure he can help me with my investigation into Eleanor's disappearance."

Bill frowns, the smile slipping from his face.

"I will anyway, with or without you, Bill," I grin. "It's what I'm being paid to do, after all."

His pale eyes study me. "You'll go ahead with this meeting, regardless of me?"

I nod.

"Well, then I will accompany you. Make sure you are as safe as possible. He was in my sights for the evening anyway. We will go ahead with the original plan."

I haul myself up from the lounge chair. "We must leave then, I think. I don't want to miss his teatime."

As I pick up my reticule from the hall table Bill takes me gently by the upper arms and turns me to face him.

"I will not be far away, and I will be watching you, but you must take every care to be safe. This Dr Blain might be the mad monster we are searching for. We are not sure what he is capable of." Concern creases his face. "You know I am not sure we are doing the right thing sending you in as bait."

I reach into the recesses of my reticule and bring out my handgun. "I will be perfectly safe. I'm not the bait, Bill, I'm the stalker."

He takes the gun from me and turns it in his hands admiringly. "What's this then?"

A smile curls my lips. "That's my muff pistol."

"Ah, Mrs Chancey, you are here already."

I look up into Dr Blain's handsome face. He takes the chair opposite mine at the table in the bay window and calls the waiter over to order tea.

"Any news today?" he asks.

"No. There is no letter waiting for me. Nothing at all. I do hope she is well and safe."

He frowns. "Yes, so do I."

He seems preoccupied with his thoughts so I drink tea in silence, wondering what he's thinking about. I crumble the stale cake between my fingers, but don't eat.

"I agree," he says, suddenly. "The tea things are not particularly nourishing this evening. A patient of mine told me today that the local park is hosting a fair tonight. Would you care to join me in a stroll to this fair, Mrs Chancey?"

"Of course I would, Dr Blain. I am sure that will lift my spirits like nothing else could."

"Do you have a maid to escort you, madam?"

"Ill. She's ill. I had to leave her in my rooms unfortunately," I prevaricate. "But surely, in such crowds and with you as escort…"

He agrees and leads me from the tavern. I draw my fur tippet over my shoulders and follow him onto the pavement. I catch sight of Bill crossing the road behind a horse and cart. The streets are abustle with office clerks returning home, women in swinging, wide hoops and any number of costermongers touting their soup, baked eels or shoe polish.

"The fair is three streets away, Mrs Chancey. Near the river."

"Lovely." We walk at a sedate pace, I assume for my benefit. "Dr Blain, yesterday you seemed very put out by that article in the newspaper about those... fallen women... being murdered."

"Yes, you are right. Working in this area, Mrs Chancey, means that I have regular contact with unfortunate women. It is a sad fact that they are attacked and used woefully, yet it angers me when I see it sensationalised in the newspapers."

"Are your medical rooms far from here?"

"Not far at all," he answers, steering me around a group of people pushing their way onto an omnibus. "I was very lucky to have attained the surgery from my uncle about eighteen months ago."

I place my hand on his forearm and peer up at him, eyes wide. "Did you know any of those girls who were written about in the newspaper?"

He smiles at me, with a patronising air. "No. Not at all."

"Really? That is a pity. You might have been of great help to the police." Has he forgotten the Dutch girl or is he hiding the fact that he had administered to her? "Apparently the last woman was foreign. Mmm... a Dutch girl I think I heard." No flicker of recognition crosses his face. "I am so afraid for my cousin's safety."

We arrive at the park, and pretty lanterns in the trees twinkle against the ash grey sky. A chill breeze wafts from the Thames, bringing a slightly muddy odour. I shiver and draw my tippet closer about my neck.

"Tell me more about your cousin, Mrs Chancey."

"Oh, Eleanor. Such a sweet child. And so pretty, Dr Blain. So fair, so ethereal."

"Yes, I remember that from the photograph you allowed me to see. Would it be too much of an imposition to show me that likeness of your cousin again, Mrs Chancey?"

"Of course you may see it." I rummage carefully in my bag so that he doesn't catch a glimpse of the handgun.

He takes the photograph almost greedily, and studies it under the light from a gas lamp. It's several moments before he hands it back. As if he was memorising every bit of Eleanor's features. He pushes his hair from his forehead so that it lies neatly against his silk hat. "No, unfortunately I have not seen her before."

The fair is arranged under looming oak trees and there are already a large number of people clustered around the stalls, exchanging pennies for hot corn cobs, tickets to gawp at bizarre humans or to play various games of chance. We stop to watch a rowdy game of skittles. The contestants have taken their jackets off and pushed their caps to the back of their heads while they noisily call each other on or moan in frustration.

As we move away, I say to him, "Dr Blain, you're a medical man, and I am a widow. I am not naïve nor stupid, but I am very afraid for my cousin. Please tell me, why is there a monster hurting these unfortunate women so cruelly?"

He's thoughtful for a moment and then says, "Maybe he thinks it is for the best. Every day I see the cruel circumstances and the tragic outcomes of how these women live. He might believe it is best if they cannot procreate."

Luckily, before I have the chance to make an ill-advised remark to the doctor he points to a well-lit area ahead. "Ah, that is where the music is coming from, I believe." He offers me his arm. "Shall we venture over there to see what is afoot?"

A Chinese bandstand, replete with a red, sloping roof and golden dragon motifs shelters a small but lively orchestra. In front of the stage, on a hard parquet floor, several merry couples dance in a swirl of motion. Blain hands coins to an usher so that we can enter and take a seat at one of the many tables arranged around the dance floor. A supper table is laden with platters of fleshy sirloin beef, capons, turkey legs, hams and tongues, which are surrounded by bowls of grapes and strawberries and dried fruits, brandied cherries and cheeses. The usher offers us champagne punch, but Blain says he doesn't touch spirituous drinks at any time.

"No, neither do I," I say. "It's very bad for the constitution, so I've heard." I watch wistfully as the usher whisks away the bowl of punch.

He makes a hearty dinner of the roast meats, while I eat some cheese and fruit.

I tap my foot along with the lively music. "They do seem to be enjoying themselves," I say, my eyes on the dancing couples.

"Yes," he says. "However, I really do think romping about like that cannot be good for you after a meal such as this."

"I am sure you are right," I say, but I can't take my eyes off the dancers.

He drops his serviette onto the table. "Well, just this once we must dance. I am loath to disappoint you, Mrs Chancey, and I can see your heart is set on a dance. But we must take it slowly," he warns.

I jump up from my seat. There are very few things I enjoy more than a frolic around a dance floor, but Blain turns out to be a very sobering partner indeed. He holds me awkwardly, well away from his chest, and the few times I peep up at his face, his chin is elevated and his eyes stare at a point above my head. His direction is stately with very slow, careful turns, which keeps us out of time with the others. Eventually, I feign a laugh and pronounce I'm too exhausted to continue.

Two broughams pull up close to the bandstand. From these well-polished carriages alight a number of fair, bright beauties. They're rouged and powdered a little too much to be lady-like, but these Cyprians of fashion conduct themselves with cheerful, yet quiet, decorum. They're heavily bejewelled and their hairstyles and headwear are elaborate in the extreme, sporting feathers, flowers and ribbon. I'm interested to see that one woman, willowy with Titian hair, has miniature, artificial birds attached to her headpiece. I must tell Amah the next time we are shopping for a new bonnet.

A flicker of distaste passes across Dr Blain's handsome face as he watches the women take their places at a table by the bandstand while their male attendants, well-dressed gentlemen with silk hats and tails, fetch them cups of champagne punch.

"Dr Blain," I breathe with contrived wonder, "Are those women what everyone refers to as... Gay Girls?"

"Yes. Well, they are a little further up the ladder than a mere gay girl," he answers, sniffing. "They, I believe, refer to themselves as 'courtesans'. Very indelicate subject, but from our conversation earlier this evening, I feel I can continue. I would have you know, madam, that I consider these 'courtesans' worse than the poor unfortunates I deal with on a daily basis at my surgery. Those poor women are so destitute and desperate they are forced into prostitution. Those women you see there," he nods towards the beauties across the way, "are nothing more than leeches with no morals who are in search of riches from those who are their betters." He stands up abruptly. "I think it must be time to return you home, Mrs Chancey."

As we walk back through the fair gardens, we pass an old man who's attired in a dirty, white shirt and tan breeches with a tatty, red scarf tied around his neck. He has a parrot perched upon his shoulder which nibbles at his silver earring with its curved beak and black tongue, and he's seated at a card-table across from a large, orange orangutan.

"Come pat Meng, my dear," he calls out. "Look at her kind eyes. Saved her from the wilds of Borneo, I did. She's almost human, she is. More human than the brown heathens I bought her from, at any rate." He laughs noisily at his own joke, and hawks on the ground.

I approach the beautiful primate, and look at its kind, almost mournful, face and put my hand out to touch the bristles on its arm. I feel sorry for this creature that has been brought from its warm, succulent home to the grey unfriendliness of London.

"Have a cup of tea with her, madam. See how refined she is," urges the old man.

Dr Blain hands the man a penny, who fills a filthy cup with a thin, dark liquid which he hands to me. I hold it in one hand and offer my other hand to the orangutan. Meng places her leathery paw, limp and cold and as long as my foot, into my hand but continues to munch on her cabbage leaves without looking at me. Truth to tell, I'm a little disappointed by the total indifference the orangutan shows in me.

Placing the cup on the table I thank the man. Taking a few steps back, I keep my gaze on the ape. A light mist of rain touches my face.

"Dr Blain, you confuse me, sir. On the one hand you are most rightly revolted by women such as those we were seated by, and you say you believe it might be best if prostitutes do not beget children, and yet you seem to feel deeply for their plight."

He also watches the orangutan. "It is like this monkey here," he explains to me. "Look at her. The man's right, she is almost human. My cousin is a naturalist and he was telling me that in the Malay jungles scores of monkeys such as these are shot down from the trees because it's imperative that their specimens are studied for the better understanding of humankind. I believe this to be justified. In this modern age some things are warranted in the name of science, I think you will find, Mrs Chancey. And while I feel sympathy for creatures killed in the pursuance of science, and I feel sympathy for the poor creatures who come to me for curative care, I cannot approve or desire to mimic their way of life."

I'm appalled by his words but also uneasily aware that I'm glad he doesn't know of my true identity. I don't want to be judged by this prig of a man. I don't want him to dislike me, or worse, pity me for who I really am.

"I am sorry, Dr Blain. I am afraid my brain is too feeble to fully comprehend what you are saying."

He smiles at me understandingly.

The rain falls in earnest by the time we leave the shelter of the oaks, and Dr Blain runs out to the road to summon a cab. I heave my skirts through the narrow doorway of the vehicle and am surprised when he climbs in after me.

"I'll see you home," he says.

"That's very kind of you." This is no good. He'll know where I live. I stare down at his square, strong hands that rest lightly on his thighs. They look like they could guide a blade with keen precision. I reach my cold fingers as close to the door handle as I dare, as we bowl along the streets. I hope Bill still has us in sight.

The rain eases somewhat by the time I run up the front path to my door, but I'm soaked through. I wave to Blain as the cab pulls away, revealing a black carriage parked a little further down the road. Breath catches in my throat. I step behind the portico column and peer around at the vehicle. Although the drizzle limits my view, I'm sure the glossy, black carriage is the one that followed me two nights ago. The coachman sits as still as last time, staring straight ahead, the rain dripping from the brim of his hat. The crimson curtains of the carriage windows open a few inches but it's too dark for me to see who's inside. My hands tremble as I untie the ribbons of my reticule and, taking my handgun out, I let the bag fall to the ground. A dark figure looms up from the footpath. I take aim with the gun, hard-put not to scream.

"Heloise, what are you doing?" shouts Bill, putting his hands in the air. "It's just me."

Cold relief washes over me as I run forward and tug his sleeve. "That carriage over there... It's following me."

As I point, the coachman cracks his whip and the carriage moves forward. Bill sprints out onto the road and although he comes close enough to rattle the locked side-door of the carriage, he has to fall back when the carriage sweeps around the corner. We watch as it bumps away. Bill turns back, collecting his hat which has fallen into a puddle.

I pick up my reticule with cold, damp fingers and unlock the front door. We both make our way into the sitting room.

"How long has that carriage been harassing you for?" asks Bill, as he makes up the fire.

"I first noticed it a couple of nights ago. I've only seen it the once, but I wonder if I just haven't observed it at other times." I bite at my bottom lip. "Whoever's watching me from that carriage now knows where I am living."

Bill stands up from the fireplace. He's as wet through as I am, and his hat looks particularly soggy. I reach up and take it from his head.

"You must take this thing off. You're getting mud in your hair," I laugh.

He smiles too. He takes a step closer to me, and slowly unties the ribbons of my hat. His fingers brush my cheeks and are already warm from the fire.

"And you must take off your pretty bonnet. The ribbons have started to droop."

I consider him for a moment. Do I dare go further? "Ah, and your coat, sir, is soaked. You must take it off." I run my hands over his shoulders beneath the coat fabric and help him shrug it away. My fingers brush along the curves of muscle in his arms, and his forearms flex as he tries to catch my fingers in his. I unbutton his waist coat, saying, "This too must come off, if you are to dry properly."

He's no longer smiling. "Madam, look at the hem of your skirts and petticoat. They are soiled dreadfully, and drenched through." He crouches down and pushes his hands up beneath my skirts. His calloused fingers lightly scratch my skin as he runs them up the back of my calves, my thighs, rest on my hips. He loosens my petticoats at the waist and they fall to the ground. Straightening up, he slides his hands beneath my silk drawers from behind, nudging his fingers between my thighs.

Chapter Eleven

"He seems like a nice man, with all his prosing on about poor women, but I don't trust him," I say of Blain. I'm lying with my head upon Bill's shoulder, leg draped over his. "It could well be him who's taking care of these poor girls. But then who's stalking me in that carriage?" My thoughts turn to Dr Mordaunt. "All doctors are vile, after all. It could be any one of them."

"And he showed an uncommon interest in Eleanor?"

I nod, sitting up against the heaped pillows. "Do you know what is strange, though? He did not once ask me why Eleanor is alone in Waterloo. Not once did he ask me why she ran away, or anything about her predicament. That's strange, isn't it?"

"You think he knows already?"

"Well, to show so much interest in her, but to refrain from asking why a young lady is roaming free in Waterloo? It seems very suspicious to me."

Bill rolls onto his side to face me, studies my pearl choker. "Tell me about this necklace you always wear."

I drop my chin to peer down at the locket resting against my chest. "It was a gift to me from my husband on our fifth wedding anniversary. The jade is from China." I don't tell him that on the other side of the jade, which I'd actually bought from a sailor in

Liverpool, is a gold amulet of a dragon with ruby eyes which was left to me by my grandfather.

He runs his fingers around the seed pearl trim of the pendant and lets his hand drop to my nipple, which he rubs softly with his thumb. He takes my other nipple in his mouth. I close my eyes and surrender to the pleasure of it. I run my hand through his hair. I'm almost gone, thoughts drifting, when Mordaunt's notebook pops into my head. I should inspect it again with Bill. I pull away from him. "Soon." I smile back.

Bending over the side of the bed I retrieve the book. "I forgot to show you this."

For the next ten minutes we peruse Mordaunt's scrawled writing.

"I think it's a blackmail book," says Bill. "Read this... *she wanted an abortion so that her husband would not find out about her pregnancy.* He's jotted the initials, A and K, the date and an address. And this more recent one... *he wanted a mixture of abortive drugs to give to his pregnant wife – but I do not believe the lady to be his wife. She seems far too young to be married to him and her pallor, despite her fair hair...* Initials E and C. And look here, he follows them to find out where they live and what they do. He must be blackmailing them."

"I wonder why the number nine is circled by every few entries," I say, pointing at the circled roman numerals. IX.

"Maybe it's code for how much money he blackmails from his victims. Nine guineas? Shillings?"

"He's revolting, that one." I fall back onto the pillows. "I'm so overwrought now, I will never find sleep."

Bill scrambles out of bed. I admire his straight back and firm rump as he leaves the room. He runs down the stairs and returns with his coat. Feeling in the inner pocket he brings out a plain snuff tin.

"What have you there?"

He crawls onto the bed and, lying on his back, he rests the tin on his chest and opens the lid to reveal an white powder. A faint whiff of violets reaches my nostrils.

"Snuff?"

He smiles. "It's a very special mixture. Take some. It'll help you relax into sleep, I can assure you."

The powder has a distinctive stickiness to it when rubbed between my warm fingertips. "Is it opium?"

He nods. He sits up for a moment and places the tin between us. Taking my hand, he dabs a pinch of the snuff onto my wrist and inhales it sharply. He sighs and lies down amongst the pillows.

Taking a pinch of the snuff, I sprinkle it on the flat, soft skin between his pubis and hipbone. Bending over, my tousled hair tumbling over his stomach, I sniff hard at the opium-laced snuff. I lick what remains with the tip of my tongue and feel him stiffen. Sitting back up, I light a cigarette and grin. "Will I have time to finish this?"

It's already late in the morning when I follow Bill downstairs to the front door. I spot the folded note on the mat almost immediately. Running forward I pick it up, and read – *You should be burnt, nay, stoned, for what you are. You are cursed.* I sink onto the bottom step.

"What is it?" he asks, seating himself next to me. He takes the note from my hand and peruses it. "Who sent this to you?"

"I don't know. They've been arriving since I first came here. I don't know who even knew I was here at first, and I've no idea why I'm being sent these letters. Maybe they're from whoever's watching me from the carriage."

He's silent for a moment. "They could be for the tenant who had this house before you."

He's right, of course. I'd had the same thought.

Standing up, he looks at his watch. "I have to run, I'm afraid. I'm late for work. We'll discuss this later." He stoops down to kiss me on the forehead. "Don't fret. Keep that blasted gun of yours at hand," he says, as he closes the front door behind him.

I'm in the middle of my toilette when there's a soft tapping at the front door. Pulling a peignoir over my undergarments I trip down the stairs. "Who is it?" I call out, and on hearing Katie Sullivan's voice, pull the door open.

"You'll have to excuse me, Katie, I'm not properly attired yet."

"You don't have a maid?"

"No, but I wish I did." I try to usher Katie into the sitting room, but she won't enter any further. She insists she doesn't have time, but in the back of my mind I wonder if she doesn't want to enter my house of sin. I can't help but feel a bit chagrined at the thought but won't embarrass her either way.

"I must get back to the coffee stall, but not bein' sure if you'd be by the park again today, I thought I'd better come and tell you my news myself."

"What is it?"

"I think I might know where that lass is. The young thing you've been searchin' for."

I feel my heart quicken. "Where is she?"

Katie shakes her head. "Now, I'm not absolutely sure it's the same lass as I saw that day in the park who was a-cryin' – the girl I sent home with Tilly – but I'm reasonably sure it is her."

"Have you seen her again?"

"Well, I think it was her I saw at the fruit markets this mornin'. She was walkin' along with that Mrs Sweetapple."

"Who is Mrs Sweetapple? I've never heard of her."

"Oh, she's a nasty one, she is. Much nastier than old Mme Silvestre," she says. "She seems genteel enough. In fact, I think she was genteel not too long ago, but somewhere in her life things have come unstuck, and now she has a very discreetly run introducin' home."

"An introducing home? I've never heard of such a term before."

"Do you not know what an introducin' home is, Heloise? Fancy me having to explain the ways of the world to you," she says, chuckling. "Well, so Mrs Donnelly explained it to me, she being a good friend of mine – who cooks and sells a very nice oyster soup not far from my stall – an introducin' house is a more refined version of what the coppers call a 'disorderly house'."

"In what way?"

"Apparently that Mrs Sweetapple 'introduces' gentlemen – real gentlemen, mind – to nice young ladies, you know the type I mean, don't you, Heloise? Not actual nice ladies. Mrs Sweetapple finds quiet, polished ladybirds. So the gentleman comes to her, tells her what he wants in particular in his lady, and she sets it all up. She has all sorts, says Mrs Donnelly. Really fat girls, old girls, foreign girls. She reckons she even had a Negro girl once. The difference is, Heloise, the gentleman gets to play families with the nice ladybird. They set up house, but without the wedding. Apparently there are many men who are either too shy to find their own bride or are too bored with their real bride, and they use Mrs Sweetapple to fulfil their peculiar little dreams. Well, that's according to Mrs Donnelly."

I can't help keep the scepticism from my face. "Very strange." Sounds a bit too good to be true, but what could this woman know of the cruelties that can go on in these sorts of arrangements?

"Yes, isn't it? And she might have her claws into that young girl you are lookin' for."

"But Miss Carter is with child. Surely she cannot sell a woman with child?"

"There are some very queer sorts in this world, Heloise. We both know that."

So, not so naive after all. I think for a moment. "Does your Mrs Donnelly know where this introducing home is?"

I dismount the burly, black horse I've hired from the local stables. In truth, even though he's a fine, tall specimen, he is sluggish and obstinate to ride and I'm relieved to tie him to a post. I'd been looking forward to a bracing ride, but really, it hadn't been worth the time. I should've caught a cab. I stand in front of a very neat house situated on a very neat street. The black, wrought iron fence gleams, just as the neighbours' fences gleam. The red and grey tiles on the doorstep are bright and clean and the front door is lacquered a dapper teal blue. I rap on the brass door knocker smartly.

The silk of my riding attire is of a severe black, and military-style frog buttons fasten the tight bodice at the front so that it is almost tunic-like in appearance. Perched towards the front of my head is a plum-coloured porkpie hat with fat, purple ostrich feathers that tickle the back of my neck. I've chosen this outfit for a purpose – I want to appear assertive, no-nonsense.

I rap on the door again, this time adding a few taps with the riding crop.

The door opens slowly and a maid, dressed in a crisp black uniform that sports a skirt almost as wide as my own, asks me how she can help.

"I'm after a Mrs Sweetapple. I have some private business to discuss with her."

"Do you have an appointment?" asks the maid, her voice uncertain.

"No, I do not. I did not realise I would need one. However, please let her know it would be very inconvenient for me to have to return at another time." I tap the riding crop against the side of my skirt impatiently.

The maid invites me into the small hallway and, after asking for my name, bids me to wait. She opens a door to the left, as narrowly as her wide skirts will allow, and closes the door behind her. It isn't much longer before she comes out again and beckons for me to follow.

The parlour is cool and uninviting, despite the over-stuffed sofas upholstered in rosy, floral tapestry, the mountains of frilly, velvet cushions and the stench of rose oil. The walls are painted a soft peachy colour and all the shelf space and table surfaces are crammed with china ornaments and crystal. By the window, at a round, oak table, sits Mrs Sweetapple. I'm surprised at how young she is, as I'd expected to meet an older, more formidable madam. Mrs Sweetapple makes a homely figure, her plump form ensconced in a striped, cerise and navy gown. Her face is quite pretty and her shiny, light brown hair is dressed simply and covered with a lace bonnet. Although she smiles sweetly, there's a calculating look in her eyes.

I've put a lot of thought into how to tackle Mrs Sweetapple. At first I supposed I might burst in upon the woman and demand the return of Eleanor, but I was quick to see the pitfalls of this plan. If Mrs Sweetapple is to prove difficult, and she does indeed have Eleanor, she might charge an exorbitant fee for her return. This doesn't worry me unduly, as I'm sure Sir Thomas and Eleanor's father would happily pay, but I'm aware that if I'm to explain the truth behind Eleanor's predicament, I'll be exposing Eleanor's family to further blackmail. As well as that, I don't want to alarm the woman. It wouldn't be any good if a whiff of the police or private detectives forces Mrs Sweetapple to spirit Eleanor away altogether. And now, looking into the other woman's watchful eyes, I realise I'd come to the right decision.

Mrs Sweetapple bids me to take a seat, and pours tea from a china tea pot decorated with blowsy tea roses. "How may I help you, Miss…?"

"Miss March." I light upon the name of the fidgety boarding-school mistress who had ruled my life for sixteen long months in Liverpool when I was young. "Muriel March. I have heard I might be able to – let us say – acquire a companion from you."

Mrs Sweetapple takes a tiny sip of her tea. "I am afraid you are wrong. I do not manage a hiring agency here."

"Yes, but I do not want to simply hire a servant. I am after something far more… more special than that."

Mrs Sweetapple gazes at me over the rim of her teacup. "And who has informed you that I can assist in this manner?"

Well, I can't say it was a Mrs Donnelly, costermonger, purveyor of excellent oyster soup. "I would rather not say. I was asked not to repeat his name."

The cup rattles as Mrs Sweetapple places it back on its saucer. She still has the insipid smile on her face. "I'm afraid I cannot help you then, Miss March."

I pause for a moment. Racking my brains for the next step.

"It was Sir Herbert Brimm." I whisper, so softly I'm not even sure if she heard me. It feels good to bandy the name of my local, Methodist magistrate about; the same man that bastard Priestly had threatened me with. Serves him right for sticking his big nose too closely into my business. "A friend of mine procured a lovely, sweet thing from you. But please, do not repeat his name. I was sworn to absolute secrecy."

A door slams up above, and I can hear female voices. I wonder how many girls this Sweetapple has squirreled away.

"And what sort of companion are you looking for, Miss March?"

"Just someone who can be useful to me at home. Maybe help me dress, attend to my needs." I stare at Mrs Sweetapple steadily, a small smile hovering at the corner of my mouth. "Someone to do what I desire. Do you understand?"

Mrs Sweetapple's eyes travel over my mannish bodice and take in the riding crop, which is resting in my lap. She nods, still simpering. "I believe I do."

"However, I have very exacting tastes in my attendants, Mrs Sweetapple. Very exacting. I am willing to pay what you require but I'm afraid if you cannot fulfil my needs, I will have to take my business elsewhere."

"Of course. Please tell me what you require, and I am sure, given time, I can supply you with what you want."

I pretend to consider for a moment. "She will need to be

slight. Very slight. I don't want a buxom lass. And fair. Not dyed, you understand?"

"Perfectly."

"For my purposes, she needs to be young."

"What do you consider young, Miss March?"

I shrug. "Sixteen, seventeen? Certainly no older than twenty."

Mrs Sweetapple nods.

"And pretty. I cannot abide ugliness."

"I am in total agreement with you, Miss March. Why waste time on the ugly?" She stands up and moves towards a roll-top desk. Opening a grey ledger, she says, "I am sure I can assist you for the right sum, Miss March."

I fiddle with my teacup. I look out the side window and straighten my shoulders. I'm hoping this sour bitch will sense my feigned embarrassment.

"There is one more thing."

"What is it?"

"I am told you can cater for even the most... unusual of requests."

She frowns for the first time. "That is correct."

I pause again and then, setting my face into a look of defiance, say, "I wondered if any of your prospective companions are with child?"

A slow smile widens Mrs Sweetapple's mouth, and her eyes harden. "With child? I am not often asked that."

"Not often. So you are asked occasionally?"

"Never by a lady. But that's no matter to me." She runs her finger down a list in her ledger. "That will cost a little more."

"How much?"

"Would you require lodgings, Miss March? To share with your companion?"

"No. I have lodgings."

"You would not be returning the young lady anytime in the near future?"

"What if she does not suit me?"

"Oh, then, certainly something will be arranged, Miss March. I would not leave you encumbered with an attendant you did not desire."

"Well, then, let's assume she will be with me for quite a while. How much then?"

Mrs Sweetapple writes some lines in her ledger. "Shall we say £20? That will ensure you receive a lovely young lady and total confidentiality."

I lift an eyebrow at the repellent woman. "Make it fifteen and I will return in an hour with the bank notes. Please have her ready to leave."

Chapter Twelve

When I return with a hansom cab to fetch the girl, I hope it is actually Eleanor Carter I will find, or else I'll be lumped with a girl I don't need and left with a substantial hole in my purse. But when I set eyes on the withdrawn, slight figure, I'm sure that I've finally tracked her down. Mrs Sweetapple holds Eleanor in a firm grip, high on her arm, and leads her forward.

"Miss March, this is Eleanor. Eleanor Gray. And this, dear, is the lady who you will accompany," says Mrs Sweetapple to Eleanor. "You have been of such great solace to me, I am sure Miss March here will not regret her choice." She makes herself clear despite the lack of malice in her voice or simpering face.

Eleanor curtsies but doesn't look at me. It's obvious from her blotchy eyes and the excessive powder on her face that the girl has been weeping. I take Eleanor's hand in mine and squeeze. "I'm sure we will get along famously," I say softly.

My voice grows curt again when I face Mrs Sweetapple. "And here's the sum we agreed upon." I hand her an envelope. "I am sure we will not need to be in further contact."

I usher Eleanor from the sickly pink house and into the cab, Mrs Sweetapple watching from the door. The girl carries a small valise. "Is that all you are travelling with?" I ask, surprised.

She blushes, and holds the valise tighter to her body. "It is all I have left. I have had to sell many of my gowns."

I pat her on the arm. "Well, don't worry about that. We will soon have you well attired again."

We settle in the cab and as the driver pulls away, she starts to cry quietly in the corner of her seat. I turn to her, take her little hand. "Hush, you goose. You are perfectly safe now, Miss Carter."

She gapes at me. "But how do you know my true name?"

"I have been hired by your father to find you. He has been extremely worried about you."

She gazes at me, and her mouth hangs open for a moment longer. "You must be mistaken, Miss March. My father is the last person who is worried about my well-being."

"My name is not Miss March. It's Heloise. And truly, I was hired through a detective agency to find you. You have led me on a fine chase for nearly a week now."

Her hand grips mine. "And I can go home?" she asks, eagerly.

"I'm afraid not, Miss Carter." She's crestfallen and looks to be about to cry again. "He wants to see you safely ensconced in Shropshire."

A stubborn look sweeps across Eleanor's face. "I will not go to Shropshire. I will not." She looks out the window, as the cab slows down to allow a group of workmen to cross the road. "I don't know what else I can do, but I won't go to that nunnery and have those dour old things grumbling at me."

"Well, let us wait and see. Maybe your father and Sir Thomas – he owns the detective agency, you know – will come up with another plan."

The cab pulls into the side of the road outside my temporary home in Waterloo. Chat's burrowing away in a neighbour's rubbish heap but pauses long enough to stare at us as we walk up the front path. I deposit the girl in the bedroom and quickly scrawl out a letter to Sir Thomas telling him of my good news. I poke my head out the front door and call to Chat.

"Can you take this to the nearest receiving house, Chat? I think you'll find it is the shop on the next corner."

The boy takes the letter and the few pennies I offer him, and is walking down the path, when I call him back.

"Chat, have you noticed that carriage again? The one that followed me home the other night?"

The boy shakes his head. "No, miss. Has it been following you again?"

I nod.

"But I seen the old prig what pushes notes through your letter slot in the middle of the night."

"Have you?"

"Yep. Few times now."

"Hurry and take that missive to the shop and then return here and tell me about it."

That evening we arrive at the Ship and Turtle on Leadenhall Street a little earlier than Sir Thomas. We're seated at a table next to the murky aquariums that line the side of the room. I'd arranged for him to meet us here instead of the musty Frazier Street house as a small celebration. Eleanor had seemed so downcast I wanted to cheer her up with a good meal and a little champagne. And as selfish as it sounds, I wanted to dress up, drink a little champagne myself, show Sir Thomas and his bastard of a friend Mr Priestly what a fine job I've done.

Eleanor stands and gazes mournfully at the slow-moving monsters swimming in the smoky, green water. "Poor creatures," she says softly, smudging the opaque glass as she draws her fingertip in a line beside a turtle's bobbing head. I can barely hear her above the din of the other patrons of the restaurant. "Living in the shadows, trapped behind glass."

Just then, Sir Thomas pushes his way to our table. "Mrs Chancey," he says, taking my hand in his, beaming. "Once again, you have not let me down." He turns to where Eleanor is standing by the aquarium. "And Miss Carter. What a relief we were able to find you before anything too untoward happened. Your father is so happy."

Eleanor looks over his shoulder. "He did not come?"

Sir Thomas glances at me, looking embarrassed. "Sit down. Please, sit down. Join me in supper," he says to Eleanor, pulling out her chair.

Sir Thomas and I keep up a patter of conversation while we order our meals. Only then does he broach the subject of Eleanor's position.

"I have a letter for you, Miss Carter, from your father," he says, taking an envelope from his coat pocket.

Eleanor takes it swiftly from his fingers, tears it open and reads. The hopeful expression on her face fades, and she replaces the note neatly. "He does not wish to see me. He insists I continue on to Shropshire."

"Miss Eleanor has told me that she is still of the same mind as when she ran away originally. She does not desire to go to Shropshire," I inform Sir Thomas.

He looks a bit startled. "I am not sure what the alternative can be," he replies.

We're quiet as our meals arrive – a plate of bread, some boiled potatoes and three bowls of steaming, aromatic turtle soup. I sip the broth, which is hearty and well-seasoned, but Eleanor, after pushing about some of the glutinous substance with her spoon, pushes her bowl away.

"I have an idea for the short while," he says, eventually.

We look at him expectantly.

"I think it might be best if Eleanor stays with you in the meantime, Mrs Chancey, until we decide what is best. At least then we will know she is safe and well-looked after and most importantly of all," he smiles kindly at the girl, "we will know exactly where you are."

It's like a pebble sinking in my chest. Sir Thomas continues to slurp up his soup and even Eleanor looks more cheerful than I've seen her all of the afternoon and evening, and starts to nibble at some of the bread and butter. But what of me? I was looking forward to this assignment being over, to returning to the luxuries of Mayfair, the attentions of my admirers. I watch Eleanor as I sip my soup. She's spent the last week or so in the company of whores, yet she still seems untouched, genteel. What a bore it will be to have to continue to look after her.

Calling for the bill, Sir Thomas thanks me again and says he must rush home to have tea with his wife. "It is the only time of the day that we meet each other," he laughs.

He escorts us out into the alleyway where a fog has crept in, as dense and hazy as the water in the turtle's aquariums. He stands by the roadside, whistles sharply and in a few moments, his coachman parks a smart, two wheeled carriage polished the colour of burgundy, in front of us.

"Ladies, allow me to take you home," he says, with a bow.

I have to laugh. "Sir Thomas, that is a very pretty carriage indeed, but it is impossible that the three of us would fit along its seat." I'm polite enough to not point out Sir Thomas' wide girth, but gesture towards our full skirts. "You are very kind, but I will take Miss Carter home in a cab."

He agrees, shouting up to his driver to summon a cab. He makes sure we're neatly packed in, pays the driver and waves us on.

"What a kind man he is," murmurs Eleanor.

"Yes." I reply absently, as I look out the window, listening to the crunch of the cab's wheels across the cobblestones. The fog is so thick now it's hard to see the people walking on the pavement. I don't know how our driver can even see other vehicles on the long drive home to Waterloo. The cab lumbers along and once in a while the driver, in a heavy, guttural accent I can't quite place, shouts directions at loiterers or other coachmen who impede his way. There's a pause in the traffic when a heavy whack to the side of the cab throws Eleanor against my shoulder. The cab lurches sideways as the sound of screeching wheels and the splintering of wood fill the air.

It's dark in the carriage and I have to feel for Eleanor's arms. "Are you alright?"

Her soft voice answers, "I think so. Although I do believe my cheeks will be bruised." I can just make out Eleanor prodding at her own face.

"Well, as long as no bones are broken." I test my own feet and legs before pushing open the cab door and hopping down onto the road. Taking only a few steps I observe that a coach, bulky and dated, from which a querulous old man, with ruddy, round cheeks is shouting instructions, has side-swiped our own cab. His coachman, a skinny rat of a man, is poking his finger into the cab driver's chest as he snarls up at him.

"You were s'posed to gi' me righ' o' way, ya grea' clotpole," shrills the smaller man.

"It was your fault," bellows our cab driver, shoving the other on the shoulder. "You'f smash't my cab. De springs on my veel is bent to buggery now, dank you fery much."

By this time a small crowd has gathered around the broken vehicles. Still holding their beers, working men find the source of the noise, having picked their way through the fog to the broken vehicles. A few vendors, holding their sacks or carts of goods, have moved in close to add to the commotion, and in the distance the thin, reedy sound of a policeman's whistle can be heard. The stragglers from the tavern let up a roar of encouragement when the cab driver strips off his jacket ready for a brawl. I'm not averse to watching a scrap, knowing full well the excitement and horror of watching two men set upon one another. However, I'm conscious of my responsibility to the young woman still waiting in the cab so I squeeze through the throng until I reach the cab door again.

"Come," I say to Eleanor. "Gather up your bag and shawl. We had better leave. Sir Thomas has paid the man, and he is of no help to us now."

I draw Eleanor through the crowd, ignoring the leers and suggestions from a couple of the revellers as we pass, until we reach a quieter part of the street.

The street lamps only give off a dim halo of light in the fog, too pale to see clearly by. There are no other bloody cabs to hire so, linking arms with Eleanor, I steer her towards the Frazier Street house. Our shoes slide on the dewy cobblestones as we walk and the fog's mist lingers over my face and throat.

There's little traffic for the road is clogged by the two damaged vehicles. The din of the cheers and the constables' whistles become quieter the further we walk. Everything is grey – the vendors who are folding away their produce and the workers who are slouching homewards. Even our own footsteps are muted by the thickness of the fog. Just as we reach the next crossroad an ominous, steady trundling of a carriage's wheels creeps behind us. I quicken my step, and fear creeps its cold fingers up my spine. I glance over my shoulder, and sure enough, its black paintwork gleaming, the crimson curtains swaying, the carriage follows us at a steady pace. Who's in the bloody carriage? Is it one man, two, three?

Ever since I first noticed the carriage following me I've been having nightmares again about that night, that terrible night those bastards picked me off the street. I was still a girl when it happened, a helpless, skinny girl. I wasn't a virgin, no, but what was forced upon me that night was not right. Sometimes I watch those young ladies in Hyde Park, strolling with their nannies, trotting along in their father's phaeton. Pretty parasols to guard their skin, servants to guard their cleanliness, tightly buttoned gowns to guard their virtue. And I could almost choke on the envy I feel. Every eye – covetous, jealous, fascinated – might now be on the alluring, incomparable Heloise Chancey, but beneath the shallow layer of make-up and expensive attire is that grubby, greedy girl who didn't even know this type of life existed. And here I am in the nightmare again, trying to flee, but never quite fast enough.

Fear rings in my ears as I pull Eleanor along, until we're nearly running over the uneven, slippery ground. She trips and asks, "Is something the matter, Heloise?"

"No, it's nothing, dear, just let's hurry." I peer over my shoulder again at the carriage, which is gaining on us.

Eleanor limps a little as we walk, slowing our passage. I support her under the elbow as she hobbles forward, and I hold back my impatience. The horse's hooves clop closer.

"Why is that carriage following us so closely?" she asks.

"I don't know," I say, and even I can hear its grim tone.

What am I so afraid of? I'm not sure if it's because I'm with Eleanor, or if the fright has fuelled my anger, but I'm fed up. I stop short. My street is a short distance away, but I know the closer we are to home, the more vulnerable we will become on that quiet, deserted road. I stare up at the coachman, who ignores me just as he has each time, and then I look hard at the crimson curtain. It twitches, which spikes my anger even more. Why doesn't the coward show himself?

I move swiftly towards the carriage door. I don't even have my pistol, but that doesn't worry me. I'm determined to see, once and for all, who is in the damned, black carriage.

Wrenching open the door, I peer into the shadowy interior until my eyesight adjusts. I'm so stunned by what I see it takes me a moment to speak. "Amah! What are you doing? You scared the arse off me."

"I am driving somewhere, as you can see," says Amah Li Leen, a defensive note in her voice.

"You're spying on me, you mean," I say. I realise my hands are still shaking with adrenalin and clamp them on my waist. "You can bloody drive us home then." I call out for Eleanor to follow and jumping up into the body of the carriage, sit down opposite Amah.

As I help Eleanor through the doorway, I ask, "Where on earth did you rustle this carriage up from? And where's mine?

She lifts her chin. "I had to hire this carriage at a considerable cost. Taff would not let me use yours."

"Didn't approve of you spying on me?"

"It would seem not," she answers with dignity. "He doesn't have your well-being at heart, like I do."

I sniff. "Well, now that you're here, you bloody well had better've brought my red petticoats."

Chapter Thirteen

It's well into the evening when the door knocker raps. Eleanor pauses in tying the ribbon of her cotton night dress and turns anxious eyes towards me.

"Do not worry, Eleanor, I am expecting someone." I look at Amah and my tone is playful when I say, "Now that my maid has decided to join us, I have sent to my home for some necessities."

"This is not your home?" asks Eleanor.

"I am surprised Miss Heloise has lasted this long here," says Amah, gingerly opening a drawer of the shabby dressing table.

"I am only here until we have decided what is best for you, Eleanor. Ignore my maid," I call, as I skip down the stairs.

I pull open the door and stand back. "Bill." I usher him into the sitting room. "I was expecting my coachman, but you will do just as well." I grin up at him. "You will never guess who I have upstairs."

"That Oriental woman who stared at me from the landing? She gave me quite a turn." He shrugs off his coat, and places it over the back of the sofa.

Casting my eyes to the ceiling, I click my tongue. "No. That's my lady's maid. She's tracked me down."

"You're very game to have an Oriental sleep under the same roof as you. You're not scared she may cut your throat from ear to ear one night, all to avenge her pagan gods or some such?"

"Don't be ridiculous, Bill." I turn away and pour glasses of madeira to hide the irritation that I know will be flickering across my face.

"How did she find you, if you didn't want to be found?"

"She knew I was in Waterloo somewhere." I grin again. "It was she who was following me in the carriage, would you believe. Scared the life out of me, the hornet."

He frowns. "That doesn't make me any more comfortable with her presence in your house. Less so, in fact."

I take a seat next to Bill and cosy up to his side. "But now you must guess who I do have upstairs, right now, in my bedroom preparing for sleep."

"Don't tell me you've found her? Miss Carter?"

"Yes." I clap my hands together. "I finally found her."

"Her family must be very happy."

I agree, thinking of Sir Thomas, ghastly Mr Priestly and the underserving Mr Carter. "She is safe. I am so relieved she is safe, at last." I tell him of Mrs Donnelly and Mrs Sweetapple and my plot that reclaimed Eleanor.

"Very clever."

"Yes, and my adventures for tonight are not done. So what with one thing and another, I cannot invite you to stay," I say to him regretfully.

"No, I am too busy to stay, as well."

"Then why are you here, sir?" I curl my hand into his, my fingers sweeping his skin. I press a moist kiss into the palm of his hand.

His eyes cloud momentarily, but he smiles as he says, "Firstly, I have a gift for you." He pokes around in his waistcoat pocket before pulling forth something small wrapped in a handkerchief. "I saw it in a shop near my home. Thought of you." He hands me a tiny, pretty snuff bottle made of cranberry-coloured glass. The ruby red vessel has an ornate, silver lid on a hinge and is strung upon a thin piece of leather. "It's just a little bit of nonsense I thought you might like." He tries to sound off-hand, yet I'm aware of his gaze upon my face, eagerly gauging my feelings for the simple gift.

And I'm touched. The pretty bauble doesn't nearly measure up to the presents of diamonds and gold (and guineas) I've become accustomed to receiving, but I'm touched he thought of me. I immediately put it around my neck with his assistance, a shiver of pleasure passing through me as his fingertips brush the nape of my neck.

"I have placed some of my special snuff mixture within it," he explains, smiling. "To help you relax when I am not around."

The cold glass of the pendant rolls against my skin. "Thank you, sweet man." I kiss him on the mouth, catching his bottom lip between mine. His moustache bristles against my skin. "What else did you want to discuss with me?"

"Well, I wanted to let you know that I couldn't find that poor woman, Prue, who you told me about."

"Oh, that's sad." I think of her greying hair, the blood she coughed up and fear the worst.

"And I wanted to ask you some questions about Mme Silvestre's."

I sit back. "Oh? What questions?"

"There's a barman there. At least, he dresses up as a woman when he works at the bar, but he is a man, nonetheless. Do you know him?"

"Henry? Yes, I've seen him. I don't know much about him. We've only really talked once and that was when he was preparing drinks."

Bill nods and thinks for a moment. He feels in his pockets and brings out a crumpled piece of paper which he presses flat on the table. "I had a hunch about him. There was something not quite right when I went to Silvestre's after the Dutch girl was found. He slipped off before I had a chance to ask any questions."

"I remember that day. I saw you there and he rushed by." I lean over to look at the piece of paper. Underneath a sketch of a man with a beard and longish, straight hair, is an offer of ten pounds.

"That man is said to have swindled a lot of money out of people in Bloomsbury when he posed as an apothecary with access to miraculous medicines. Said he could cure all kinds of things but he was especially interested in women's problems."

"What problems?"

Bill shrugs. "Hysteria, mania, regulatory."

"For women who didn't want a baby?"

"It would seem so. But it was soon found out that his famously expensive tonics were nothing better than sugar water, although one pill he sold as a regulator was made of irregular amounts of arsenic and herbs which caused severe and life-threatening symptoms in the women. In fact, one woman did die, hence the end of his career in medicine and his flight from the law."

I squeeze his hand. "Yes," I say. "I'd forgotten. Tilly was telling me the other day that the girls in Mme Silvestre's brothel do not always go to the doctor to be..." I almost say 'scraped', but think better of it, "regulated. Sometimes they rely on Henry and an evil tasting draught he gives them."

I pull the picture to me again. "Henry's eyes are very like those in this picture – a little sunken and dark. And his nose is straight, just as it is here. I guess it could be him." A memory snags so that

I slap the piece of paper and bounce up from my seat. "Now I know who he is."

"What do you mean?"

I'm so excited I can barely say the words sensibly. "I saw him. Henry. I didn't know who he was. I mean, I recognised him, but couldn't place him. Without his curls. Of course. He was leaving Dr Mordaunt's premises."

"When?"

"That day I pinched the notebook." My thoughts rush ahead. "Do you think he could be in this with the doctor?" My voice is hushed with triumphant hope.

"Well, that is now what I am wondering," he says. "Might he be venturing further into the world of medicine? His tonics have failed. Has he turned to surgery?"

Suddenly I remember Agnes whinging about the messy sheets. Were they nastier than a night of dissipation could account for? However, I can't deny I find it a little hard to believe Henry could be a part of this butchery. But, of course, if he is under the sway of that bastard, Mordaunt... "He seemed quite nice, though, at Silvestre's."

Bill smiles and tucks the flyer back into his pocket. "You women will trust anyone."

The poor thing really has no idea.

"Well, I won't do it, Miss Heloise," says Taff, backing out of the kitchen. "I won't'm."

"You must, Taff, you foolish man," I snap, bearing down on him. "Give me that sack at once."

I tug the bag from his hands and peer inside at the screwed up pieces of clothing.

"I would never have bought those old rags if I knew'm what you had in mind, Miss Heloise," he says, shaking his head slowly. He looks over at Amah Li Leen. "What do you think, Amah?"

The older woman's mouth is pinched at one side. "She always does what she pleases."

"Well, if I'm to wait out on the street in the dark," I say, looking out the window, "and it's well past midnight already, I cannot be dressed as a woman. I will blend in best if I am disguised as a man." I pull out a tattered pair of trousers. "A vagrant, no less."

"Why don't you just let'm me do it, Miss Heloise?" asks Taff.

"Because I want to feel the thrill of the catch, not have it relayed to me," I answer, stepping out of my shoes. "Taff, we won't need you again tonight, so take the horses home and rest. We might need you tomorrow." It's only when I curl my stockings down from my thigh to my ankle, determined to undress in the kitchen, that Taff stops hesitating and leaves.

Amah and I hear a soft voice from above. I say, "Go attend to Eleanor, Amah. Nothing can be simpler than dragging on a man's attire."

The patched trousers are stiff and I hope that no fleas or lice lurk in the threadbare fabric. I pull a rather musty shirt over my head, shrug into a flannel vest and pull a cloth cap over my hair which has been pinned flat to my head. I have to put my own little boots back on but it's dark outside anyway. Nobody will be looking at me closely. Finally, I tuck my handgun into the back of my trousers and, grabbing a half empty bottle of brandy, I slip through the back kitchen door. I stand very still in the darkness and listen, my ears attuned to the distant voices of drunks and working men plodding home. I creep down the narrow easement between my house and the next, letting out a low whistle as I tread. Almost immediately, Chat pops out from behind a small shrub across the way, and I cross the road to join him.

"Are you sure I am not too late?" I whisper to the boy.

"Nah. I 'aven't seen anything yet."

"Let's walk up and down so we just pass for a couple of drunks." I take a swig of the brandy which burns my throat but warms my flesh, and pass the bottle to the boy.

He takes two swigs, screwing up his face. "Cor it doesn't 'alf scratch yer throat on its way down."

We bump against each other as we trudge along the road.

"Why are you around here so late at night?" I ask him.

"Me da' and I doss down around this corner." He pulls me along and points to a rickety lean-to huddled in the shadows away from the light of the gas lamp. "Used to be a goat in there," he says. "Bu' thankfully it died and we been there ever since."

"Where's your father? Is he there now?"

The boy shakes his head as we turn back onto Frazier Street. "No, 'e sometimes gets work cleaning up at the tannery late at night. Cor, 'e reeks when 'e comes 'ome. That's why I stays on the streets this late. I feel a bit afear'd when I'm by meself in our shack."

I look at the boy, his gaunt face marked with dirt and privation and I feel sad for him, just one shadow amongst so many.

We trudge along the path again, slurping noisily from the brandy bottle, and then pretend to settle down to sleep on the steps of a boarding house adjacent to my own residence. A good half hour passes and apart from a straggle of men making their way home, heads down, hands shoved deep in their trouser pockets, all is quiet. No lights flicker behind windows, there are no sounds of human movement. A chill breeze tickles my exposed ears and I'm just wishing I'd brought my fur tippet when Chat whispers, "'Ere comes the gorbellied, ol' cow."

We watch a large figure noiselessly leave a house three doors down from my temporary home. The heavily cloaked individual shies away from the gas lamp and then, turning abruptly, makes its way up my path. I pad across the road as noiselessly as a cat, and hear the faint clink of the front door's letter slot.

"What the hell do you think you're doing?" My voice is loud and determined.

The intruder tries to push me aside but is tackled to the ground by Chat, who sits on top of his prisoner. The front door opens and Amah stands in the doorway holding up a lamp. "Did you capture him?"

I take the lamp from her and, holding it over the figure struggling and shrieking on the ground, reveal a plump woman with greying ringlets falling from her crooked bonnet. "Well, we captured her."

"How dare you hold me like this, you harlot," screeches the woman.

"How dare you leave nasty notes, you dog-hearted wretch." I bend over and pick up the note the woman has left behind. *Jezebel. Whore. May God pierce you with his sword, and the Devil turn you aflame.* I read it through twice, and then laugh. "I cannot believe I was afraid. This is nothing more than nonsense."

I watch as the woman totters to her feet. I smirk. "'May God pierce you with his sword,'" I quote, poking the woman in her side. "Is he going to stick his cock in me? Is that what you mean? You saucy wench. Where did you find such filth?"

"How dare you?" gasps the woman. "I only read the Bible like all good people."

By now the neighbours have awoken to the noise and are peering out their windows.

"There is no cause for alarm," I call out. "We have just found an intruder. Peeping in on us, she was."

The woman clasps her hands to her droopy cheeks. "I never was. I never was. You are an evil trollop and you and your like should be punished."

My eyes narrow. "I will summon the police right now if you do not leave my doorstep. And do not deliver me any more of your nauseating notes or I'll tell all the neighbours you're harassing me 'cause I stole all your best johns."

Chapter Fourteen

I endeavour to sleep through the rest of the night in the sitting room upon the lumpy sofa, but only manage snatches of rest 'cause I can't straighten my legs or turn over on my side in the improvised bed. When I do finally sleep, I dream that my gun fails – that I need to, am desperate to, shoot a dark shadow of a man who's intent upon attacking me, but my gun refuses to shoot. A short knock on the front door, followed by its opening squeak, wrenches me from an uneasy sleep and I peer over at Amah, who's slept on the carpet in front of the fireplace.

"That must be Agnes, the chargirl from Silvestre's," I whisper. I collapse back onto a cushion and rub at my bleary eyes. "Agnes," I call. "Agnes."

The girl pops her head around the door and gasps and ducks back when she sees Amah, who's groaning as she sits up.

"Who's that, miss?" Agnes asks.

"That is my maid. You may call her Amah. Don't stand there gawping at her. It's rude." I press my hands on the small of my back to stretch. "And I have a lady guest upstairs in my bedroom. We are a full house this morning. Would you put some water on for tea, please?"

"Yes, miss," says Agnes. "For 'er too?" she asks, nodding towards Amah.

I frown upon the girl. "Tea for everybody, thank you, Agnes."

"Yes, miss."

Once she's left, I grin at Amah. "Still scaring the natives, I see."

"Pah!" She shakes her head, straightening her blouse. "I will never be bothered with what the likes of her think of me, Heloise."

"I know," I say, pulling on my peignoir. "That's what's so amusing."

We trudge up the stairs to the bedroom and I push open the door slowly. Eleanor's sitting up in bed, and she has opened the curtains so that weak sunlight filters unevenly into the room.

"How are you this morning, Eleanor?" I ask.

"I am well," answers the girl, although there are dark smudges under her eyes and her face is pale. She smiles shyly at Amah and watches as the older woman takes a pale celeste-blue gown from the cupboard and places it on the bed at Eleanor's feet.

"I had this brought for you to wear, madam," she says to Eleanor. "It is one of Heloise's day dresses, but she has grown too large for it." She throws me a sly look which I note but choose to ignore. "The colour will suit you nicely."

Eleanor kneels forward and strokes the shiny taffeta. "It is beautiful." She continues to watch Amah, as she unpacks further toiletries from a trunk. "Are you Spanish, Amah?" she asks curiously.

"No."

Eleanor picks up the blue gown and holds it against herself. "Maybe you are from India?"

"No, I'm from a land further away than that," Amah says. "You would not have heard of the place."

"I might have," says Eleanor. "I was born in Delhi, you know. That's where my mother died, so they sent me home to boarding school when I was twelve years old. Father returned to London not many years after that." She stares at a spot on the blanket, plucking at the weave with her fine, tapered fingers. "I was so happy in India."

Amah stares at the girl for a few moments and looks to say something, but thinks better of it.

"Has there been any word from Sir Thomas or my father?" Eleanor asks me.

"No. I believe we have them at a standstill," I answer. "Not to worry. I'm sure between the two of us, we can arrange something you might be pleased with."

Amah helps us dress. With me, she's merciless, hauling in the stays of my corset, her bent knee pressed firmly into my back as she pulls. But she's gentle with the girl.

"How far along are you now, Eleanor?' I ask.

Blotches of red flush Eleanor's face and neck. "I'm not entirely sure. Four months maybe?" She places her hand on her slender stomach, the slightest of firm curves the only hint that she is with child.

I watch the girl as Amah tugs away at my hair. I wonder if Eleanor knows of her options; if she knows she might have had a chance to rid herself of the child. In her days being passed from one place to another in Waterloo, surely someone had mentioned the possibility of an abortion to her.

When Amah's finished with my hair, having fixed it in a more intricate manner than I could ever achieve by myself, she starts on Eleanor's. The old harridan brushes Eleanor's hair softly, as if her fair locks are a sacred halo. I roll my eyes as I slide my silk hose onto my feet and up over my knees. I slip my feet into white, kid boots and go to the kitchen in search of breakfast, finding Taff seated at the table having a cup of tea with Agnes.

"Ah, Miss Heloise, I have returned because I have'm a missive for ye," he says, handing me a neat, square card. I recognise the writing on the egg-shell white, stiff paper at once.

"Agnes, could you please take some tea up to Miss Eleanor and Amah?" I ask as I take a seat at the table. I wait until the girl has left the room before I open the letter.

I'm shining with excitement when Amah joins us in the kitchen. "I have left Agnes to moon over Eleanor," she says, pouring herself a black tea. "She is admiring the girl's prettiness and helping her with her toilette." She pauses. "What do you look so pleased about?"

"I have a message from Lord Hatterleigh. He is back from the country and wants to take me to the opera tonight."

"Is that where he's been?" she says. "I wondered what he thought had become of you. You're not thinking of going are you? You cannot leave Miss Eleanor."

"But it's Faust, Amah. You know how much I've been longing to see Faust ever since Sir Berry described it to me."

"But what about Miss Eleanor? I will have to stay with her."

"No, I'll need you to help me prepare," I say, biting my lip. "And I'll need to go home to Mayfair for the night, of course."

"We can take Eleanor."

"Take Eleanor? Amah, we cannot take Eleanor. How strange she would find it when she sees that Lord Hatterleigh is to stay the whole night, and how strange he will find it that I have an unfamiliar girl in the house." I worked bloody hard to get where I am. I'm also well aware that it's been a small miracle I've pulled it off. So the idea of sharing my Mayfair home with another fair beauty… No, I won't share the attentions of my lover and patron, Hatterleigh, just yet, either.

Agnes and Eleanor descend the stairs. Agnes is regaling Eleanor with a story about Mme Silvestre's cat. "Vomited the pearl right up on Silvestre's bosom, it did," she finishes, triumphantly.

I swivel around in my chair to face the chargirl. "Agnes, I will not be able to keep Miss Eleanor company this evening. Neither will Amah. We'll both be out for the entire night. Do you think Mme Silvestre can spare you? So you can stay here with Miss Eleanor?"

Agnes looks pleased. "I'm sure she'll allow it if you was to 'ave a word with 'er."

I smile broadly. "That will not be a problem. I will write a short note to her right now and you must deliver it at once."

Eleanor seems so wan I decide to take her for a walk, ensuring we each carry a parasol to guard our complexions from the sun. I try to set a quick pace but Eleanor pauses to admire every flower or pat every dog or talk to each small child. Eventually I have to draw her arm through mine so I don't leave her too far behind. As we pass Mme Silvestre's establishment, Eleanor averts her gaze, but once at the corner we both look back on hearing a commotion. Mme Silvestre herself, as well-stuffed and tightly buttoned as an ottoman, bellows obscenities from her front doorway while Mr Critchley holds her back from pounding a young policeman over the head with a shoe.

Spying Tilly standing by the front gate I leave Eleanor for a moment and approach her. "What's she carrying on about?" I ask.

"The pigs have come around looking for Henry." She points at my purse. "You have a cigarette for me?"

I bring out my cigarette case, hand her one. "Where is he?"

"Don't know," she shrugs, blowing out smoke. "But they're heading around to Mordaunt's now."

This I want to see. If the police are going to take in that rat Mordaunt, I want to be there. I race back to Eleanor, and tug the girl behind me all the way to the doctor's cul-de-sac. We're just in time to see Mordaunt led out through the front door between two constables. Crowded upon the front terrace are several surprised patients. The doctor's assistant is so shocked he can only gabble noiselessly, rubbing the palms of his hands down the shiny breast of his suit-coat.

Walking behind is Inspector Kelley, who's mightily officious in his black frock coat and helmet. Then comes Bill, his bowler hat in hand, and Henry, who's shed his gown and is dressed in his plaid brown suit, hands manacled behind his back. Bill acknowledges me with a nod and they all climb into a police buggy which is parked in the road.

Eleanor clutches my arm nervously so I lead her away. I choose a route that's in the opposite direction to The Old Trout and we walk in silence for a few minutes.

"I've seen that man before somewhere, the one in the brown suit," says Eleanor.

"Yes. He's the barman at Silvestre's."

"There was no barman on the night I was there." The memory of the place quivers across her soft features.

"Yes, he was. You cannot remember a rather big lass tending bar? Wearing a frock and an over-abundance of rouge and powder?"

"With brown hair?"

"That's him. He was dressed as a woman. Those rich ringlets on his head were from a very tidy hairpiece, I wouldn't wonder."

Eleanor stops walking for a moment, a look of aghast wonder on her face. "He was dressed as a woman?"

"Yep," I grin.

A small crease puckers the girl's eyebrow. "I am sure I have seen him somewhere else, though." She straightens her shoulders. "Although I was not thinking clearly the night I was in that horrible place. I was so dizzy I was sure I was going to faint."

She looks so upset I direct her notice to a mangy cat sitting atop a fence post but then I have to spend the next bloody minute deterring her from fondling its patchy coat.

I buy us each a plum from a street vendor and we wander onto a scrap of parkland and settle on an old log that's lain here so long the grass and weeds snake over its bark. I bite into the tart skin of the plum catching the sweet juice with my hand. Its nectar runs down my chin so that I have to bend well over my billowing skirt. I suck the juice stain from my lace gloves. Eleanor doesn't bite hers, just holds the plum lightly in her lap with one hand and, with the other, snaps up pieces of grass.

"What is to become of me?" she asks.

"What do you want for yourself, Eleanor?"

She shrugs her thin shoulders and the tip of her nose becomes red with the exertion of holding back tears. "Do you know what I'd really like?" she eventually whispers.

I shake my head.

"I would like to live in a cosy little cottage. Somewhere I could just stay and be left alone." She lifts her face to the sun and shuts her eyes. "Somewhere like Cornwall. I went there once before on an excursion with my school, you know, to stay by the sea. Oh, it was so lovely, Heloise. And by the water there were quaint little cottages, whitewashed with thatched roofs. I would dearly love to live in one of those cottages with my baby. Just me and the baby." Her eyes open again and she stares ahead.

"No gentleman?"

"No," she answers immediately. She rests her chin on her hand and watches an ant crawl across her boot. "No gentleman. Although I think I would be happy with a maid. A maid like your kind Amah."

I laugh, a snort escaping my nose. "Even Amah would be surprised to hear herself described as kind."

A light mist hangs in the top branches of the young plane trees muting the light.

"How did you know the French man you tried to find in Charing Cross?" I ask her.

"Oh, Mathis? He was my viola teacher. Of course I was supposed to call him Monsieur Baudin, but he became my Mathis when we fell in love."

"You were in love with him?"

"Yes. He was so sweet. He was not exactly handsome – his nose was too large and he was too stout to be considered handsome – but he had lovely, brown eyes. I loved him and he loved me too."

"So... why are you not with him?"

"Well," she says, a grim smile on her serious, little face. "I cannot believe he was terribly thrilled at the idea of being saddled with a pregnant girl." Her face becomes sad again. "But he was going to do the right thing by me, which is more than the others were willing to do."

"So, he didn't throw you over?"

"Oh, not at all. He was willing to marry me and take me to France."

"Then why in heaven's name did you not take him up on his offer?"

The mist lifts from the trees and silvery sunlight clears the air again, but Eleanor trembles and covers her face with her hand.

"It is not his baby. And although I do not know what I am to do, I could not make such a good man pay for my sins."

I try in vain to find out the name of the father of Eleanor's baby. She becomes white with the effort of holding onto her sobs until she starts to retch. I put my arm around the girl's heaving shoulders and wait for her to quieten down.

I don't know Eleanor well enough to speculate on who the man might be. Surely the French music master was the most dangerous of risks to enter the sheltered world of a young lady fresh from boarding school? Has Eleanor any brothers? Brothers who have other young gentlemen to visit? I'm not sure, but from listening to her earlier it'd seemed she was an only child.

A grey wood pigeon wanders before us, pecking for crumbs. Not too much longer another pigeon, with white tufts on its neck, joins its partner.

Unless it was her father. Eleanor's face rests against her folded arms and I study the barely visible, flaxen down on the curve of the girl's pink ear. Maybe Eleanor's own father has left her with child. It's not unheard of, especially in the back-rooms of brothels.

Li Leen

In some ways I am like Eleanor. I sometimes think back to my time in Makassar and wonder if that was the happiest period of my life. The earlier years, that is, the years before Tiri came into our lives. When Mother still combed my hair with her tortoise-shell comb and fed me tripang with her sandal-wood chopsticks. Before Tiri's gaze inched so heavily across my skin that I allowed my hair to fall across my face while I looked to the side, pretending he was not there.

The only respite I had was to work in Tiri's shop that fronted our living space. Mostly I sat by the cash box, counting the comings and goings, while Tiri's serving girls assisted the customers. At the back of the shop stood two large aquariums, the water moss-green and cool, in which glistening, tiger-striped gourami bobbed sluggishly waiting for a customer with a yen for fresh fish. A girl from the Dutch governor's kitchen taught me how to handle and fillet the fish. For this I had a special scaling knife with which I pierced the gill of the flapping fish and waited for the wet shiver of death, a coat of viscous webbing shiny on my fingertips. I then cleaned and scaled the fish, before handing its fleshy carcase over to the customer. When possible, I kept the fish head for Mother to stew in ginger and garlic so that she could offer it to the Chinese gods of her tiny red and gold shrine. We well knew how much the gods delighted in fish head.

Chapter Fifteen

Amah Li Leen sets the kitchen table with bread, cold meats and cheese for our midday meal.

She's testy with Eleanor, who only nibbles on a few berries.

"How can you nourish yourself and your young one if you are not to eat?" she says. "Look at yourself. You are so thin I can almost see through your white skin." She tuts and scowls at the girl but carefully assembles a neat cheese sandwich with wedges of butter and thin slices of pickle. She then removes the crusts and cuts the sandwich into bite size squares. This she places in front of Eleanor next to a cup of sweet, milky tea. "Eat, eat," she urges.

She pinches me on the elbow and gestures towards the spread of food on the table. "You eat too. None of this fasting before your big night out at the opera. I did not trudge through the dirt and haggle with those smelly hucksters for you to both starve yourselves."

We eat obediently as Amah washes the dishes, occasionally popping a morsel of food into her own mouth. When Eleanor is finally finished, having only eaten half her sandwich, Amah sniffs but takes the plate away.

Since there are no books in the house, or musical instruments or even, thankfully, needle-work to be done, I endeavour to engage Eleanor in conversation. We sit upon the sofas in the sitting room and, being curious about how the young woman had fared for her few weeks of solitude in Waterloo, I slowly draw the story from her.

"I did not realise my money would last such a short period."

"The owner of the boarding house made you leave?"

"Oh, yes," she says. "As soon as she understood that I could no longer pay her any board she almost pushed me out of the house." Colour tints her cheeks. "What an abominable woman she was. You know, she made me take my shoes off when I entered the house. And she only allowed us one cup of tea in the morning. She guarded the pot like it was a chest of gold, and I'm sure it was not even tea. I'm sure it was just muddy water from the drains."

"And then?"

"And then Tilly took me to Mme Silvestre's." She thinks for a moment. "It's strange. It was over a week ago that I was at Silvestre's but I seem to have learnt a lot since then. I am not sure if that is a good thing or not."

"But you did not stay there?"

"Oh, no, I could not. It was so warm there and seemed so merry but when that man placed his hand on me and all I could see was his wet mouth..." She shudders.

I grin at her. "Yes, you need to grow a very tough skin for that kind of thing."

She looks across at me and then lets her gaze fall. "Did you ever work somewhere like Mme Silvestre's?"

"Yes. I worked there for a short time when I was about your age. There are worse places to work." I laugh at the horror on Eleanor's face, although I do feel a tiny, tiny flicker of irritation. "Although I will refrain from telling you the particulars. So tell me, what did you do then, before that ghastly woman, Mrs Sweetapple, sank her claws into you?"

"It was awful. Awful. I found myself near the bridge and it was very dark and I was so frightened I eventually begged a room from an Irish woman. The lodging was no better than a hovel and the room cost two shillings a week, and yet I could not even come up with that. She had me help her launder men's shirts and breeches for my board but after a few days her niece arrived so she asked me to leave. I would have gone to the workhouse, but I did not even know where it was, and I was too ashamed to ask. So that first night I hid in a stairwell not far from here. Luckily it was not a terribly cold night, but I still did not manage any sleep."

"I can imagine you didn't. Your hiding place wasn't discovered?"

"I was so afraid I would be found. So many men, so many women, passed by. I did not know what would become of me. I hoped that if I was found it would be by a woman, a kind woman who would assist me, but I have learnt that the fairer sex is not always as charitable as I had been brought up to expect. I was sick with worry. I assure you, if I had eaten anything that day, I would have passed it up." She leans forward and with shaky hands she grips her teacup and has a sip before carefully placing the cup down again on its saucer. "I only had the one gown left by that stage and it was terribly soiled and crushed. And my hands – I had thrown away my gloves by then, they were in such a sorry state I could not bear to keep them. I think that was when I realised there was no going back for me to a normal life." She gazes down at the palms of her hands, and rubs at them with her lace handkerchief. "My hands were so dirty. I could not wipe the grime away."

"How did you meet Mrs Sweetapple?"

She hides her face in her hands. "It is so mortifying to have to tell you this part." She looks up again and there are red smudges around her eyes where her hands have pressed. "I was so hungry. I was more hungry than I have ever felt in my life. At first I asked a coster who looked friendly enough if I could have one of her apples, having no money, but she told me if she was to give me an apple, she would be obliged to give all the vagrants an apple, and then where would her business be? She did not say it nastily, but she was very firm. I was too afraid to ask again after that. Then I noticed a cart of chestnuts. The man was serving an old lady, so I walked past and tried to sift my hand through the nuts," she makes the motion with her hand. "I tried to take one without being seen but a beastly little girl told the old woman and then the coster looked around at me too. I could have sunk into the ground I was so embarrassed. I just stood there, the chestnut in my hand, unable to explain myself, when Mrs Sweetapple took it from me and told the costermonger that she would buy it for her niece – she was referring to me, you see."

"How clever of her."

Eleanor nods slowly. "Yes. So when she offered to take me home, and she seemed so kind, of course I went."

"Of course."

"Of course," she repeats. She stares down at her cup of tea, and I let her be.

Amah and I are packing some of my toiletries to take with us for the evening, when Agnes appears at the bedroom door.

"There's a gentleman here for you, miss."

"Do you know who it is?" I tuck some stray hairs behind my ear.

The girl shakes her head. "Nah. Never seen 'im, miss. Looks like a toff though, all straight and proper, 'e is."

I follow the girl down the stairs and am surprised to see Dr Blain, attired in evening dress, standing by the hall stand.

"Dr Blain. How do you do?" I'm not entirely able to keep the astonishment from my voice.

"Mrs Chancey." He takes my hand in his gloved one, drops his hat, and upon gathering it up again, says, "You must find it very strange that I have called upon you, but I have not seen you again at the Lion's Inn since we visited the fair."

I smile politely, and assure him I'm delighted to meet him again. Knowing Eleanor to be in the sitting room, I'm unsure as to whether I should invite him in or whether to continue our uneasy conversation in the hallway.

"I see you are going somewhere special tonight," I venture, gesturing towards his tailcoat.

"Yes, yes," he says, distracted, picking at the rim of his hat. "I have an engagement to attend with my aunt." He swallows hard. "The thing is, I was wondering if you have found your cousin yet, Mrs Chancey?"

I'm just about to tell him that I haven't yet found Eleanor when the girl herself walks out from the sitting room.

"Dr Blain?" she says. Her face is flushed pink as if she has sat by the fire too long.

Blain stares at her, then rushes forward to take her hand in greeting. "You are well."

"Yes, I am well. Heloise has taken such great care of me."

He glances back at me. "But how did you find her?" He looks again at Eleanor. "Where were you?"

I stare at the two of them. She was his patient after all. I'm not quite sure what to say so I usher the two of them into the sitting room to give myself some thinking time.

"A kind lady not far from here allowed Eleanor to board with her," I finally say. "The woman who owns the coffee stall knew I was searching for Eleanor and, having heard of this kind lady taking in a young woman, she thought to tell me of it." I hold Eleanor's gaze for a second. "Luckily it was my cousin Eleanor, after all."

We each take a seat. Blain sits next to me so that he's facing Eleanor. He stares at her for a few moments before his eyes fall to his hat which is resting in his lap. "And you have been well, madam?" he asks me.

"Yes, thank you. And your work, Dr Blain – has it kept you very busy?"

"Yes, yes it has," he says, glancing again at Eleanor. "That is to say, no, actually. It has been slow lately. Which is a good thing for my patients as that means cholera is not rife, yet it is not so fortuitous for my livelihood."

He smiles tremulously at Eleanor and a blush creeps across the skin above his stiff collar and bow-tie. Jesus. He's besotted with the girl, not stalking her. I press my lips together to stop from grinning. Poor Eleanor, who's unpicking the lace border of her handkerchief, seems to be oblivious to his attentions.

"Let me arrange for the tea things to be brought in," I say, standing.

"No, no. Please do not bring them on my account." Blain also stands. "I really must be going. I have to collect my aunt very soon. I only came to enquire after Miss Carter." He jerks out a smile at Eleanor then walks from the room.

I follow him into the hallway and he turns to take my hand. "I suppose you will be returning to your own home soon?"

"Yes, I will," I wonder if Eleanor will be averse to seeing the nice doctor again. "I will provide you with my address." Oh dear, I'm going to have to find lodging for the girl in Watford now.

"No, that is not necessary. I am afraid this may be the last time we meet under these circumstances."

"But surely you will visit us again?"

He gives a short shake of his head. "No. No, I don't think I will. In fact I know I will not."

"But..." I say, confused. "But you seemed so... glad to see Eleanor again."

"Mrs Chancey, your cousin came to see me as a patient. I know her predicament."

"But why didn't you say earlier? Why didn't you tell me she had been to see you?"

His eyes drop from mine. "I had to protect her privacy in this matter. The unpleasantness..."

I feel the expression on my face flatten, tightening my mouth and brow, as I realise what he means. "Ah. Therefore, even if you desired to do so, you could not bring yourself to know Eleanor better?" I say.

"No. It would not be right."

The smile on my face is fixed, as I open the front door. "Well, we must be thankful for the generosity of spirit that allowed you to check on Eleanor's well-being. You are a true gentleman."

"Heloise," calls Eleanor from the bedroom doorway just as we're leaving for the night.

"Yes, Eleanor?" I look up at the young woman.

"I've remembered where I saw Henry – you know, the barman from Silvestre's."

"Where, dear?"

"It was on the morning after I slept in the stairwell.." She curls her fingers over the banister. "It was still quite dark and I wandered by the river. I was so sick and dizzy with fatigue, but I'm sure of it. That's where I saw him. He was standing over a woman who had fallen in the road beside the fishmongers." She frowns. "No, that's not right. It was almost as if he had dropped her there. I thought she may have fainted or else maybe she was the worse for wear from gin."

"And you're sure it was him?"

She nods, although her eyes are worried. "I think so."

Chapter Sixteen

I'm bursting with contentment as I dab scent behind my ears and between my breasts. If I was a cat I'd be purring. How satisfying to be back in my luxurious home in Mayfair. It actually irks me to know I'll have to return to Waterloo again to organise Eleanor's affairs. How pretty my boudoir is, with its creamy, thick carpet and the glossy, ornate furniture. The bed, with its canopy of heavily embroidered gold and black velvet and its crisp linen sheets is especially inviting. Everything smells fresh and clean – no musty mattress, no tallow candles. My beauty accoutrements are spread across the surface of the mahogany dressing table – crystal jars containing fragrant ointments and oils that nourish my skin and assist in keeping it fashionably pale and free of freckles; lip salves and fragile bottles of tinted cream to enhance what nature has neglected; and ivory-handled brushes to groom my hair and apply powder to my face and body. I choose a pair of heavy diamond earrings from my jewellery case. As I look around my room I can't help but think of Eleanor's last words.

"I have to tell Bill what Eleanor told me of Henry. The timing fits in with when the poor Dutch girl's body was left by the side of the fishmongers," I say to Amah. "Can you fetch me paper and pen?"

"No, I cannot, Heloise," she snaps at me, as she twines my hair into a full, loose braid that tapers down my back. "I need to finish your hair for tonight, and what with that and dressing you, there is no time for letter writing."

I sigh loudly with frustration. "Alright. I suppose I can let him know in the morning. Hopefully they'll keep Henry at the station."

"Did they arrest him?" Amah asks as her nimble fingers pin diamante stars into my hair. Towards the nape of my neck, at the top of the loose braid, she inserts a glittering diamond and pearl comb.

"Yes. At least, I saw Bill and other bobbies taking him off in their buggy," I murmur, as I trace charcoal across the corners of my eyelids. I turn my face from side to side to admire my handiwork.

"You know, where I come from they say beauty fades with each moment you admire yourself," says Amah, inspecting me from behind.

I laugh. "What rubbish, Amah. I'm positive you just made that up. And besides, beauty fades each moment anyway. That's why I need all these unguents," I say as I rub tinted cream onto my cheek bones.

In the reflection of the mirror I notice Amah shake her head.

"Which of your new gowns will you be wearing tonight?" she asks.

"Bring me the two gowns Worth sent from Paris."

Amah pauses on the way to my dressing room. "I'm sure I saw Sir Thomas' friend outside the Waterloo house this morning. It was when I was on my way to the markets."

"What man?"

"You know – the one with the big ears," she says, holding her hands up to her ears and flapping them.

"Mr Priestly? No, you couldn't have."

"Yes, I am sure it was him. He walked past the house in Frazier Street," she insists.

I'm puzzled as to why Priestly would be loitering around the house, but lose all thought of him when Amah returns from the other room and drapes a gown of silk taffeta the shade of champagne over a plump armchair. The bodice is cut to reveal the shoulders and fine, intricate lace flows from below the bust-line and around the upper arms. The outer layer of the flowing skirt is neatly parted in the front with a swathe of lace and a run of neat bows. The other gown, made from a burnt red and gold silk brocade, she places on the bed. The fabric is so sumptuous that besides a short train, further lace and furbelows are unnecessary.

I press my hands to my cheeks. "They are simply ravishing. I'm sure I cannot choose."

"Well, I must say, Worth dresses you well," says Amah grudgingly, her hands on her hips as she scrutinises the dresses. "He knows what colours suit you too. None of that ghastly purple you favour so much."

I roll my eyes but refrain from saying anything. "I think I'll wear this one tonight," I say, gently rubbing the brocade of the red dress. "If the old hags are going to cut me, I might as well give their husbands and sons something to look at."

As she replaces the other dress Amah calls out, "Yes, but at least you can be sure that tomorrow all those same ladies will run out and command their cheap little dressmakers to copy your gown."

I half-smile at myself in the mirror, my cheek dimpling. "Yes, that is some consolation," I say. I step into my crinoline and petticoats with Amah's assistance. Together we pull on the gown, which is gratifyingly heavy. I adjust the bodice so that it is low enough for the fullness of my bosom to swell. I arrange a black, lace mantilla shawl around my shoulders. Its scalloped edge swells over the back of my gown, although my straitened, tiny waist can be seen through the sheer lace.

Amah tidies my hair again and then kneels on the floor to help me step into my delicate shoes. She rests back on her haunches. "There. You're ready. You look beautiful." Her voice holds satisfaction, but her smile is tight.

I sway against Lord Hatterleigh as his carriage hurtles through the London streets. The carriage is as well-sprung as money can buy and is upholstered in dark leather and plush, maroon velvet. He hands me a crystal goblet of cognac. "Drink up," he says, as he throws his own cognac back. The glass clinks against the decanter when he pushes it back into its small cabinet. I sip the pungent liquor and settle my other hand on his thigh, which he covers with his own large one.

Lord Hatterleigh is the heir to an earldom, and owns fine estates in both Ireland and near York, although it cannot be denied he has more the look of one of his gardeners than that of an earl. He hasn't got a fluted, aristocratic nose, and his complexion isn't so fair that canals of blue veins are visible. He's a thick-set man, without being too fat, with dark hair and a meaty face. He has fine, smiling eyes though, which are brimmed with dark lashes.

"What have you been doing with yourself, my dear, while I have been rusticating?" he asks.

I place my head on his shoulder, careful to not mess up my hair. "I have been waiting for you, Giles, of course."

He lets out a shout of laughter and slaps my thigh so smartly that, had it not been amply covered with layers of fabric, would have stung. "You jade. Now, tell me the truth."

I pinch his arm and grin. "I've been working for Sir Thomas again."

"That rogue. What has he mixed you up in this time? You haven't managed to sneak into the Prussian embassy again, have you? There'll be hell to pay, love, if you're found out."

"Nothing so glamorous. I've been hunting for a girl in Waterloo."

Hatterleigh pats my hand. "Be careful of the hoi polloi down there, Heloise. Don't want to pick up one of their fevers."

The carriage pauses in front of a terraced house in a small lane off Tottenham Court Road. A middle-aged lady, wearing a blue dress which is tightly buttoned to her neck, its only embellishment being a lace collar, strides towards the carriage and climbs in after waving away the groomsman's helping hand.

"Good evening, Mrs Forrest," I say.

"Good evening, Heloise." Mrs Forrest takes the cognac Lord Hatterleigh offers her and finishes it in three determined sips as the carriage pulls forward.

Mrs Forrest's, wiry ginger hair is pulled into a neat chignon under a lace head covering and above her bulbous, pink nose she wears large glasses which accentuate the creases on her pinched face. She's a distant cousin of Lord Hatterleigh's and he pays her well to exude her air of conventionality when she chaperones us on public outings.

The carriage halts by the imposing entrance to the Covent Garden Opera House. A throng of people are gathered in front of the theatre but it's not so hectic because it's out of season. We press forward with the assistance of the theatre manager and make our way through the outer columns into the foyer. My heart thrums a little faster once we're amongst the other opera patrons who chatter loudly under the bright and glittering light thrown from the chandeliers. The gentlemen are neat in their tailcoats and silk top hats, while the ladies display astounding tastes in flounces, silks and hairpieces. We make slow progress up the curving, carpeted staircase to our box so that Hatterleigh can greet his friends along the way. I know several people myself, of course, whom I greet with a grin and a quick word. Many others pretend to ignore my presence when they're not actually staring at me.

A man, leering so that his yellow teeth flash all the way to his pallid gums, breathes "*Paon de Nuit,*" as I pass. I have to turn my head away from his foul breath and attention, but when a handsome, young woman hisses, "There she is. The Peacock of the Night," to her plump, overly-frilled companion, I give those witches a serene smile and a quick curtsy of acknowledgement. They look affronted and hide behind their fans.

"I don't know why everyone insists on calling you a peacock, Heloise," complains Mrs Forrest. "A peacock is a male bird, after all. Although, to be sure, a pea hen is a drab, brown creature, more along my lines, really. The Pea Hen of Soho. Ha!"

I smile as we take our seats in Hatterleigh's box. The orchestra strikes the first thrilling notes. The box is on the second tier which has an excellent view of the stage and as the lights dim to accentuate its splendour, I have to marvel at the magnificence of the newly restored theatre. All is fresh and sparkling; there are no faded, moth eaten curtains and no persistent stench from the water-closets. It's a far cry from some of the theatres in which I've performed.

I enjoy the first act, amused at Faust's self-important transportations. I can just imagine Amah's eyes cast to the ceiling in disdain at the man's conceit and my own lips lift in agreement. I've known many men who would be as easily corruptible as Faust. It then occurs to me that maybe I'm a bit like Faust. It's a sobering thought I decide not to dwell upon.

During the interval Hatterleigh and I leave the box for the narrow corridor. He goes in search of refreshments while I relish the relief to be had from standing upright. Those damned corsets stick into my ribcage something rotten. Several gentlemen pass me on similar missions to that of Hatterleigh, and a few boxes down two ladies stroll arm in arm along the corridor.

I'm about to enter our box again when Dr Blain marches up and glowers down at me. His face is flushed and his usually neat, brown hair is as dishevelled as I've ever seen it.

"Dr Blain. I didn't realise you were at the opera too."

"Mrs Chancey," he says, grinding on the word 'Mrs'. "If that is your real name."

I glance towards the other women in the corridor, but they have turned to perambulate in the opposite direction. "I'm not sure I understand your meaning, Dr Blain," I answer, smiling politely.

"I am here tonight with my aunt, I'll have you know, Mrs..." Blain stops, apparently unable or unwilling to repeat my surname.

"Yes?"

"Yes. And my aunt knows more of society than I do, Mrs..."

"Please, just call me Heloise if the name Chancey is sticking in your throat," I reply, exasperated.

"I would prefer not to refer to you at all. My aunt has told me all about you."

"Ah. Is she an acquaintance of mine?" I ask, lightly, mischief stirring my blood. "You must bring her here so that I can greet her."

He glares at me. "My aunt is a good woman. It distresses her to be in the same theatre with you, let alone in the same room."

I can no longer keep up a friendly façade and the smile vanishes from my face. "Indeed. Then how can she know so much of me, sir?"

"You are infamous, madam."

I'm silent for a few moments as I try to dampen the anger rising in my chest. I can feel that Liverpool street-girl close to the surface, the one who can scream blistering insults until her throat feels scalded. "What is your point, sir?"

Blain runs his hand through his hair. "What of Eleanor? What is to become of her?"

I feign a look of surprise. "What concern is that of yours, sir? You washed your hands of her mighty quickly earlier today."

"Yes, yes, I did." The skin around his lips is white. "And it almost kills me to do it. I cannot marry a woman who is already with child to another man, but it is almost worse to think of her residing with a woman such as yourself. I would prefer her dead."

"Stop your hysterics, sir," I say through clenched teeth. The ladies further down the corridor now watch us over their fluttering fans. "I can assure you, Eleanor is much better off with me than lying dead in a doss-house somewhere, no matter how noble you think that end might be."

Blain takes a step closer and thrusts his face close to mine. I don't back away.

"Madam, just because you are well known at the opera, live in a fancy house and own expensive steeds does not mean you are anything better than the harlots on the streets of Waterloo," he chokes out, his eyes bloodshot with the exertion.

"I am a woman of independent means, sir, and she will be just fine in my care."

"You are a prostitute."

"I am a courtesan." I feel foolish as soon as I say it. My hand clenches into a fist and I'm sorely tempted to clout him on the cheek.

"Who is this, Heloise?" asks Hatterleigh.

Blain and I were so absorbed in each other we hadn't noticed his approach. I take a deep breath and straighten my fingers in their soft, white gloves.

"Nobody," I answer, smiling stiffly up at Hatterleigh. "Nobody at all. I believe he is lost."

Hatterleigh opens the door to our box and says, just loudly enough, "I did advise you to stop mixing with the hoi polloi, my dear."

Faust falls to his knees, his hands clasped in prayer while he watches despairingly as Marguerite is lifted into the heavens of the theatre. The grand curtains close upon the scene and the audience applaud, some men standing to cheer.

Although sympathy for Marguerite's plight swells in my chest with each rising note, so that I too hold my breath through the final moments of the opera, it doesn't take long for common sense to steady my heartbeat. I gather up my mantilla and wonder how Marguerite had killed her infant. Smothered with a pillow? Quickly with a knife? She would've been better off using the blade on Faust than begging for God's forgiveness.

Mrs Forrest also stands. Her glasses are fogged over and she sniffs hard.

"Wonderful opera, Giles. Very French, but wonderful, none-the-less," she says to her cousin. "Where are you young people off to now?"

Hatterleigh looks to me. "Motts?"

I wrinkle my nose. "It's become a bit boring, don't you think? Let's try somewhere new."

"Why don't we try that dance hall old Trickett was telling me about?" he says, as he guides us down the stairs to the foyer. "It's quite smart, apparently. A mix of all the right people and those who are a little more audacious. You'll enjoy it, my dear, having grown accustomed to the riff-raff of Waterloo."

The Clipstone Street Hop is tucked behind a timber yard in Fitzroy Square. A cool wind has picked up between the tall buildings on the street, whisking my hair into my face as we walk briskly from Hatterleigh's carriage to the small assembly room. We join a noisy crowd of revellers gathered around the entrance to a squat building. Progress is slow as those desiring entrance to the Hop, which is situated in the loft, have to reach it by ladder. The spectacle of gentlemen either shoving the ladies in their cumbersome skirts up the ladder, or needing to duck out of the way of those same undulating appendages, only adds to the merriment.

Finally, we manage to squeeze into the club. Despite its humble entrance, the Clipstone Street Hop is flash and aristocratic. The lighting from the gas lamps, being warm and low, casts a flattering glow on the complexions of those out carousing so late in the evening. The carpets are dark, and the surrounding furnishings are made of well-polished timber and marble. A long bar runs across one side of the room behind which glittering glass bottles full of whiskeys and wines line the wall, and on the other side of the room a violinist and harpist play upon a stage next to a small dance floor. Amongst the crowd we recognise many of our friends from the opera who canoodle with fair ladybirds and sleek lotharios.

I gulp down several glasses of champagne in quick succession and dance the quadrille with a number of my admirers and, although I maintain a cheerful front, my irritation with Dr Blain and my own reaction to his words still gnaws at my spirits. The champagne only heightens rather than dispels this mood, until a headache hammers at the back of my head leaving me feeling giddy, as I weave back and forth amongst the other dancers. Blain's a pompous arse. Mooning about over Eleanor, like she's a tragic figure in a play, while blathering on about the difficulties of poor, fallen women. Thinking he's as good as a mortal god, like all the other doctors I've ever met. What the hell did he know about my life?

I make my way unsteadily through the crowd until I reach Hatterleigh. "I'm not feeling too well," I shout in his ear, over the din of the music. "I think I'd like to return home."

He looks surprised. His eyes are bleary and his nose has turned red. "That's not like you, Heloise." He drains the last of his whisky. "Not to worry. I'll take you straight home."

The night's turned nippy and, once Bundle lets us in, Hatterleigh settles in front of the fire in the drawing room with a fresh tumbler of scotch in his hands. I still feel a little light-headed from the champagne and find Amah waiting in my bedroom. She helps me shed my petticoats and the stiff crinoline.

Even without the hoop, the skirts of my gown remain full and heavy, and I sway from the room, tripping over its hem. I poke out my tongue at Amah, who tuts and shakes her head.

Returning to the drawing room I sit by Hatterleigh, who lifts his glass to the portrait where I'm dressed as a Javanese girl.

"I've always liked that painting," he says. "I can imagine you as my little native girl."

I grin as I pour myself a scotch. "Would you like me to wear that costume one day?" I curl my legs up against him and stroke the corner of his mouth with my thumb.

Amusement lightens his heavy features. "That would be a bit of fun. I could unravel you slowly, like a sweetmeat from a wrapper." He brushes a tendril of hair from my neck.

I swallow my drink and press up against him. "I could be your exotic lover." I lean in and nuzzle in the crook of his neck. I pepper soft kisses across his throat until his body becomes pliant. He tastes of sweat and the sharpness of cologne and, when I flicker my tongue into his ear, I can smell the musky scent of his hair oil.

He slides his hands beneath my petticoats, along my thigh, and when I close my eyes, I can still feel the remnants of the headache click away irritatingly. His hands are large and strong, but his skin is smooth, unlike Bill's. I feel a pang of pleasure when I recall Bill's body against mine, and I keep my eyes shut to stay absorbed in the moment. Hatterleigh grasps me firmly by the hips and pulls me to him so that I straddle his lap. I bring my face close to his, gently bite his bottom lip, drawing it into my mouth. I squeeze his full cheeks and rub my thumb across the stubble around his mouth. I'm so bloody fond of this man, this man who takes such good care of me. But I don't love him. I know better than that.

For where would love have gotten a girl like me? I would've had to settle for a dismal life in some back alley or country village. Maybe long hours in a dark room, stitching others' breeches, or worse, sewing ball gowns for other women who were more happily provided for. Working every day, while my intended toiled equally long hours until we could afford to marry. And look where love has gotten poor Eleanor.

I can't help it, my thoughts turn to Blain again. I tense at the memory of his obnoxious words. Arrogant bastard. I unbutton Hatterleigh's shirt and, pushing back the fabric, kiss his chest. Entwining my arms around his neck I kiss him on the mouth, my tongue teasing his. I close my eyes again and picture the tall doctor dangling by the neck at the end of a piece of rope. How I'd enjoy it if he were found guilty for the murders of those poor doxies, but somehow I can't believe it of him.

I help Hatterleigh shrug his trousers down and kneel between his knees. He groans as I run my tongue firmly along the ridge of his cock and then I settle into tickling a pattern with the tip of my tongue. This I continue for a few moments until taking him fully into my mouth. I count the seconds in my mind, easing into the rhythm, one-buttercup, two-buttercup, three-buttercup, four-butter... Usually I allow for five minutes or so, or until the muscles around my mouth ache, but I find myself hoping that the police discover the evidence they need that will prove Henry is the Waterloo monster after all. I really hope that the horrible deaths will stop with his arrest. And what's old Silvestre doing, meanwhile? I almost feel sorry for the old cow, but I'm relieved it'll all be over soon.

I've lost count, but Hatterleigh pulls me into his lap again and enters me beneath the canopy of my brocade skirts. My head falls back and for a few moments my eyes follow the scrolled patterns in the pressed ceiling. I will myself to relax and enjoy the waves of motion as I would normally, but I can't. I rock against his thrusts and, just as he reaches climax, I remember Dr Mordaunt's diary. Has Bill investigated Mordaunt any further? He's another man I'd like to see hanging from a rope. I slump against Hatterleigh and bury my face in his neck.

"Is something the matter, Heloise?" He holds me lightly by the nape of the neck and kisses me on the chin.

I climb from his lap and reach for the crystal whisky decanter again – anything to numb the thoughts that drum away in my head. I lean against his arm and take a sip of the amber spirit. "I still have that headache." Finishing the whisky, I allow the glass to roll from my fingers onto the carpet.

Hatterleigh stands, pulling his trousers up. "Let's get you to bed then, my love."

Chapter Seventeen

Hatterleigh's left by the time Amah pulls the curtains apart to wake me in the morning. She flicks on the gas lighting because the day is gloomy, and heavy rain streams down the window's glass. I bury my face into the pillows and groan. My headache's shifted, now stabbing at the area behind my eye sockets, and my mouth is sour and dry.

"Too much champagne, as usual," she says. "I do not know when you will learn."

Shut yer mouth, shut yer mouth, shut yer mouth churns through my mind, but I don't have the energy to utter the words. There's the tinkle of a silver teaspoon against china. Amah's preparing a cup of hot, sweet tea for me, but I'm only enticed from the depths of my swansdown pillow by the smell of toast.

When she sees my face she pretends to look frightened and then laughs heartily, covering her mouth as she chuckles. "Ah. You look like the warrior god, Zhong Kui, with his beady, red eyes and ferocious frown."

I grimace at her and take a sip of tea. "Hush your mouth, or I'll hack up all over the carpet and you'll have to clean it up."

Amah cheerfully butters the toast and hands a thin slice to me. "Monsieur Agneau made your favourite eggs, so make sure you eat them up. You know what he's like," she says of my cook. "You leave a morsel and he'll be offended."

I slump back against my pillows. "Can't you eat them for me? I can't face it."

Amah places a fork between my slack fingers. "You eat them. You'll feel better for it," she says, firmly.

"Between you and Monsieur Agneau I get no peace. I'll be as large as a sow at this rate," I grumble. "I need a little puppy so that it can eat what I don't want."

"Except I'll be the one left looking after it," says Amah, as she moves towards the dressing room to prepare my wardrobe for the day.

I nibble at the toast, licking the butter from my bottom lip. I feel up to trying a few mouthfuls of the fluffy eggs, and the herbs are tantalising, reviving. How I've missed Monsieur Agneau's cooking.

I watch as the rain drizzles against the window. It dampens my spirits to think that I have to return to Waterloo. Hell, it dampens my spirits that I have to leave my cosy bed.

Amah returns with a jewellery case, in which she deposits my diamonds. She glances sideways at me and smirks. "I know why you're so grumpy today. You don't want to return to that mouldy house in Waterloo."

I lick egg from the fork and shrug. "Do you think we could just send Taff to pick up Eleanor and the rest of my clothing? Bring her here?"

Amah places my dratted corset and petticoats upon the foot of the bed. "Well, it depends on what you have planned for the girl. I don't know what you and Sir Thomas have arranged."

"Nothing yet." I rub my face and turn onto my side, almost upsetting the plate of eggs. What to do with Eleanor? It's true that

I've received no further word from Sir Thomas or Mr Carter as to the young woman's fate, and Eleanor can't stay under my wing indefinitely, after all. I roll onto my back and drape my arm across my eyes, to think. What to do with a pregnant girl? I've a great many acquaintances and friends, and even quite powerful connections, yet I don't have any contacts in the field of good works, who would be of use in this matter – I don't know any Christian, charity workers or benefactors who could find a home and employment for a young woman such as Eleanor. And what of her? Do I really want to deliver her into a world of condemned drudgery for the rest of her life? The only community that I can think of which would be likely to take on a young woman in Eleanor's plight is the type to be found in houses such as Mme Silvestre's. I know of many women from nice households such as Eleanor's, who had fallen – through financial necessity, rape, seduction or ignorance – into the brothel trap. I myself had been much younger than Eleanor when I'd first stumbled into this way of life. But, damn it, I didn't have a father who could pay my way like little Eleanor does.

And what of the child? Either way, Eleanor will not be able to keep the baby.

I think of Blain's words, how he was revolted at the idea of Eleanor residing with me. Bastard. It will serve him right if I keep young Eleanor, here, in my den of immorality. Yes, and it will also serve as a slap in Mr Carter's face, to have his fair daughter traipsing around town on Heloise Chancey's arm. Hasn't Hatterleigh mentioned time and again that I need to have a chaperone? And the baby. I think I'd quite like having the pink, chubby creature in the house. Oh, how that'll show all those bloody bastards.

"What are you grinning about under there?" asks Amah, her voice suspicious.

I sit up, purposefully pushing the covers from my knees. "I've decided what is best for Eleanor," I announce.

She puts her hands on her hips. "And what is that, Heloise?"

"She will stay with me. She will be my companion and we will hire a nursemaid to look after the child."

Amah's silent for a few moments, her mouth agape. "Have you finally lost all your sense, girl?" she gasps.

I don't know what's twisted her garter. I know she's fond of Eleanor and I'd been sure she would agree whole-heartedly with my plan. "But it's a perfect plan, Amah. Can't you see?"

"You're thinking of the baby, aren't you? You think it will be all sweetness and joy to have the little beast in the house."

I plonk myself down in front of the dresser mirror and tug the brush through my tangled hair. "And what of that? Poor Eleanor will not be able to keep the child any other way, Amah."

"And what if you grow tired of her company?"

I cock my head to the side, considering. "If that time comes I'll think of something else, no doubt."

"She's not a pet monkey to bandy around, Heloise," Amah says, her tone abrupt. "What are you going to do? Pass her on to a friend when you become tired of her like you did with the parrot Sir Winsome brought you from the Americas?"

I purse my lips together and glare at her. Amah's always known just how to sting me like a noisome mosquito.

"Thankfully, this is my household, so I may do exactly as I please." I have the satisfaction of seeing Amah's mouth twist in anger.

Bundle opens the front door just as my carriage arrives. The pair of chestnut horses toss their heads against the steady trickle of the rain. A whiff of earthy peat rises from the pavers as I stand in the doorway, waiting for Amah to fix her black hat and veil over her head.

"I don't know why you persevere with the veil, Amah," I say. I watch as the older woman pulls black gloves over her hands and a black cape around her shoulders. "You look like a villainous, black moth."

"If you were stared at as much as I am," she replies, "for all the *wrong* reasons, you too would find solace behind cover."

We lift our skirts and trip across the neat path and with Taff's help, climb into the carriage. The journey back to Waterloo isn't too arduous since it's the middle of the morning. The houses become decreasingly elegant the further we travel.

"You have not changed your mind about Eleanor?" asks Amah. She doesn't turn to face me but rather stares out her side window as she speaks.

"No. No, I haven't." I too gaze out my own window at the buildings, coaches and people we rumble pass. I'm still miffed with her, so I can't admit that since her words of warning I've experienced doubts about my plan. But I honestly can't think of anything else I can do with Eleanor.

The roads have turned to mud from the incessant rain so I start to place pattens over my kid shoes. The carriage bumps its way along Frazier Street and just as it pulls into the side of the road, Chat hurtles out through the front door of my Waterloo abode. His face is the colour of curd and his mouth hangs open in a distressed maw. He stumbles down the path, grasping unsteadily at bushes and the fence. He glances at the carriage but I don't think he recognises me, and then he runs off down the street.

"What's happening here?" I cast the pattens to the floor of the carriage and leap to the wet ground before Taff can help me alight. I hurry through deep puddles of water, drenching both my shoes and the hem of my gown in the process. The front door is ajar.

The house feels as cold and barren as that first night I'd arrived. No warmth from the fireplaces, no aroma of tea or cookery. Dread tickles down my backbone and I pause in the hallway.

"Check the kitchen, Heloise," whispers Amah, from behind. "I will check upstairs."

Taff and I rush into the kitchen. Upon the table is a loaf of bread, the knife sticking out from it awkwardly, where it's been left, mid-slice. One of two teacups is upset, the dark liquid spilt across the table cloth. The fire is out in the blackened range, and dirty water and plates fill the sink. I push a chair aside and sprawled across the floor, behind the kitchen table, lies Agnes. Blood, as sticky and rich as toffee, mats her hair. We both crouch over her body, but even before Taff presses his ear to her chest and then shakes his head slowly, I know from the chalkiness of the girl's skin and the blue tinge around her mouth that she's dead.

I pinch at my bottom lip, aghast, and then spring up so quickly my head spins for a moment. "Eleanor."

I hurry up the stairs and hear a short moan from the bedroom. At first I'm glad for the noise because it means Eleanor is alive, but then, bile rising in my stomach, I realise the moan comes from Amah.

"Amah, Amah," I call. My voice is hoarse. "What's happened?"

Amah tries to bar my way at the bedroom door. "No, Heloise, no. You must not see her."

But I'm taller than her. Peering over her head, I can see Eleanor's body laid out across the bed. I push Amah aside and slowly approach what is left of my young ward.

Eleanor's face is so waxen it appears to be a mask of her true self, except for the marks of faint bruising around her mouth. A rosy blush no longer tinges her cheeks, and her bloodless lips are barely discernible against the glaucous pallor of her skin. There are rags twisted through some of her hair but she will never see the ringlets unfold. Her tiny body is hidden beneath the white sheet which is pulled up to her chin, but at the tips of the slight mounds that were her breasts, crimson blood is etched into the fabric, the blood's stain accentuating its weave.

I can't breathe. My fingers pluck at my bodice, trying to loosen it. Amah mutters in a foreign language behind me. I lean over the girl's body and lift the sheet near the top of her thighs to reveal a pool of blood under her pelvis, resinous rivulets seeping down the side of the mattress. My knees give way.

I squeeze my head with strong, hurtful fingertips as if I can purge the ghastly image from my mind. "Horrible. Horrible." The intimate stench of blood and another, almost familiar, sweet smell, makes me gag. Amah grips me by the upper arm and yanks me to my feet.

We stagger to the landing, and I take in two long breaths and sink down upon the top step. Taff starts up the staircase but I shake my head. "Just fetch the police, Taff. Go now."

I press the heels of my hands into my eye sockets until it's too painful. Poor, poor Eleanor. I know I'll never be able to erase the image of the girl's mutilated body from my mind, and nausea fills my mouth with saliva, and my breakfast eggs roil in my stomach.

"That boy couldn't have done this, could he?" asks Amah.

"Of course not," I say, my voice choking. "The monster who's been cutting up prostitutes did this." I punch the stair railings with my fist until the skin on my knuckles split open.

"Stop that," says Amah, holding my wrist. "What will that achieve?"

"It'll stop me from screaming, at least." I allow myself one long groan. I then get to my feet, holding onto the bannister to steady myself. "I must find Chat. I must find out what he knows."

"But the police will be here soon, Heloise," says Amah, also standing. "What am I to tell them?"

"Tell them I will return shortly." I rub my forehead. "I'm not sure what to tell them yet. You can just act like you don't speak much English."

I run down the stairs and out onto the street, turning left towards the goat-shed the boy had shown me on our night of adventure. I crouch low and pull aside the ragged material that functions as a doorway. Chat is seated cross-legged on the ground, his grubby face blank. He glances at me and then looks away.

I shuffle into the small shed as far as my skirts will allow, but I can still feel the wind and rain brush against my hind quarters.

"Chat?"

He turns his head more to the side and doesn't answer. I reach over and gently take hold of his frozen, stubby fingers. "Chat? What happened?"

Still the boy says nothing.

"Won't you talk to me, Chat?"

The boy gives an almost imperceptible shake of his head.

"But you must, my dear. Aren't we friends, after all?"

"I don' wanna talk 'bout it," he mumbles. His bottom lip trembles.

We sit silently for a minute, until I finally say, "What did you see, Chat? Please tell me. You might be able to help."

"I seen her dead on your kitchin floor. She 'ad blood on 'er 'ead."

"Did you see anything else?"

"Nah. I scarpered when I seen 'er. You saw me."

"Did you see who did it, Chat? Who killed her?" I hope, desperately, that he can identify the girls' attacker. But Chat just shakes his head again.

"I didn' see nuthin," he says. "'cept that chargirl of yors dead on the floor."

"But what made you enter my house?"

"The door was open, wasn' it?" he answers. He stares down at his knee and picks at a dry scab until a dot of blood appears. "I wondered why your front door was wide open, so's I went and called fer you but got no answer."

"So you went in?"

He nods. "Wish I 'ad'nt now." He scowls. "You probably think I wanted to nab yer stuff, but I didn'. I wouldn' nab from you. I was just checkin'.'"

I pat him on shoulder. "I know, Chat. I know." I watch him and then say, "You're a brave boy, Chat."

He straightens his skinny shoulders. "Well, it's not the first dead body I seen, is it? There's always a dead 'orse or dog by the side of the road. Sometimes I've even seen dirty, old codgers lyin' dead for anyone to sees." He shrugs and says, loudly, "I was just shook up, is all, when I seen 'er lying dead in your 'ouse. There was so much blood on 'er 'ead." His eyes dim again.

"I wasn't at home all last evening, so I don't have any idea what happened. You didn't notice anyone going into or out of my house?"

He thinks for a moment. "Nah. It was a quiet night. My da' left before dawn to beg for work at the tannery, and the only thing I saw was a cart go past. Nothing else."

"What sort of cart, Chat? Was it coming from the direction of my house?"

"Yes. It was a 'orse an' cart like those at the markets."

"Did you see who drove it?"

"Nah. A man, though."

It's not much to go on.

"But I seen a man yesterday walking up and down the street, staring at your 'ouse."

"Really? What did he look like?"

"Skinny. Dressed like a toff. Looks like the vicar what gives us free food late at night if he gets to feel your ballocks at the same time. But this toff 'ad bigger ears."

Anger tightens my chest. Amah was right. What the hell was Mr Priestly doing here the day before? "Is that right?"

Chat nods. "That's all I seen out of the or'inary."

"Well, like I said, you're very brave."

His eyes are still bright with distress, but there's a sternness about his mouth.

"You do have a lot to deal with, don't you? Do you ever cry, Chat?" I ask.

"Nah," he says. With his thumb he smears the smudge of blood from the scab into his skin. "What's the use?"

Li Leen

As I sit in this desolate house waiting for Heloise's return, I realise the heaviness of sorrow I feel for poor, dead Eleanor is half borrowed from the recollection of another's death.

I woke well before dawn on that terrible day, when the evening buds of the sedap malam *flowers were most fragrant. I was still young then, still foolish. I sat at the kitchen table and helped myself to a bowl of sweetened black rice, adding coconut milk for its saltiness. I had eaten most of it when my mother's maid ran into the kitchen, fell to the floor, and wrapped her arms around my legs.*

"She is dead. She is dead," she wailed.

Mother had placed her Chinese gods in a circle on the floor and had hanged herself so that they were watching over her. I vomited up all the black porridge, a torrent of sorrow and regret and vileness. I gagged on my sobs, and my eyes grew so swollen I couldn't see for days. My mother, my mother, had left me behind. She had written me a short note. I am sorry, daughter. The shame is too great. The shame of what? I did not know what she meant.

After that I moved into Mother's room, and I didn't bathe and rarely ate, just as Mother had behaved in her last few weeks. I hoped her meaning would become clearer to me if I lived like her. But as I watched myself in the mirror I realised I was a half white-ghost, and I wasn't sure if her gods, still gathered around her tiny shrine, would respond to me. Her maid brushed my hair, just as she had brushed Mother's hair, and whispered in my ear of devils and ghosts and vengeance. I was too numb to listen, too weak to respond.

Chapter Eighteen

When I get back to the Frazier Street house there are uniformed police in the garden, in the living areas and upon the stairs leading to the bedroom. I find Amah seated in the sitting room, a monstrously tall constable standing to attention close by.

"He's guarding me – he's making sure I don't escape," she says, with that twist of her mouth. "Your policeman friend thinks I am the best suspect so far."

"How foolish." I reply.

Bill enters the room. I'm relieved to see him. "Do you really imagine that my maid had something to do with this... butchery?"

He takes me by the elbow and draws me to a quiet part of the hallway where we can't be overheard. He holds me by the upper arms and shakes me slightly.

"Where were you last night?" he asks. His face is rigid with anxiety.

"I went to the opera. I didn't return here, I stayed at home."

He pulls me into a quick, tight embrace, and then holds me at arm's length again. "Do you realise that if you were here you could have been murdered just as these two poor women have been?"

I stare into his bloodshot eyes. It hadn't yet occurred to me that I'd been at such risk too. I flinch at the thought of that sharp blade which had gone to work on Eleanor.

"And what of that heathen servant of yours? Where was she last night?"

I shake my head to clear it. "Don't be ridiculous, Bill. She was with me, anyway."

"All night?"

I'm anxious, can't keep the annoyance out of my voice. "No, of course not. I was at the opera, and when I returned home, she slept in her own quarters. But whatever you're suggesting, it's ridiculous. Amah did not sneak out in the middle of the night to murder these poor women."

He crosses his arms. "Well, I'm not so sure."

"You're wasting your time." I press my fingers to my temples. "Let me think." What was it I wanted to tell Bill the night before? My mind feels spongy, my thoughts skittling out of reach. Something about Henry? "Where's Henry? Mordaunt?"

"We still have Henry locked up, but we never really arrested the doctor. He was free to leave last night."

I stare at him, aghast. Free? "Then he has done this."

"That's a possibility."

"But why else was Henry at Mordaunt's so often? They're obviously in partnership."

"Well, Henry says it was just to clear up a case of the clap."

"Can't you see that's just a cover up?"

Before he can answer, a tilbury, drawn by two horses snorting with exertion, creaks to a halt outside the house. Arranged across the whole length of the bench seat, arrayed in festoons of velvet the shade of moss, is Madame Silvestre.

"Get me 'Eloise," she shrieks at a constable. "Where is that dratted woman?"

I snatch up a parasol and hurry to the carriage, Bill on my heels.

"What are you doing here, Mildred?"

"What 'as 'appened 'ere? Quick. You must tell me." Silvestre's neck and face are flushed puce, and as she gasps out the words, her bulbous bosom heaves. "What 'as 'appened to Agnes?"

As I hesitate over an answer, Bill steps forward. "How do you know something has happened to Agnes, madam?"

She sniffs in anger and her eyes become as hard as cold, glass marbles. "You 'ave 'alf the constabulary 'ere, and you ask me 'ow I know something is amiss? Are you simple? You'll 'ave 'alf the neighbourhood 'ere soon wanting to know what's 'appened."

Even as we speak, a crowd of people gather along the road. Women wander out from their homes, children in tow, and labourers and clerks stop on their way to work to peer in at the commotion. They stare at us curiously, and crane their necks over and around each other the better to see the house and the attendant police.

A young constable runs out from the house and calls for Bill. The sergeant seems loath to leave us but, on being called upon again, reluctantly leaves.

"Well, 'Eloise, what 'appened?"

I grip the side of the tilbury as I look into the madam's face. "I'm sorry, Mildred, but she's dead," I say quietly, so that only she can hear me. "She was hit on the head."

"Do the police know why?"

I glance at the people who hover close by. "There was another girl murdered here too." I say, keeping my voice low. "She was butchered like the others." I watch Silvestre's face closely for her reaction. When I'd originally asked her about the gruesome murders of prostitutes in the area, she'd laughed it off, but I find it puzzling that a woman of the madam's stature in the world of prostitution did not know what was happening in her own vicinity.

Mme Silvestre's fat face is expressionless. The high colour slowly drains from her cheeks and throat. "Their lives were taken by the same person 'oo murdered the others?"

"Yes." I fold the parasol down as the rain has petered out.

She relaxes against the back of the seat. "Therefore the police must know that 'Enry could not possibly have killed them as 'e spent all last evening and today safely in their gaol." A satisfied smile settles on her face. "Which means the police must now know 'e could not 'ave killed the others either."

An enterprising costermonger drums his pot of eel soup as he wheels his cart through the watching throng.

Silvestre sits forward again, peering over my shoulder. She says, over the din of the costermonger's call, "It looks like they've finally nicked the real culprit. I'm not surprised either. Dirty chink."

I spin around. Three uniformed constables march a shackled Amah along the front path to a waiting police buggy. My legs weaken and I stumble across the cobblestones towards her. "What's happening?"

The crowd jostle closer and murmur 'yeller' and 'coloured'. Amah gives me a telling look and, the chains of the shackles rattling, she draws the black veil over her face. I reach for her, but Bill stands between us.

"She had a switchblade on her," he says, in a low voice. "It was secreted away in a pocket of her bodice."

"But you're mad." I frown up into the sergeant's stern face. "She didn't use it to murder these women. Amah uses it to slice fruit or to cut off loose thread. She would never hurt someone with it."

"Until we've examined it carefully, and interviewed her, she must stay in our custody."

"Well, I must accompany her to the police station," I answer, pushing forward towards Amah.

"That will not be necessary, Heloise," he says, holding me back by the arm.

The constable who's leading Amah opens the door of the police buggy and as Amah lifts her skirt to climb in, a fresh, foul wad of manure plumps against her chest. A lanky boy with boils spotted across his chin and the filthy evidence smeared across his hands whoops with delight. Some of the crowd noisily approve and a squat woman with greasy wisps of hair falling from her bonnet picks an egg from her basket and prepares to pelt it.

For a short moment I'm frozen in shock. Then a fierce, blind rage takes over. I pitch my parasol at the boy, clocking him on the forehead with the handle. I fly at the woman, but Bill catches hold of me around the waist and holds me at bay. "You bitch," I holler, clawing at Bill's hands to free myself. I manage to swing my leg forward, kicking the woman's basket to the ground, where the eggs smash upon the muddy cobblestones. In amongst all this commotion the constables bustle Amah into the waiting buggy and Bill drags me into the house where he firmly pushes me down onto a chair in the sitting room.

"You must calm yourself, madam."

I struggle to get back on my feet, the weight of my wet skirts and petticoats slowing me down. "You should be out there arresting those bastards who assaulted my maid," I shout.

"If that were the case, I should need to haul you down to the station too, for attacking bystanders."

I collapse back against the chair's cushions and fold my arms. I glare at the empty fireplace.

He waits a few moments and then says, "You have a fine throw, Heloise. Great precision. You could have taken the lad's eye out if you'd tried a little harder." He crouches down in front of me, and tugs my skirt until I shift my gaze to his face. "And that kick... Such a pretty fighter belongs down at the London Boxing Club." He's smiling at me now.

But I'm too anxious to smile back. I know he's trying to placate me, and I realise it's in my best interests – in Amah's best interests – if I calm down, if I charm him again. I lean forward and grasp his lapels. "Can't you see how ridiculous it is to suspect my maid of these murders?"

Bill sits back on his haunches. "Heloise, we have to investigate her just as we would any other suspicious character."

"But these murders are obviously connected to the others." Eleanor's wounds flash to mind. I press my eyes shut. "Obviously."

"That hasn't been confirmed yet. And what of Henry then? Are we to set him free? For if this is the work of the man mutilating prostitutes, then obviously he is innocent for he's been locked up all night."

He's right. I cover my eyes with the heels of my hand, my fingers kneading at my hairline.

"Inspector Kelley will be here soon with the doctor," Bill continues. His voice is kind. "I must go to the morgue now and make sure they are prepared, but I'm afraid you will need to stay here so the Inspector can have a word with you about Eleanor."

"But if Eleanor has been murdered just as the other women were, then it couldn't have been Amah who murdered them."

"Are you so sure, Heloise?"

"Of course I am. What reason would she have, anyway, to butcher these poor girls?"

"If I provide you with the dates of the other murders, do you think you can vouch for her movements? Provide evidence of some sort."

"Of course. I'm sure of it." I swallow as he leaves the room. I'm not sure at all, but I'll have to try.

I push myself into my seat. There's no-where to go. Poor Agnes' body is still in the kitchen, and what's left of Eleanor – my heart skips a beat – still lies above. I stroke the cool glass of the cranberry pendant Bill had given me. How nice it would be to sniff some of its relaxing elixir of opium and forget the ghastliness of the morning. I could lie down and fall asleep, oblivious to the misery that's ready to engulf me. Better yet, I could return to Mayfair and hide away in the folds of my bedcovers with the rosy bottle of snuff clutched to my nose. But I can't do that. It would leave me too bleary to find a way out of this mess. I close my eyes, wishing the fire was alight to dry my cold, damp skirts.

"What are we to do'm, Miss Heloise?" Taff asks from the doorway.

"I don't know." I reply, truthfully.

I stride across the room and fill two glasses to the brim with madeira. "Here, take one," I say, holding a glass towards Taff. I throw my own wine back in one swallow and, clinking the decanter noisily against the wineglass so that a crack slithers down its side, I fill my glass again. This too I gulp down, until I feel the familiar warmth in my chest and my stomach's initial recoil. I hold the decanter out to Taff who sweeps his half-finished drink away, placing it on the low table.

"It's no help to Amah if we sit'm here and get corned, Miss Heloise," he says, softly.

I rub my face. "You're right." I lean both hands on the side-table and feel the wine quicken my senses. "It's so frustrating. I need to return home and find some way to prove Amah was not responsible for these deaths, yet I have to wait here for Inspector Kelley." I turn to the coachman. "You must follow Amah to the station and find out what's happening. Take the coach."

Taff nods and rushes from the room, leaving me at a loss for something to do. I fret over Amah's predicament for several minutes, pacing back and forth in the small, cramped room, until the unpleasant sensation of my soggy petticoats penetrates my anxious thoughts. Kneeling on the hearth, I arrange kindling in the fireplace and I'm just ready to light a heavy log when I hear the sound of a carriage and voices from the road. I run to the front window and, peeping past the muslin curtains, see Inspector Kelley alight from a coach. He's closely followed by an elderly man with grey whiskers, who wears a tweed cape and carries a plump, leather doctor's bag.

The two men greet the constable who guards the front door while another constable comes forward and guides them to the kitchen where Agnes' body remains. The Inspector exclaims and the doctor tuts. They are some time, murmuring between themselves. I pop my head around the sitting room doorway in the hope of hearing what they're saying, but encounter the stern gaze of the young constable on duty.

"When may I see the Inspector?" I ask with a friendly smile, to account for my curiosity.

"I'm not sure, ma'am," he says. I wait for more, but he continues to stare at me in a baleful manner.

I wait several more minutes before hearing voices in the hallway. The Inspector directs the constables to help the undertakers remove Agnes' body from the kitchen, and he and the doctor make their way up the stairs. As I stand by the doorway of the sitting room I remain unnoticed amongst the flurry of activity. There's a moment of quiet while the constables are in the kitchen assisting the undertakers when I hear the Inspector swear loudly from above. Revulsion rushes through me, and I want to cover my ears, my eyes, in the hope of blotting out the horror I know the Inspector is witnessing at this very moment.

The constables and undertakers march past with poor Agnes' body upon a stretcher. Her apron is draped over her head to conceal the wounds. She's anonymous, finished with. She will never again have to scrub the dolls' sheets, never be a doll herself. Whatever life she had before her has ended.

The hallway's clear, so I step forward. Peeping out the front door I spy the constables, gathered around the undertaker's carriage, smoking. I climb the stairs to the bedroom, moving slowly to minimise the creaking of the stairs and the rustle of my gown.

About three steps from the top I hear the Inspector ask, "But why on earth mutilate them in this way, Dr Featherby?"

"Well..." replies the doctor slowly, "well, there's been an interesting theory put forward lately by a set of physicians who believe that relieving women of a certain part of their sexual apparatus helps them become more whole – more rational – able to live fulfilling and sedate lives that hitherto had evaded them. Ever heard of the surgeon, Isaac Baker-Brown?"

"No."

"Have you ever heard of a clitoridectomy? Or, for that matter, of the woman's clitoris?"

"No," says the Inspector, sounding flummoxed.

The doctor makes a grunting noise. "Well, this Baker-Brown and his crony – Ivor, Isaiah, something like that – Xavier were taking 'em from women against their will. Looks almost like you have an imitator here. Except Baker-Brown and Xavier managed to keep their patients alive."

"Could one of them be causing these deaths?'

"No, that's not likely. Baker-Brown was discredited by the medical fraternity and I think he may have moved across the Atlantic to a more sympathetic audience. And Xavier hid himself in the wilds of Wales, then took his own life. The disgrace seemingly too much."

I'm so immersed in what the two men are discussing I fail to notice they've moved closer to the bedroom's doorway. Almost too late I realise that they are upon me, at which point I pretend to be hurrying up the stairs.

"Mrs Chancey," says Inspector Kelley, looking down at me in surprise. He's paler than the last time I'd met him, and he mops the back of his neck with a handkerchief. "I did not know you were still here."

"Oh, yes, Inspector, I have been waiting all this morning. Sgt Chapman informed me that you would need to have a word with me." I touch my brow. "I was just coming up to ask you if it would be alright to collect some of my belongings before I return home."

"Of course, of course," he answers, taking my elbow and guiding me back down the stairs. "But first let us go into the sitting room. You don't want to go into the bedroom with... er... the... right now."

We return to the cold sitting room.

"Terrible business, Mrs Chancey, terrible business," he says, wiping his handkerchief over his face. "It must have been quite a shock to find… er… her. Your cousin. In such a state." He peers at me with concern.

I take a seat on the chair that faces the doorway. "I've never seen anything so ghastly," I reply, honestly. I watch the doctor lead the constables and undertakers up the stairs.

"Sgt Chapman told me you were out last night?"

I drag my eyes from the other men back to the Inspector. "Yes. I returned to my home in Mayfair so that I could attend the opera. I only came back here this morning."

"And this foreign woman that Sgt Chapman has in custody? She is your maid?"

"Yes, that is correct. But she could not have murdered these girls. She was with me all evening." My voice rises with agitation. "When I return home later today I will find some way to prove she could not have been in the vicinity during any of the murders." I pause, for over the Inspector's shoulder I can see the men come out from the bedroom at the stop of the stairs. Between them they carry the stretcher down awkwardly, but this time the body is completely shrouded in a white sheet.

We both watch in silence as Eleanor is carried from sight.

I wonder what's to become of her small body, and when I'm going to have a chance to inform Sir Thomas of this disastrous outcome. How could I have left the poor girls alone? My heartbeat skips uncomfortably again. Maybe the police have already told Eleanor's family. My thoughts lack coherence as I gaze at the Inspector. "Sorry, what did you ask me?"

"What was it you needed to find in your room, Mrs Chancey?" he repeats.

"Only some personal belongings. Toiletries. Clothing." I draw my distracted thoughts back to the moment.

"Please," he gestures for me to follow him. "Come, we'll go together to fetch your things."

We trudge back up the stairs. I hesitate only a moment on the landing before entering the bedroom. My eyes rest on the bed, which is now stripped of all its bedding. The mattress, already soiled with bygone cloudy patches, carries a dark stain so large and deep it couldn't possibly be removed. I collect my brush and hair pins from the dresser, placing them in a case. My fingers are trembling. Gazing through the open doors of the wardrobe I survey the gowns within. I'll leave them behind. I never want to see them again, or remember this terrible place. But behind the dove-grey gown I catch a glimpse of fresh, pale blue, and pull out the taffeta gown Amah had given Eleanor. I slip it from its hanger. This I will take. I'll make sure Eleanor is dressed in it when... Or, at the very least, I'll keep it in memory of the girl.

I stoop to pick Eleanor's handkerchief from the floor when I remember Dr Mordaunt's diary. That I must retrieve. It will look very strange indeed if the police find it in my possession, in this room. I look on the bedside table and under the bed and behind the dressing table, but I can't find it.

"What are you searching for, Mrs Chancey?" asks Inspector Kelley.

"A book I was reading." I'm puzzled. "It does not seem to be here. Do you think one of your men might have moved it?"

He shakes his head. "No. They would not have moved anything without my express permission." He glances around the room. "Maybe you left it in the sitting room?"

I agree, and force a smile to my lips. Maybe Bill had removed it when he was inspecting Eleanor's body. "Yes. It is nothing. I'm sure it will turn up."

The Inspector escorts me to the front door. "Do you have a carriage, Mrs Chancey?"

"Yes, I do, but my coachman has taken it to the police station to hear word of my maid."

"I'll have someone find a cab for you," he says, before calling over one of the constables and giving the instruction. He turns back to me, taking a notebook from his pocket. "Mrs Chancey, do we have any way of contacting you if we have further questions?"

I think quickly. I consider giving him a false address but know it will be easy enough for the police to trace me eventually. I should've made up a fake name at the beginning of all this mess. What was one alias compared to another, after all? Cursing myself, I give over my Mayfair address to the Inspector and climb into the waiting cab.

Chapter Nineteen

My study is tucked behind the staircase in my Mayfair home. It was previously used as a lady's parlour by earlier residents and although I've kept the rustic green wallpaper, I replaced the pretty table, chairs and lace coverings with furniture more suited to an office. Against the furthest wall stands my desk next to a large glass-front cabinet, filled with books. My library includes novels, poetry and works of science suggested to me by past lovers and patrons who attend my evening soirees, but I also own tales of romance and murder, and one of my favourite books is the outdated *Newgate Calendar*. I just love its lurid illustrations.

The one concession to comfort in the room is a chaise longue by the sash windows and lying upon it, face down, is the book by Wollstonecraft I've been reading. It seems like months ago I last picked it up, but actually it's only been a matter of nine days or so. I open it and read from the page I've earmarked: *Taught from their infancy that beauty is woman's sceptre, the mind shapes itself to the body, and roaming round its gilt cage, only seeks to adorn its prison.* My eyes roam the rest of the paragraph, resting on words such as *insignificant, slavery, sensuality of man*. I struggle against seeing myself in these words, but recognise their truth too. But surely there's more to my life now?

I close the book and move to the filing cabinet. I know exactly what's to be found in each of the twenty-four, slender drawers. The bottom drawer to the right holds the deeds to my house in Brighton and a couple of annuities. Two of the top drawers hold my latest receipts for a range of goods, from my evening gowns to horse shoes, while the third top drawer houses bills still to be paid. The drawer third from the bottom contains intimate letters from lovers; letters that I still cherish when I'm feeling sentimental. The other type of intimate letters I've received over the years – the ones that I keep as insurance of one kind or another – are safely locked up in the bank.

I pick at my bottom lip for a moment, staring at the filing cabinet. What can I find here to help free Amah? I pull out the second drawer from the top right side. Within are my receipts for payments to the servants and a small ledger. Although there are amounts made out to the butler, the cook, the housemaids and the groomsmen, I know there will not be any formal receipt made out to Amah. I yank out the fifth and sixth drawers, where I keep my travel documents. I'd visited Paris for a sennight not five weeks ago. Of course Amah had travelled with me and if only I can find evidence for this, maybe I will prove that Amah did not have the opportunity to murder the earlier victims in Waterloo. But searching through my paperwork proves fruitless. Although I have travel documents in my own name, any tickets or rooms that Amah had occupied have been left anonymous.

I sink down onto my desk chair. I can't think of any other way to prove Amah was at home or abroad on the nights of the murders.

Is Amah in a cell at this very moment? Is she cold, thirsty? I pluck at my lip again until it hurts. Is she scared? That would be almost worse than anything else.

And is Amah allowed to keep her veil lowered, hiding her dark features? It's never been more evident to me why Amah likes to be invisible to the world of London, and that it is necessarily so.

My fingers clasp the familiar shape of the snuff bottle again. If only I could have a sniff. But as Taff had said, being delirious on the sofa is of no help to Amah. I take a cigarette from my purse and light it, drawing the smoke deep down into my chest. I flick the ash into the grate and draw in another, quick breath of smoke. Suddenly I know exactly what I'll have to do, and I have to stop wasting time wallowing around. I can't prove Amah's not the killer, therefore I'll have to prove that someone else is.

I think for a few more minutes, until the red tip of the cigarette burns my fingers. I toss its remnants into the fireplace. Pulling writing paper to me, I scrawl a note to Sir Thomas telling him the horrific news. My pen hovers above the paper, as I quell a surge of shame. Eleanor was in my care, and I'd let her down.

I call for Bundle and hand him the letter to send.

"Any word from Taff?" I ask. "Is he back yet with the carriage?"

"No, Mrs Chancey. No, I have heard nothing from him and the carriage has not yet returned. Shall I find you a cab?"

"Yes, thank you."

I fold Eleanor's blue dress into a large hatbox and, grabbing a parasol, shawl and my reticule I walk briskly out to the waiting cab. I direct the driver to take me to the hospital in Waterloo and, once there, bid him wait for me. I'm not sure if Bill is still at the morgue or back at the police station, but I don't want to miss him.

The undertaker's coach is still parked outside the building, and I peer gingerly down the morgue's sterile corridor, hoping I won't encounter the girls' bodies again. I catch sight of Mrs

Dawkins' familiar iron-grey curls and call out to her from the doorway.

The cleaner bustles over. "Mrs Chancey. Such a terrible business. Terrible." She folds her arms and shakes her head. "Terrible, it is. I'm sorry for your news."

"Yes, yes, it is terrible. Thank you." I offer the hat box to the older woman. "Mrs Dawkins, do you think you could make sure Eleanor Carter is dressed in this gown? I believe she admired it so."

"Of course, my dear. Of course." She pats my arm. "I'll make sure it's done, even if I have to do it myself."

"Thank you, I appreciate that. You haven't seen Sgt Chapman have you?"

Mrs Dawkins looks over her shoulder. "He's still in the back room with Mr Pike and those young 'uns." She shakes her head again, sadly. "He's worked so hard on this matter. I've never met such a diligent young man."

"Do you think I could have a word with him?"

"I'll go check for you."

I only wait a couple of minutes before Bill strides towards me. He beckons me outside, and we stand on the kerb by a coffee stand.

"What is it, Heloise?" he asks. He looks less exhausted than he had earlier that morning, and I sense a tremor of impatience in him. His pale eyes are especially cool. "The inspector released Henry from our custody a little while ago."

"I don't care about him. What of my maid?"

"I'm sorry, I have no news of her." He buys us each a cup of coffee. "Have you come with proof of her whereabouts on the nights of the murders?"

"No. No, unfortunately I could not find anything." I watch his eyebrows lift, as if he expects as much. I tamp down a frustrated desire to regale him with the unfairness of a maid's – a foreign maid's – lot. "But I have remembered two things that I need to discuss with you." I sip the tepid coffee which leaves a sour taste on my tongue. I throw the remaining coffee into the gutter and return the cup to the stallholder. "But first, tell me, did you take Dr Mordaunt's diary from my room in Frazier Street?"

He shakes his head. "No. I can't remember seeing it, as a matter of fact." He pulls his pocket watch out and glances at it. "I only have a moment, Heloise."

"What of Dr Blain?" I say, quickly, catching hold of his sleeve. "I've not told you of his visit to us yesterday. He seemed very taken with Eleanor, but in a very odd way."

"What do you mean?"

I can't tell him of my conversation with Blain the night before at the opera without compromising my own story, so I prevaricate. I remember Blain's actual words, though, and turn them to my use. "I almost think he was obsessed with the girl. Almost as if he would rather see her die than not be with him. He said as much." I realise, if the sergeant were to interview the doctor, Blain will inform him of my true character, but what is that in comparison to Amah's safety? He would have to know sooner or later, anyway, if he is to visit me in Mayfair. But that test is for another time.

His expression hardens as he watches me. "You really do consider yourself the little detective, don't you? But you must remember that I am the real detective. I'll have you know that I have already thought of our Dr Blain and questioned him not an hour past."

Ah. Now I see. Finally I can peer through those pale eyes into his mind. For I've seen this disdain before. This abhorrence that tightens the muscles around the mouth. The sense of betrayal that hums behind each word.

"And?"

"And he spent the whole evening at his aunt's house last night. Escorted her to the opera, I believe."

So, he won't reveal what he now knows of me. I wonder if that is for my benefit or for his own. I join in the game even as my chest burns with disappointment. "But he could have sneaked out from there, surely? In fact, it'd be a good cover for his story if it was thought he was at his aunt's house rather than in his own home near here, alone."

"Heloise, she lives in Marylebone. It would take him an age to get to Waterloo. He's hardly going to slip out in the middle of the night, do his dastardly deeds, and return there again."

"But that's exactly what you think Amah did," I argue.

He just shakes his head. "What was the other thing you wanted to discuss with me? I really must be getting back."

He turns from me. No fare-well, no crooked smile. I pull my shoulders back, bite down on my jaw. I have to keep my mind on Amah. And my other idea is almost more far-fetched than the one featuring Blain. But I'll bloody well investigate it on my own..

Chapter Twenty

Hopping down from the cab I pay the driver and watch as the carriage's large wheels rumble away. I pause for a moment in the middle of the road, and tap my foot against a cobblestone, thinking. I stare ahead at the pine-green door. My heart's racing and I take two deep breaths. I've wanted this confrontation for years – for so many years – but I shake my head abruptly. That is not why I'm here. I've come here on a new mission. A mission to find out who killed Eleanor and the other women.

The black, wrought iron gate creaks noisily as I push it open. I close it with a decisive clang, and march into Dr Mordaunt's office before my resolve flags. The bell above the doorway tinkles and the doctor's oily assistant looks up from his work.

"I'd like to see Dr Mordaunt please," I say, my voice haughty.

"Do you have an appointment, madam?" asks the assistant, his voice just as haughty.

"No, I don't."

"I will see when he is free." The assistant makes a great show of perusing his ledger.

I roll my eyes at his greasy pate. The door to the surgery is open, the room empty. But the doctor's office door's shut and I can't hear any murmurs or movement coming from in there.

I really want to search his office again. I need to find out if the notebook is back in his possession. If the diary is back in its hiding spot, then I can be sure that it was Mordaunt who'd taken it. Who else would have wanted to steal the diary? I can't think of anyone else. And I know that if he'd stolen back the diary, it also meant he'd murdered the girls.

But what if he's disposed of the notebook? What if he'd taken it home, not to his surgery?

Then I'll have to follow him. I'll have to ransack his home, and hope against hope that he hasn't destroyed it. I'll have to keep searching for clues against the man so that I can free Amah.

"I am afraid he was called away to a patient for the rest of the day," says the assistant. The sincerity of his tone is unconvincing. "He will not be returning here until tomorrow morning."

"That is a pity." I pull a face of disappointment. "I will return another time."

"You don't want to make an appointment?"

"I will take my chances, thank you."

Returning to the cul-de-sac, I make my way to the next corner. I wait by the same fence I'd stood by last time, but after a short while I feel conspicuous. The street's busy and men ogle me as they pass. Keeping a watch on the mouth of the cul-de-sac, I stroll along the road, returning when I judge it too far to see when the assistant makes his way home. This I continue with for an hour and a half, stopping only to drink a ginger-beer and avoid the cold drizzle that dogs my surveillance. Sighing with the tedium, I've almost come to the stage of making excuses for myself to leave, when the assistant walks towards me from the doctor's street. I duck behind a water-cart, pretending to scrape mud from my soaked shoes to keep my head averted until he passes by. I hesitate until he walks on down the street and turns left near the cross-roads.

Stepping swiftly across to the doctor's street my pace drops to a stroll when I notice a young mother and her baby standing upon a neighbouring doorstep watching me curiously. Smiling sweetly, I greet them, and continue to amble to the end of the cul-de-sac. I wonder what the hell I'm to do when, luckily, the woman re-enters her narrow abode.

I go to work on the doctor's front door lock and enter as easily as I had the time before. Tiptoeing into his office, I close the door and lean my back against it. I must be very careful. If I'm to find the diary and the doctor suspects as much, he will move or destroy it. It's imperative that if I find it, the diary remains in the same place so that once I've informed the police, they can return and discover it for themselves. Surely, once I explain the timing of its disappearance from the Waterloo house to Bill, he too will see that Dr Mordaunt must have killed the girls.

I rifle through the drawers of his desk, careful to replace objects exactly where they are. I glance over the books on his bookshelf and flip through the papers in his filing cabinet but cannot find the diary.

This time, being so focused on my investigation, I don't hear the bell's tinkle from above the entrance.

Dr Mordaunt swings the office door open. He holds a half-empty bottle of whisky to his mouth. Liquid dribbles from his bottom lip when he sees me.

I'm startled, but only for a moment. My dislike for him is so great I can't prevent a sneer from lifting my lip.

"A bit early in the day for a doctor to drink, isn't it?" I ask. "Although I do recall that you were at your most active in the middle of the night."

"What the hell do you want?" He sets the bottle down on the desk.

I'm by the filing cabinet and the doctor's between me and the door. I know there'll be no fudging my way out this time. My hand snakes down into my reticule.

"I came here to discuss your diary." I note with satisfaction how his hard eyes widen. "You know – a black, leather notebook. Red ribbon."

"So you took it, you little bitch." He lurches towards me, his wide hands stretched towards my neck.

I yank out my handgun and level it at his chest. He halts and stares at it for a few moments then gives a derisive snort. He slumps down at his desk and takes a mouthful of his whisky.

"Well?" he says, eventually. "What do you want to discuss?"

"I want to know where the diary is."

"What do you mean? I thought you had it," he says, looking up at me.

"I did have it. But it went missing last night and I think you took it."

"How the hell was I supposed to know where you were with my diary? I don't even know who you damn well are," he shouts. "Yes, I guessed it was you who took it after I caught you in here last time, but I certainly didn't know how to trace you. In fact, I've been waiting for your return." He laughs humourlessly, and takes another swig from his bottle. "Waiting. Waiting." He turns a nasty face to me. "And here you are, as expected."

I lean against the hard edge of the cabinet, my gun still trained on him.

"What do you mean you were waiting for me to return?"

"Well, I assume you read the thing."

"I glanced through it enough to see it held detailed records of your... more prohibited activities."

He gulps from his bottle. "And now you've lost the notebook too. You've lost your nice little money-earner. Well I'm not sorry for it."

"Money-earner?" It takes me a moment to realise what he means. "I wasn't going to blackmail you with it. Why would I try to extort money from you?"

"Well, what the hell did you take it for?" He pounds the desk with the flat of his hand. "What the bloody hell did you take it for?"

"I wanted to know what you were up to." I manage to keep my voice and gun steady.

"And what did the diary tell you?"

"It told me you were still doing your special favours for the women in the area."

His eyes are fixed upon me. "But you're not here to blackmail me?"

"No. I wanted to show the police that diary."

"What for? There's nothing actually incriminating in there. Just a list of former patients."

"Who you've been following," I point out. "That's pretty sinister in itself."

He shrugs. "What of it?"

"I'm going to prove to the police that you were behind the deaths of local prostitutes."

"What deaths? You don't mean..." He frowns at me, starting up from his chair. "The murders written up in the newspapers?"

I nudge the gun in his direction. "Yes. I mean the girls you've been slicing up and leaving to bleed out."

He stares at me through his thick glasses, his mouth ajar.

"I don't know what you think I've done," he says, eventually.

"I think you weren't satisfied with scraping babies out of girls like –" I almost say 'me', but clamp my mouth down on the word, "– like the street girls and the parlour girls. I think you went one step further and ensured they'd never bear children again. And you snipped off their bits that made it bearable to be grinded by all you bastards. But being the incompetent culley you are, the poor women bled to death."

"You're mad," he says. "Hysterical. I should have you committed."

Always an arsehole's ultimate threat, that one. Oh, I've detested and feared this man for so long. Suddenly, my hatred for him is almost blinding. "You really don't recognise me, do you?"

"I told you last time that you looked familiar, but a lot of women come through my doors." He looks me up and down. "You are covered in fine clothes and costly jewels now, but you girls never quite lose the shine of your former life." He clicks his tongue in exasperation. "What do you expect? I see too many of your type."

"But do you leave all of them barren, like you left me? Do you scour them out so that they lie in a fever for days, only to waken to a life of never being able to conceive a child again?"

"That's always a risk," he says.

"You should have told me."

"And what? You would have kept the baby? Where? How? In the backstreet brothel where you worked day and night on your back?"

I glare at him, but my fury won't allow the tears that are scorching my chest and burning my eyelids to surface. I'm speechless, as both anguish and the acceptance of the truth of his words grapple inside me. What indeed would I have done with the child, had I had her? What choices did I have then? Not many at all, and not one of them enticing. I was so young, and alone, and I'd had the abortion as routinely as the other girls did. But that didn't mean I didn't hope for a future of abundance and stability and love and babies. Scrapes were supposed to be temporary, not for life. I remember Amah's words to me when I announced I'd keep Eleanor and her baby; how that old harridan knows me so well. Amah had immediately guessed that I wanted a child in my household. That I wanted to feel the baby's fat fist grasp my finger. That I wanted to cuddle her when she was asleep. But maybe Amah was right. I'd be bored with it soon enough. And it's never to be, anyway.

"And do you know what else I think?" I say to Mordaunt, finally. "I think one of your last entries in the notebook was about the young woman who was the latest victim."

There's a flash of hesitation in his eyes. "What woman?"

"The one in the photograph I showed you last time. Eleanor Carter. I'm sure you did know her, even though you denied it when we spoke."

"Latest victim?"

"Yes. She was murdered last night." There's surprise on the doctor's pugnacious features, and I feel a flicker of doubt. "But you knew that already."

Mordaunt ignores me. He lifts the bottle of whisky to his mouth but pauses over it. "The poor young lady."

"So you did know her?"

He drops the bottle to the desk again with a clunk. "Yes. Mind you, I did not know her as Eleanor Carter. She was introduced to me as Ellen Campbell."

"How did you come to meet her?"

"She came to me about five or six weeks ago. She was in trouble."

"But you didn't..."

Mordaunt shakes his head. "No, not at the time. She was extremely agitated. There was nothing I could do then, but they were supposed to return when she was in a calmer frame of mind." His words are becoming slurred and he rests his forehead in his hand.

"I wondered when I read an entry about a fair, young lady if it could be about Eleanor. Or the girl you knew of as Ellen. Why did you follow her?"

He waves his hand briefly before resting on it again. His gaze is unfocused. "As you can imagine, many of my patients stay... anonymous. Which was fine by me, I assure you." He takes one last drink from his bottle of whisky, and tosses the bottle into the second drawer of the desk where it rattles against other empty bottles. "But then a charming fellow a few years back blackmailed me. I'd performed a procedure on his wife – if we can call her that – and he made it clear to me that he was willing to disclose to the police what I had done." He looks up at me. "But for a tenner, he'd shut his mouth and move away."

"And you paid him?"

"Of course. I might be a – what did you call me? – an incompetent culley, but that's how I make my living, after all. However, you have to keep in mind that what he was willing to report to the police endangered his own position too. It was just as illegal for his woman to have the procedure as it is for me to perform it. But I didn't know who he was, or who his woman was for that matter, or else I could have turned the tables on him and reported them to the police for soliciting an abortion from me." His mouth slackens. "Therefore, in order to cover myself from blackmail, I make sure I know exactly who I operate on. And if I'm suspicious, I get Ignatius to follow them to find out their true circumstances. You know? My assistant?" I think of the doctor's obnoxious clerk. "Hence the diary."

"So you have power over them?"

He shrugs again. "Yes. But I don't use it."

I run my eyes over him: his bulky shoulders and large, meaty hands, the hard mouth wet from alcohol.

"I don't know if I believe you."

"It doesn't matter what you believe because you don't have the notebook anymore," he jeers. "And if she really was murdered last night, then I couldn't have done it. I was attending an old patient of mine in Newington. I was with him most of the night." He grabs paper and, spilling ink as he scrawls upon it, says, "I'll write down the name and his direction so that you and your precious police can verify my whereabouts."

He holds out the scrap of paper and I snatch it from his hand. I keep the gun on him as I edge my way to the door.

He watches me from below his thick eyebrows as I back out of the room. "You blasted girls. You blasted girls." He bends forward and grips his head in his hands once more. "You come hollering at me when you get in trouble and then you treat me like the devil when it's over." He lifts his head and jabs a finger at me. "Where would you all be if I hadn't helped you out? Where? It's bloody dangerous for me to go on, you know. It's only a matter of time before a blasted moralist reports me to the police. And I can assure you I don't do it for the measly money I get out of it either."

"Well, what do you do it for?" I stop in the doorway, curious despite myself.

The doctor leans back in his chair and sighs. I can smell the alcohol on his breath from where I stand.

"It's just part of my life now. I'm used to it." He gives a drunken shrug and almost topples from his chair. "And what would the girls do if I didn't operate on them or give them medicine? They're a lot safer with me, I can assure you, than with the old sow in the alleys who pierces them with a rusty knife."

I don't want to feel sympathy for this man. I drop my gaze and, teasing the cords apart of my reticule, I put away my gun. My voice is level when I speak.

"You said 'they'. When you were talking about Eleanor, you said 'they' were supposed to return. Who was she with?"

"He said he was her husband."

There's derision in his voice. "You didn't believe him?"

Mordaunt shakes his head.

Who'd brought poor Eleanor to this place for an abortion. Was it her father, as I'd suspected? Or Eleanor's music master?

"Did he have a French accent?"

Again the doctor shakes his head. "No, he spoke his English as well as you or me," he says. "Better, in fact."

"Do you think he could have been related to her? Her father perhaps?"

He frowns, concentrating. "No, I'm almost sure he was not, although he was old enough to be. Ignatius reported that they didn't reside together, for when he followed them, the gentleman escorted Miss Carter to a house near Russell Square after which he went on to another home in Goodge Street. Ignatius found out from a newsvendor that he lives there with his wife and five children."

"What did this older gentleman look like?"

The doctor leans his head back against the chair-back and closes his eyes. "Thin prig of a man. Big ears."

Li Leen

Finally, hollowed, I decided to bathe. Mother had been dead for exactly twelve days when I peeled aside the stubborn frog buttons of my smock and lay it beside the mandi. *I washed with the cold water, shivering with each splash and when I returned to my mother's room and Mother's maid brought me a clean smock I told her I would not wear it. "Fetch me a sarong. A sarong like the village girls wear. I do not want to answer to your Chinese gods anymore. Bring me a sarong and I'll be a local girl." The maid laughed at me at first, and then grew impatient, but in the end she had to do what I asked. She brought me a brown sarong, made of the plainest weave and a kebaya for my bodice, although the fabric was so sheer my dark nipples and the curve of my breasts whispered against the silk. I sat slumped on the side of the bed when my stepfather entered the room and sat by my side, his bulbous weight pressing the mattress down so that I leaned in towards him. I hadn't seen him in days. Since before my mother passed.*

"What is this I hear? You won't leave your room?" he asked.

I didn't answer.

"You won't come out into the world, so I have to come to you," he persisted.

Still I said nothing. I had nothing to say.

"Beloved, are you afraid of what will happen to you now that your mother has died?" he asked, his toad face serious, the saggy bags under his

eyes drooping. He waited a minute then continued. "I have a plan. Stay with me, my little fox-fairy. You can take your mother's place in the house. Won't that be the best way?"

He reached across and slipped his hand through the opening in my kebaya and drew his fingertips slowly across my bare midriff. It felt as though his fingertips had burnt a trail across my skin. I was surprised they didn't leave a welt in their wake.

Chapter Twenty-One

I peel off my soiled gown and petticoats and kick them aside. The warmth from the fireplace is a comforting relief after such a cold, long day. For once I ignore the sheer, silk peignoirs I would normally drape around myself and pull on a cosy, velvet dressing-gown, dusky grey with swansdown ruffles. I make my way to the drawing room on the floor below and pour myself a scotch.

"Mrs Chancey," says Bundle, from the doorway. "Monsieur Agneau would like to know if you are in need of supper."

"Thank Agneau for me." I take a sip of my drink. It's almost painful how the heat of the alcohol relaxes the muscles in my shoulders. "And let him know a light soup would be welcome." Really, I can't stomach a thing but I know the cook must be impatient to create a menu after so many days idle.

"Also, a note arrived for you not long ago from Sir Thomas," says Bundle as he leaves the room. "I left it on your desk."

I hurry to my desk and snatch up the missive, tearing it open at the edges.

My Dear Mrs Chancey,
What truly distressing news you conveyed to me earlier this sad day.
I have since had the difficult task communicating between the police

*and poor Miss Carter's father. I have not time to go into much detail
here, but please know that due to the police's involvement in this case,
Mr Carter does not believe it is necessary to prolong your services. I
am truly sorry you had to be a part of this tragic situation. I blame
myself for involving you in a man's business. I really do pray that this
violent event has not forever damaged your womanly, delicate senses.
I will call upon you as soon as I am able.
Yours Sincerely,
T.A.*

I read through Sir Thomas' letter, and I take a large gulp of
scotch, and then another. I've truly bungled this affair and
sweet, young Eleanor has lost her life in the bargain. Sitting
down at my desk, I read the note over and over again. Sir
Thomas really is a fool. I've seen more horrifying things in my
short life than he would ever know, although I have to admit
the sight of Eleanor's gouged body was one of the worst. I
frown over the letter once more then crumple it into a ball.

I tap my fingernail on the desktop and swing lightly, to and
fro, on the swivel chair. How is it I've always had to follow the
directions of the men in my life? Have I accumulated all this
wealth and security for nothing? Certainly the pleasure's gone
from this detecting game, but I'm not ready to stop just because
Sir Thomas and Eleanor's father have ordered it so. Just because
Bill has turned his back on me. I feel a dip of regret that I hadn't
had the chance to ease him into my life, but what can I do?

And what of Amah? I won't be left at home, wringing my
hands and sniffing smelling-salts, while I can help Amah. I'll keep
searching for the murderer. I know I have as good a chance to
catch him as any of the others. And when I do – I curl my fingers
into a fist until my fingernails leave crescent marks in my palm

– I'm going to shoot a big, deep hole into the bastard, in a very manly fashion.

Pulling open the side drawer I take out a wad of paper and dip my pen in ink. The pen hovers over the page and a drop of the ink plops onto its surface.

For me, before I'd found Eleanor, the butcher who was murdering pregnant prostitutes could have been anyone in the vicinity. Anyone. But now, with Eleanor's death, I'm sure I must know the murderer personally. How else would the murderer have known Eleanor was in the house on Frazier Street, and that she was pregnant? Guilt worms its way through my stomach again, but I resolutely press on with my thoughts.

And who took Dr Mordaunt's diary? The only person who makes sense is Dr Mordaunt himself, although I'm almost persuaded he was telling the truth when he denied taking it. Regardless, I write his name down.

Under this I jot the name *Priestly*. It has to be him who Mordaunt had met with Eleanor in his rooms, and hadn't Chat and Amah seen him watching the Waterloo house? I write these points against Priestly, wishing I'd taken more notice of Amah's words. But what of the other women who were murdered? Surely Priestly's not responsible for all the deaths? But he did know of the methods used to kill the earlier victims... Could he have copied the earlier murders to get rid of Eleanor? But why? Why would Priestly want Eleanor dead? I stare at the wallpaper of my study, my eyes following the line of the branches, leaves and the occasional blue bird, until a possible motive for Priestly becomes clear to me, which I write against his name.

I sit back. Who else knew of Eleanor's presence in Waterloo? Of course Tilly and Katie Sullivan knew, but I swiftly dismiss them. I write down Dr Blain's name, ignoring Bill's assurances of his innocence. I'm bloody sure the doctor had the opportunity to murder all the women. I list this against a note of his passionate reaction to Eleanor. I write of him as I consider the dreadful Mrs Sweetapple. She'd also known of Eleanor's predicament. Could she be involved? The woman's detestable, but I'm really not convinced that she had a hand in the murders.

And what of Mme Silvestre, sitting high in her tilbury.

"I have laid out a tray in the drawing room, Mrs Chancey, by the fire," says Bundle from the doorway.

"Thank you, Bundle." I add the madam's name to my list. Gathering up the pages, I move into the drawing room. On a low table by the sofa in front of the fireplace, Bundle has set out a fine repast. Next to a miniature, china tureen is a plate of chicken quenelles. I feel a little forlorn as I lift the lid of the tureen, releasing the clear consommé's fragrant steam. Agneau has prepared one of my favourite dishes and I've absolutely no appetite for it. What will Amah be eating in her cold, damp prison cell?

I reach for the crystal decanter of claret and pour myself a generous amount before sinking onto the sofa. Taking a few sips, I glance over the list I've made. My eyes rest upon Mme Silvestre's name. Was it smugness I'd seen spread across the madam's large face when we both realised that Henry had been locked up during the latest murders? Or was the madam hiding something all along? I can't be sure. I take another sip of the dark wine and close my eyes to recall my last encounter with Silvestre. Immediately I feel the pull of sleep, all thoughts of Mme Silvestre slowly dispersing. My hand twitches, spilling some of the wine onto my dressing-gown, and I'm awake again.

Not having a pen and ink at hand, I trace the name *Henry* upon its surface with my fingertip. Henry. I mustn't forget that Eleanor had recognised him – that she had seen him with one of the victims. And Bill was sure of Henry's guilt too, before Eleanor's death. What if Henry was the real murderer and someone had murdered the girls in Frazier Street to cover for him? Someone like Silvestre. Or bloody Mordaunt. I always come back to him.

Swallowing the last of the wine I lean forward to pour some more. The warm alcohol leaves a sudden void in my belly and I kneel in front of the small table and pick a quenelle up between my fingers and take a bite from one end. I lick the warm sauce that streaks down the side of my hand and then take one more mouthful before dropping the rest back onto the platter. I feel around in my pocket for Eleanor's handkerchief I'd salvaged from the house in Waterloo and wipe my fingers. Picking up my wine glass, I lean back into the sofa.

Silvestre. Would the old cow go that far to free her lover? I can't bring myself to believe it. I'm sure the old woman's callous enough to tolerate a certain amount of violence inflicted upon her girls, but these mutilations? And the thought of Silvestre exerting herself to go to the extreme effort of murdering and butchering two women? It's laughable.

Which leaves Henry in jail at the time of Eleanor's murder, and most probably innocent of the other deaths.

So maybe Eleanor didn't see him standing over the Dutch girl's body after all. But then where did she see him? Was it just at the brothel? Or was she mistaken? I swallow another mouthful of the wine and lie my head back against the sofa. My thoughts are unfocused and I just want to sleep.

Lifting the cranberry snuff bottle to my nostrils, repulsion sweeps over me. I can't just lie here and inhale my way to oblivion, and the faint, sickly scent of violets with which Bill drenched his snuff mixture makes my stomach quail, which reminds me of

Eleanor, enshrouded in her own blood. I sweep a hand across my eyes to blot the image, and take another gulp of wine.

The handkerchief lies upon my lap and the embroidered letters in one of the corners catches my eye. *XI*. I hold it before myself. An X and I. It's not the handkerchief Eleanor picked at, after all. And it's certainly not mine. XI? I toss it onto the floor. It must belong to one of the policemen who tramped around that bedroom. Or maybe it's Dr Featherby's – the doctor who attended poor Eleanor's body? Inspector Kelley's? I think of their conversation about the vile men who stole women's pleasure. That B, B man – something Brown? And the other one. Xavier. I nudge the handkerchief with my toe. Flip it over. IX. Someone Xavier. I Xavier. And I think of the last time I noticed these letters. The number nine. The roman numerals circled in Mordaunt's notebook. But this Xavier Dr Featherby spoke of is dead. He said he died of shame.

Gazing out the long windows into the inky darkness, I wonder if Bill is still at the morgue or the police station at this time of night. I must tell him of my ideas. I think of his strong hands, his crooked smile. Really, I shrink from seeing him again, but I must. I need to look him in the eye, let him see that I am unaffected by his disdain for me. I must find him as soon as possible, but the warmth of the fire and the wine, and maybe even the muddled insights forming in my mind, leave me feeling unusually languid. I hope no more girls will die violently overnight while I sit here paralysed with uncertainty in my comfortable drawing room. Surely the killer will not strike again with Amah safely tucked into a cell acting as scapegoat. Pulling the sheets of paper against my breast I resolve to make a plan of action, but promptly fall fast asleep amongst the sofa cushions.

Chapter Twenty-Two

The police station's chilly entrance hall is so crammed with men – some bleeding, all caked in dirt – that I'm jostled on my way to the front desk. Muddy boots tread upon my skirts, interrupting my progress, and at one stage I have to duck out of the way of a falling body. The constables' batons weave through the air and the prisoners, stale liquor on their breath, holler abuse.

I'd woken in the middle of the previous night, shivering on the sofa. I had a crick in my shoulder and a beating headache from the wine. Finding little rest since then, I filled the intervening hours with determined plans to free Amah. As soon as the milky morning light filtered through the curtains I made my way to the police station. The sight of the unruly mob in its vestibule did not dampen my ambition.

I finally see a uniformed policeman at the station's front desk. He's a young man with cropped brown hair and earnest eyes and as I reach him, I grab his sleeve and tug.

"Madam, this is no place for a lady," he says. His baby face looks horrified on my behalf. "Allow me to take you away from this commotion." He leads me past the closed doors of the back offices and into a room that appears to be a makeshift kitchen.

"Why are there so many men here?" I ask. I widen my carefully accented eyelashes and pretend to be fearful of the filthy men being led away by the constables. I sense the young policeman expects a certain level of femininity from me. "Who are these brutes?"

I allow him to settle me into a chair, away from the melee.

"Don't worry about them now, madam. I wouldn't sully a lady's ears with their doings in any case," he answers.

I peer around the open doorway at the departing captives, guessing they were participants in an overnight brawl or fighting match. "Where will they be taken?"

"They'll be confined in the lockup out back."

"But, how many lockups do you have?"

"Just the one," he says, leaning against a table. "One space is enough to cram those thugs into."

"But this won't do." Alarm has made my voice strident. "My maid is confined there. She cannot be expected to wait amongst those men."

"Your maid?" He looks confused.

"Yes. She was brought here on ridiculous, trumped up charges yesterday. I have come here to ask for her release." I draw a sheaf of paper from my reticule. I know most of this paperwork is next to bloody useless, but I've forged Amah's names onto one ticket of passage and against two receipts. "I have brought what I can to try to prove her whereabouts over the last few months." I twist around in my chair and look around the station. "Where is Sergeant Chapman? William Chapman? He will know why I am here."

The young constable gapes at me for a few moments. "Do you mean the foreign woman who was here last night?"

"Yes."

"She is your maid?"

"She is."

He stares at me some more, before shaking his head slowly. "She's murdered many women, madam. There will be no freeing her."

"But you don't understand." I shove the papers I have crushed between my fingers towards him. "She did not murder those women. I have brought proof. She cannot be left with those drunkards." I can't think of any other way to free Amah. It's been years since I've felt so utterly helpless. Anxiety constricts my chest as I think of the older woman, wondering if she's frightened or just plain angry at me for not getting her out of this mess. I imagine her cowed in the corner of the cell surrounded by the pack of abusive men.

The young policeman looks dubious. "Madam, you will have to wait for the Inspector to be free as he is the only one you can speak to of this matter."

"Well, where is he?"

"He is interviewing a witness at this very moment. He could be a long while."

"Can you at least have my maid wait in here? With me? Have her wait with me for the Inspector."

"I am sorry," he says, averting his eyes from mine. "Our orders are to leave her in the lockup and, come this afternoon, she will appear before the magistrate and then be sent to Newgate."

I slump back into the chair as I squeeze my eyes shut. I feel sick to the stomach. Amah will be tried for murder and hanged before we know it.

The policeman moves to my side swiftly. "Madam, are you ill?"

"I must be strong," I say. I allow for a staged, tremulous note to creep into my voice but, truth be told, maybe it wasn't all acting. "I have had so many frights lately, but your Sgt Chapman has been such a friend to me." I look up at the young man, my eyes pleading – 'shimmering pools of melancholy, making thy heart ache' after all. "Do you think he is available to see me now?"

"I will check for you." The policeman returns after what seems only a few moments.

"I'm afraid he isn't," he answers, apologetically.

I bite down on my lower lip and taste blood. I can't be sure if Bill really can't meet with me or if he just refuses to.

Leaving the papers, the handkerchief and a note for the Inspector in the policeman's care, I summon a cab to take me to an address in Waterloo. The initials on the handkerchief have given me an idea. I'm going to hunt the killer down to his own lair. I know I should have someone accompany me, but the police have proven of no help and I don't have time to track down Taff. Briefly I think of taking Chat along with me, but I can't upset him any more than he has been already. I have something far more useful anyway. My hand folds over the handgun which is now in a hidden pocket of my gown, its bulk reassuringly heavy against my thigh. The only thing on my mind is the immediate release of Amah, which means I have to find the murderer. And shoot him, if I'm lucky enough.

As yet, I've not actually shot at anyone with my handgun. A young lover gave it to me two years ago and had trained me in its use at his hunting box in Essex. Before that I'd made do with a pretty, pearl-handled switchblade. Amah had taught me well in the use of that blade, but today I feel the handgun is more favourable.

The cab driver lets me down on the corner of where Emery crosses Morley Street. Pulling an organza veil over my face, I pass a horse yard and stables until I reach a row of small shops. Between a milliner's and a tobacconist is a butcher's shop, its wide shopfront filled with gleaming, pink carcasses hanging from hooks. I pop into the milliner's, which sells cheap, unfashionable headwear, and ask directions from the young shopgirl, who points to the alleyway that runs down the side of the horse yard.

The brick wall of the shop looms high to one side of the alley, while on the other side the tall, timber fencing of the stable yard cuts out most of the grey light. The alleyway is so narrow my skirts brush against the side walls, and a brisk wind whooshes past my exposed neck, making me shiver. The rims of my shoes stick in the mud as I pick my way through to the row of small, two-storey dwellings that are adjacent to the rear of the shops. The stench of the cluttered yard grows stronger as I approach – the smothering sweet smell of open flesh and manure mixes with the pungent odour of rotten meat. I press a handkerchief to my nose as I round the corner. The dripping end of a newly-slaughtered sheep nudges my shoulder from where it hangs over a bucket. A stream of fresh, port-coloured blood streaks through the filthy cobblestones and two more sheep tethered to a stake watch me, dancing on skittish hooves, ignoring the hay at their feet. A skinny lad carries a straw cage of chickens to a chopping block. He looks enquiringly at me as he lifts a hen by its feet from the cage. Its squawking and flapping make conversation difficult so I just point at the house nearest to the butcher's.

Knocking on the front door, I'm not sure if my rapping can be heard over the screeching of the chicken. The din stops abruptly with a loud thud so that my second round of knocking rings out loudly across the small yard. I wait through the raucous deaths of two more chickens, but no-one answers the door. Turning the door handle, I find it locked. I watch as the butcher's lad carries the chicken carcases through the back entrance of the butcher's shop, and quickly pick the lock. Stripping my gloves from my hands, I stuff them into one pocket while pulling my handgun from the other. I slip into the small house.

I find myself in a large, dimly lit area. There's only one small window at the back of the room, the daylight muted by a grubby, muslin curtain. The furniture, although aged, is surprisingly fine in its dreary surrounds and the two paintings upon the walls appear quite valuable. A lovely crystal bowl encrusted in dust stands upon a side-board, yet the table is set with cheap crockery. I'm still as I survey the room, my senses heightened to hear any movement from behind or above. Along the wall is a make-shift bookcase, constructed from bricks and planks. My eyes are drawn across the spines of the books, reading the titles – there are several university anatomy books and home doctor journals – and my breath catches as I glimpse the book at the end of the row. It's black without a title across the spine, and a red ribbon pokes out between the pages. I spring forward and, lifting the notebook, open its pages. It's Dr Mordaunt's missing diary.

My fingers tremble as I replace the book against the others. The uncomfortable beating of my heart echoes loudly in my head. I'm in the right place. I've tracked down the man who's murdered all the women; who's murdered poor Eleanor. Where is the bastard? I grip the handle of my handgun, my fingertip resting on the trigger.

I gently step across the grimy floorboards, pausing to look at a framed document upon the wall. *Royal College of Surgeons* curves across the top of the page, over a coat of arms. At the bottom of the page, written in curling script, *1830. Ignatius Xavier.*

The name of the surgeon the doctor had spoken of; the surgeon who thought he could operate on women bits to keep them from hysteria. I mouth the name – Ignatius Xavier. If only I'd caught on earlier.

I move across to a poky stairwell, and peer up into the shadows. I can't see the half of the staircase that turns off from the landing. I place my foot on the first step, quickly withdrawing it when I notice the dark smudge ingrained into the wood. I crouch low in order to see it more clearly. The thickish stain runs down the middle of the lowest four steps. Is it blood?

Someone shouts in the butcher's yard, and a cow clip-clops its way across the cobblestones, lowing. I grasp the stair's handrail, listening. Another male voice joins the first. Perhaps the butcher and his assistant? The sound of steel scraping across whetstone muffles their voices. Feeling a little reassured at their close proximity, I stare up into the stairwell again and begin to climb the steps, keeping to the side to avoid the stains.

I reach the landing. It's even darker than it is below. Turning to my right I look up the remaining stairs. At the top is a door, ajar.

The cow is bellowing in earnest now. I can just hear it over the loud whooshing of my heartbeat. Perspiration prickles the skin above my upper lip and at my hairline. I make my way slowly up the final stairs, gripping the handgun so tightly I have to be careful it doesn't go off prematurely. I reach forward. Lightly push open the door.

In the centre of the room, illuminated by a single lantern, is a chair – just like the one in Dr Mordaunt's rooms – a reclining chair with stirrups.

I gape at it for some moments before I notice the baleful silence. No voices, no cow.

By the time I hear a rustle behind me, it's too late. He pries the gun from my grip as he holds me in a strangle hold with his other arm. He presses a wad of linen soaked in a familiar, acerbic substance to my mouth and nose. I struggle in his arms, scream, bite and scratch, but the more I try to call out, the more I breathe in the ether. My heartbeat clamours in my ears and I feel I might be sick, when all goes black.

Chapter Twenty-Three

I heave back into awareness. I struggle to sit up but my ankles are bound in the chair's stirrups and my wrists are tied to its arms. I'm groggy, panting with the effort of righting the spinning room.

Ignatius steps in front of me. Mordaunt's slimy assistant. He smiles, and his wet lips make my skin crawl with loathing. "Awake?" He points my handgun at me. "If you dare make a noise I'll finish you so quickly your screams will be taken for a hen's squawk."

"What the hell do you think you're doing?" My mouth's dry from the ether, my tongue numb, sunken in my mouth, slurring the words.

"I think you know exactly what I'm doing, Heloise." He holds my gaze until I know what he means. "How did you find me?" he asks.

"I watched you leave Mordaunt's. You always turned into this alleyway." My words come slowly.

"Well, what a lovely surprise to find you here. How do you like my humble abode? It suits me very well, I must say – the noisiness from the slaughter yard, its remoteness from others. But do you know the best part?" He breathes in deeply. "The smell. That metallic stench of blood. Of course, mostly it's from the cows and the sheep, but once in a while the blood from a whore's body mingles with the rest."

"You're a bastard."

An ugly expression settles across his smooth features. "I'm no bastard." He moves to a side-table. "I can account for both my parents, which I'm sure is more than you can do." He neatens some objects on a cloth, metal jangling against metal. "In fact, my father left me these," he says, holding up a scalpel, shiny in the yellow lantern light. "They're instruments from his surgery. He had no more use for them, and then he died anyway, so I have appropriated them." He places the scalpel back on the cloth and picks up what appears to be a butcher's knife. "Have you worked out that part yet?"

I nod, the words sticking in my throat. I stare at the mottled grey of the knife. "Yes. Ignatius Xavier. Baker-Brown's associate. The one discredited for mutilating women. I assume you're his son," I finally croak.

His jaws clench and he stabs the point of the knife into the table top. "I didn't ever train to be a doctor, you know. I wanted to be on the stage, trained to sing opera in Venice. But when the pricks struck my father off, leaving him with no income, I had to support myself. Had to find work in a fucking doctor's office." He scowls, moves to my side. "I found my father's body, you know. It had rotted away for weeks before that. The poor fellow had been deserted – deserted by his friends, by his family, by the medical fraternity – all because he tried to help you crazy women."

I long to turn my head away, shut my eyes, but I'm mesmerised by his knife hand. I can barely comprehend what he's saying.

"What gave me away? What brought you to my home?"

"I found your handkerchief. I noticed the monogram. Same as in Mordaunt's notebook."

His eyes narrow as he gazes at me. "Clever little bitch, aren't you? Now you know the real me. Of course, I've known the real you for a while now too. When you first came into Mordaunt's office I thought I'd seen you before, but I couldn't place you. I only truly recognised you when I glimpsed you eating supper at the fair by the river. It was when you stood amongst all the other fancy-pieces in their gaudy jewels and painted faces, that I realised. I saw it then. She's the infamous *Paon de Nuit* of the stage and of the bed, I thought. Heloise Chancey. Peacock of the Night. The woman who ventures out in all her finery to attract and trap unwitting suitors." He reaches down and caresses between my legs with his free hand. I squirm to the side so he tweaks me hard and laughs at my yelp of pain. "I've seen you often at the opera, my dear. But of course, I don't venture past the lowly stalls. You would never notice the likes of me." He's still smiling but there's an unpleasant glint in his eye.

"Why are you doing this? Why mutilate all those poor women?"

"I couldn't let my poor pater's work go unfinished. He can no longer fight for himself, but I can seek justice for him."

"That's justice, is it? Slaughtering young, defenceless women?" I ask.

"They weren't just normal young women, though, were they? They weren't decent ladies, at home, minding their families. They were diseased. They were immoral. A wound, an infection, in our society."

"That's nonsense," I whisper.

He places the heavy knife on my stomach and with his free hand he strokes the loose hair from my face. "Your desire for pleasure causes too many problems, Heloise," he says in a low voice, close to my ear, his warm breath on my face. It has the sourness of rancid milk, of decay. "Disease, illegitimacy, madness. I decided to further my father's work. Cut pleasure from whores' lives and cut the risk of procreation out of them while I was at it. This wanton desire of yours is dangerous. It needs to be destroyed. Have you read any of Darwin's fascinating work? But of course you have. I've heard of your Mayfair evenings with gentlemen of science and culture." He strokes my hair some more until I toss my head away. "Let's say my method is more akin to artificial selection than that of the natural sort. Instead of choosing the good, Heloise, I am choosing to cull the bad."

"But do the girls have to die?"

"Well, I'm not a doctor, like I said. Although I have learnt some rudimentary surgery from the good Dr Mordaunt. Not that he knew of it. He's usually too far gone with whisky to know I'm skulking in the background." He smirks down at me. "At first I meant for the tarts to live, but most of them didn't which I realised wasn't so unfortunate after all. I was quite excited when I found out one had survived and how she didn't return straight back to the streets. But I had to finish her off too, although she was surrounded by a sentinel of infernal whores. What with her ghoulish account and the other whores' deaths, my actions might mean an eventual end to prostitution."

"Why don't you just chop off your cock? And the cocks of all the men in London? Then there'd be an end to prostitution," I mock, unable to stop the bitter words.

His eyes narrow as he looks down at me. He returns to his side-table and pulls something from the doctor's bag. He holds up a rounded, metal contraption. "Do you know what this is?"

He punches my face as I breathe in to scream. In the following blinding moments he rams the gadget into my mouth, securing it behind my head. "It's called a choke pear, meant for shutting you women up. My father had it specially designed for my mother when she finally succumbed to her hysteria. I've found it very useful in my work."

A scorching pulse of pain beats beneath my cheek as I gag against the choke pear. I fold forward, fighting rising nausea.

He presses my head back against the chair and, waiting until he has my full attention, he flourishes the butcher's knife. He slowly rakes its blade at an angle down the skin of my throat and across my bosom.

"I fucked 'em all first, you know. Although I had to... cajole that young woman staying in your house." He clutches the knife in his fist, and hacks at the bodice of my gown, slicing an opening down the middle. "I saw she'd recognised me outside Mordaunt's the day he was arrested. I remembered her too from the morning I disposed of that blond girl's body. I had to make sure she didn't expose me. She wasn't exactly a whore, but clearly I had work to do on her too."

I think back to the bright, sunny day Eleanor and I watched the arrest outside Mordaunt's. Think of how we watched Bill escort Henry past Ignatius to the police buggy, surrounded by all the uniformed policemen and the Inspector. Think of how they each had on a brown suit. How stupid of me. My breaths come in noisy gasps, my chest spasming up and down so that he nicks my skin. A patch of blood blooms through my white chemise.

"So I followed you home. You had no idea. I've had a lot of practice shadowing people for Mordaunt, after all." He shook his head at me. "But a chink? You had a dirty chink there. There really is no end to your depravity, woman." He pulls the fabric of my gown apart. "And I see you found Mordaunt's diary downstairs. Handy that I saw it in the bedroom when I killed that girl. My initials are against some of the entries, after all.

And, of course, if I want to continue with my work in the future I need only peruse that notebook for the whereabouts of all the whores in Waterloo."

He sweeps his hand over my breasts, cupping one, the knife's cold edge resting against my skin. "I've noticed how much pleasure you women receive from these. I thought the only pleasure was ours." He squeezes my breast so that I wince. "My usual experiences with whores are mere romps – bent over a table, a quick one on a musty bed." He's thoughtful for a moment. "Although I do prefer a hard one against a wall."

He licks my nipple before sucking it into his mouth. I feel nothing.

"So I sliced 'em off," he says, straightening up. "It's a pity you weren't home the night I finished off the other two. I was like a fox. I was going to clean out the whole hen house – her, you, your chink, the whore-house maid. After all, finishing you whores is not unlike killing chickens – a lot of squawking, then blessed silence." He pulls his snuff box from his pocket and inhales, his eyes shut in momentary contentment. He turns back to his surgical instruments and picks up the scalpel.

My eyes water as the choke pear stabs against the roof of my mouth with the slightest of movements. I try to shrink as far back into the chair as possible when he approaches me again.

The scalpel hovers above my bare skin. "I'd like you to survive. You'd be a perfect specimen of chastity versus pleasure, and its terrible outcomes. But, alas, despite my negligible medical skills, you definitely have to die. You are more dangerous than the rest, my dear, because you think you are entitled to the freedoms of a man."

My bladder loosens as the wretched scalpel lowers to my breast. He presses the sharp point to the edge of my nipple, and the blade slips easily into my flesh. I scream against the choke pear. I flinch from the keen, searing pain, knocking his hand aside.

He lifts the scalpel away. "This won't do. I cannot do a neat job with you struggling against me."

Pulling the tie from around his neck, he binds my upper arm with a savage tightness. Once the make-shift tourniquet is secured he turns to his instruments and, after some moments, returns with a syringe.

"In America they use opium in this form to relieve you feeble women from your special pains," he says, as he forces the needle's point into the vein of my arm. "I hope I have the dosage right – although I hardly think it matters."

I sink into the morphine almost immediately. I feel weightless, at peace, a lovely warmth engulfs my body. I retch against the choke pear, hot vomit rising in my throat. As darkness surrounds me, a great, black moth envelopes Ignatius, its wings beating furiously.

Li Leen

"Your skin is as smooth as polished ebony, dark and tight," Tiri said, as he ran his finger down my forearm.

I trembled and pulled back. "Please stop touching me," I said.

I stood to get away from him, but he followed and stepped close, so close my breast almost touched his.

"How full your lips are, you tempting little fox-fairy, and when you open your mouth, yes, like that, your mouth is pink, as pink as the flesh of a fig."

I felt his breath on my own so I moved back again and said, "Please, leave my room, Tiri."

He laughed. "Beloved, this is my room in my house, and now you are mine too."

I stared at him, but he wasn't really looking at me. All those times Mother pleaded with him to stop staring at me, he was not really seeing me. He was availing himself of my body with his eyes, those same eyes that now followed the lines of my breasts, and lingered. That flickered over my waist line, over my hips, down my tightly clad limbs. The fear I felt melted away until a sore hardness stiffened inside me. He was so blinded, he did not see me draw out my scaling knife. I slid the blade into his throat, under the jawline.

Then he looked at me.

His warm blood sprayed my skin as softly as a spider treads, and he sank to the floor. The life shuddered out of him, and all his gore, and words, and rapacity seeped into Mother's special Persian rug. I wiped the knife on the side of my sarong and gazed at the beads of blood on my arm that glistened like ripe pomegranate seeds.

And here I am again, many years later, wiping the drops of another man's blood from my skin. I still wonder what it was that tormented my mother so greatly that she felt she had to take her own life. Was it her husband's lust for me? Her daughter? Or was it that I was her accursed, yet beloved, half-gweilo, who burdened her with bad luck? Perhaps she knew that it would be impossible for her to keep me safe from Tiri's attentions.

It can be difficult to protect a daughter.

Chapter Twenty-Four

"Heloise... Jia Li... Heloise, my child, wake up."

I stir, but I'm only forced to open my eyes when slapped across the cheek. "Bloody hell," I protest, pressing my hand gently over my wounded cheek. The effort is almost too much. Morphine-induced lethargy weighs upon my limbs.

Amah gathers me into a sitting position. "We have to get out of here, Heloise. You must get up." She tears away a strip of my ruined chemise and wipes the vomit from my chest and chin.

I lean into Amah's bosom. The horrors of the past hour come back to me in dizzying clarity. I'm no longer bound, no longer choking on the mouth-piece. I let out a sob and clutch at Amah's arm. "Where is he?"

"You're safe now, Jia Li," replies Amah. We both look down at the cuts to my skin, and Amah clicks her tongue. She carefully draws my bodice together and tucks her own cloak around my shoulders.

I bury my face in Amah's shoulder. "Oh, Mama, I was so scared. So scared." I sob dryly.

"I know, child, I know," says Amah, patting me on the back. "But no good will come from sniffling over it."

My face is still pressed against her chest, but I manage a weak grin. "Can't you be tender just this once?"

"What good would that do?" she says. But her cold, bony fingers grasp me closer.

We stay like that for only a matter of seconds before she says, briskly, "Come. We must leave." She pulls my veil back in place before covering her own face. Placing the handgun in her reticule, she takes me by the arm. "The police may be here at any moment."

"But that's a good thing, surely. We can tell them who the murderer is."

I lean heavily against my mother as we stagger from the room.

"Not such a good thing," she answers. She pauses for a moment and nods towards the floor on the other side of the room.

On his back, his white shirt shredded with several gaping, crimson slashes, lies Ignatius, quite dead.

"The police will work out that he murdered all those young women," says Amah. "But they need not know that it was I who had the pleasure of murdering him."

Taff helps us climb into my carriage which he's parked around the corner.

I lift the veil from my face and rest my head against the cushions. "How did you two find me?"

"We followed you."

I frown. "Followed me? But you were locked up."

"Taff freed me."

"What?" I lift my heavy head to look across at Amah.

"He provided me with an alibi. We were with the Inspector most of the morning."

I shake my head in wonder. "So when I was at the station, the Inspector was with you, all along?"

"I suppose so."

"What was the alibi he gave you?"

She lifts her chin and gazes steadily out the window. "He just told the Inspector he knew of my whereabouts for the whole evening of Eleanor's death." Her ears turn plum as she speaks.

"Well, how's that convincing? I told them the same thing, but they didn't believe me."

"He said he was with me... with me," she stresses the words, slowly. "For the whole night." Her hard, dark eyes widen defensively.

It takes my drug-impeded mind a moment to catch on, and then I hoot with laughter.

"So, Taff pretended that he was with you, under the covers, for the whole evening?"

"Yes."

"I didn't realise he was so brave." I continue to chuckle, my eyes on my rigid mother. "The police think you two are living in sin? Under my roof?"

"Yes."

I press my lips shut, only allowing myself a little smirk, until a troubling thought occurs to me.

"It's bloody lucky for me that you followed. Did you see me at the station?"

"The Inspector had just released me when we saw you hopping into a cab. Taff collected your carriage and we followed. We assumed you were returning to Mayfair."

"If you were following me, why did it take you so long to save me?"

"We lost you for a few minutes. We asked for you in the tobacco shop and the butcher's, but it was not until we spoke with the milliner that we found out where you'd gone. Even then we weren't sure where you'd disappeared to from that slaughter yard."

By the light from the carriage window I can see the damp, dark patches upon the black wool of Amah's gown, and a fine spray of blood on the skin of her throat. I turn my gaze out the window. My thoughts are drawn into a loop of the nightmare I've narrowly missed. A tear slips from the corner of my eye.

"I know, I know. Snivelling will get me nowhere."

Chapter Twenty-Five

I scrutinise my face in the mirror. The bruises to my mouth are clearly visible by the sunlight that shines past the open curtains. There are dark smudges under my eyes, although I slept well and dreamlessly after drinking the dose of laudanum Amah mixed for me the night before. I'm finding it difficult to stop shivering even though Bundle has repeatedly stoked the fire. I tenderly dab cream and powder around my lips to hide the blemishes, and apply a smidgen of tinted lip colour. Testing a smile in the mirror, I flinch at the sting that shears through the split in my upper lip. Well, I won't smile then. God knows, I've nothing to smile about today, in any case. I pull open my peignoir and grumpily scrutinise the bandages Amah has wrapped around my wounds. I've no idea how I'm to explain them away to Hatterleigh. In fact it might be best to go away for a couple of weeks. But first I have things to deal with.

The blue dress I'd left for Eleanor at the morgue lies across my bed. The girl's detestable family sent it back to me last night and while Amah and I had discussed what to do with it, Amah came across a crumpled page of paper in the gown's pocket. It was a letter from Eleanor to me.

I pick it up to re-read. Fury makes my head ache.

A glint on the carpet catches my eye. The cranberry glass snuff-bottle. Sweeping it up in my hand, I wrench open the window and hurl it out onto the cobblestones. For several minutes I stare at the sparkling pink shards scattered upon the road.

"What are you thinking, Heloise?" asks Amah from behind.

"That I might retire."

Amah snorts. "Retire? Where would you go? What would you do?"

I watch Amah pull a chemise and petticoats from the dresser drawers.

"I have enough money to live comfortably for a while. Perhaps it's time I move to my house in Brighton – that would cut costs." I sit back down at the dressing table and stare at myself in the mirror. What other options do I have? I'm not that good an actress that I could live off my wages. Not in this style anyway. Seamstress? It isn't worth the hardship. Governess? Nobody would have me. The only other option I can think of is marriage, but aren't the freedoms of my current situation preferable? "Maybe I could just continue with Sir Thomas' work."

"That wouldn't pay for the champagne," says Amah. "You'd be back at it soon enough, Jia Li."

"Maybe not." I step into the petticoat that she holds out for me. I then wait patiently while she buttons my chemise.

"Why do you think like this now?" she asks, as she lifts an embroidered gown over my head. A new delivery from Worth.

I think of Eleanor and the other dead women. I think of the despicable Silvestre and Tilly and all the other renters I know. It isn't that I'm scared. It isn't even that I'm sorry for them. I'm angry. Angry that we're all vulnerable to the whims of all manner of men.

Before I can answer Amah there's a sharp rap at the front door.

I pick up Eleanor's letter and tuck it into my cleavage. "This will be very satisfying, Amah. You should watch through the peacock's tail."

Mr Priestly is standing by the fireplace when I enter the drawing room.

He waves a letter in my direction. "What is the meaning of this missive, with its sly undertones and almost threatening tone?" he demands immediately as he sees me.

I sit down on the sofa and spread my skirts neatly around myself, patting down the creases. "Ah, a threatening tone. You noticed that, did you?"

"I most certainly did." Blotches of colour mottle his skin. "How dare you send for me in this way."

"Well, why did you come then, sir?"

His jaw bobs up and down as he tries to answer. "Well... I was curious, I suppose. Curious to know what a little trumped up tramp would have to say to me."

I manage to keep my temper in check because I know I've got the upper hand. "Why don't you take a seat, sir, so we can discuss this matter in a more – I was going to say friendly, but let us say – businesslike manner."

He remains by the fireplace, until finally, finding no response from me, sits down opposite in a deep lounge chair.

"Well, what is it?"

City noises – a horse trotting past, a dog barking and the clink of the letter box – fill in the moments we stare at each other.

"I want you to donate £500 to the Euston Reclamation Home for Fallen Women. I hear they do good work there with women unfortunate enough to be with child outside wedlock."

"I will do no such thing."

I tilt my head to the side. "Oh, I think you will."

He sits back and folds his arms, smiling. "And how are you going to make me do that?"

"Well, if you don't, I will tell the police about how you were following Eleanor in her last days. I believe I might convince them that you are the one who murdered her."

"But you're mad. I didn't murder her. I spoke to Sir Thomas just this morning. The police have found the culprit who murdered all those prostitutes."

"Yes, but there's no proof he murdered Eleanor. And I have two witnesses who saw you shadowing her on Frazier Street on the day she died." Of course, it's best not to mention that one witness is of foreign blood while the other witness is a homeless child. "And you are also mentioned in Dr Mordaunt's diary, which I believe is in the police's possession at this very moment. I know that Dr Mordaunt can definitely identify you as the man who accompanied poor Eleanor to his surgery, so that you could be rid of your baby."

"What do you mean by that?" he asks, through bloodless lips.

"What I mean is I know that you were the father of Eleanor's baby." I feel an absolute thrill of triumph when wrath sweeps across Priestly's face.

"Take that back, you harlot."

"I will not." I allow a smile of victory as I slowly withdraw Eleanor's letter from between my breasts.

He licks his dry lips as his eyes follow my every movement. "What is that?"

"A letter from Eleanor," I reply, as I unfold the sheet of paper. "In which she names you as the man who raped and impregnated her."

Priestly makes a sudden lurch for me, but I hold up my hand, pointing to the doorway where Bundle stands with a sword stick held casually against his thigh. "Ah-ah," I remonstrate. "Come closer, and Bundle will cut you."

Priestly glances at the tall butler and settles back into his chair. He turns his face back to me.

"What do you intend to do with that?" he asks.

"I haven't quite decided yet." My eyes scan the letter. "But I do believe it would make interesting reading for Eleanor's father. Although I am not sure I could put even Mr Carter through the repugnance of reading Eleanor's account of how much she loathed your touch." I re-fold it and poke it back into my bodice. "It will go straight into my safe at the bank and, of course, if anything dastardly were to happen to me, this letter will be sent to Mr Carter and a copy to the police."

"You will never convince the police that I murdered her," he says, his voice hoarse.

"Probably not. But tell me, how would you like this letter and the witness accounts smeared across the newspapers for your wife and esteemed friends to see? Think of your children, Mr Priestly. Be sure, the damage will be done, even if you are not prosecuted for murder." Priestly's mouth gobbles away at words that will not come. I have to suppress a bubble of laughter. I haven't felt so good in days.

I stand up. "So, I expect my friends at the Euston home to inform me within the week that someone has given them a large amount of money in Eleanor Carter's name. If the money does not appear, I will simply send this letter to *The Times*."

Priestly hauls himself out of his chair with difficulty. He leans upon its arm. "But that amount of money will break me."

I dimple, but my eyes are cold. "Sir, that is not my concern." I turn my back on him and gaze out the long, sash window.

As soon as Bundle sees Priestly from the premises he returns to the drawing room to hand me a letter.

"This arrived while you were engaged with Mr Priestly."

The butler walks from the room passing Amah in the doorway.

"How do you know of this Euston home for prostitutes?" she asks, joining me by the window.

"I had Bundle make some enquiries when Eleanor was still with us," I murmur as I rip open the seal on the letter. "It's from Sir Thomas." I read from it out loud.

"*My Dear Mrs Chancey,*

I hope I find you in happier spirits than the last time we corresponded. You have, yet again, cleared up a mystery that puzzled even the police. Of course, they may never have solved these murders had you not pointed them in the direction of their evil culprit."

"So they know it was this Ignatius Xavier," says Amah.

I nod. "*I have just arrived back at my office from a meeting with Inspector Kelley. He told me that as soon as he received the message you left with him at the station stating your suspicions of Dr Mordaunt's assistant, he gathered a small force of men and went directly to Xavier's home.*"

"What did you write?" asks Amah.

"I wrote that Eleanor had recognised him as the man with the dead girl. And that I'd found his monogramed handkerchief next to... you know." I continue to read. "*I do hope that what I am about to relay to you does not leave you faint, but the Inspector and his men found Mr Xavier stabbed to death. They are convinced he lured another prostitute to mutilate but was most likely overwhelmed and*

murdered in turn by her or an accomplice. – Well, that much is true,"
I say, wryly. "*There was sufficient evidence in his house, of which I
won't sully your senses, to prove that he was indeed the man killing those
defenceless women. Also, they found a curious diary, which they assume
is a list of past or future victims.*" I look up at Amah. "He must
mean Mordaunt's diary. *Dearest Mrs Chancey, although I earnestly
apologise for the grief caused by Miss Carter's death, I am truly thankful
we retained your investigative services or this despicable affair would
not be over. Please find enclosed a promissory note. I think you will find
that Mr Carter has been quite generous. I hope to visit you soon.*" I stare
down at the cheque, my face blank. "Well paid for my excellent
service, yet again."

Amah takes the note from me, and her eyebrows lift as she
reads the amount. "Very generous. That will take care of the
servants' wages for the next six months. I will put this note on
your desk with your other banking tasks."

I watch my mother, dark and tightly bustled, walk from the
room. How horrified society would be if it found out that the
celebrated Heloise Chancey, *Paon de Nuit*, is a true exotique. Not
that it matters who I am actually – what matters is what society
thinks I am.

I glance across the room at my portrait, at the façade I call
Heloise Chancey. It's just one of my many roles. Can I really leave
it all behind? I have my independence, thanks to my shrewdness
with the riches that have come my way, but do I have any real
choices that are not already carved out for me?

Maybe it's time to give up the pretence. The artifice of allure,
and the constant pursuit of luxury, is exhausting.

Although, doesn't pleasure count for a lot? Thinking back to
the stupor and pestilence of poverty that was once mine, I know
that it does.

There's a knock at the front door and peeking out the window I see that Sir Ripon and his friend, the rich Mr Burke, have come to visit. The word's already out that Heloise Chancey is receiving guests again. I rustle over to a small, cloisonné mirror on the mantelpiece and pinch my cheeks and neaten my hair. It's time to perform.

Acknowledgements

I would like to thank Tom Chalmers, Lucy Chamberlain, Robert Harries, Allison Zink and everyone at Legend Press for believing in Heloise and Amah Li Leen. Likewise, thank you to Alison Green and all the lovely people at Pantera Press. Particular thanks to Lauren Parsons. I have appreciated her continued support and graceful editing of my work.

Big thank you to the people in my writers' groups who have helped me shape this book over the years: Trudie Murrell, Janaka Malwatta, Jonathan Hadwen, Catherine Baskerville, Rohan Jayasinghe, Tamara Lazaroff, and especially to the crime fiction work-shop extraordinaire, Emma Doolan. Thank you to Susan Carson, Sharyn Pearce, Lesley Hawkes, Sarah Holland-Batt, QUT Creative Industries, Sisters in Crime (Aus), Queensland Writers Centre, Laura Elvery, Penny Holliday, Andrea Baldwin, Sarah Kanake, Madeleine Bendixen, Chris Przewloka, Mark Piccini, Joanna Hartmann and Stephen Smith. I have learnt from you all. Huge gratitude to those who have cheered me on: Ellen and David Paxton, Tina Tjia, Liam Tjia, Damien Riwoe, Amy Tjia, Fiona Kearney, Yasmin Cameron, Rebecca Dann, Cindy de Warren, Helen Curcuruto, Ann Cleary, Tina Clark and Kevin Boland.

Special thanks to Marele Day and Byron Bay Writers Festival for the mentored residency that helped me find my way; and to Varuna, The Writers' House – parts of this novel were taken from my wonderful time writing in Eleanor Dark's studio.

From my heart, thank you to my papa, a constant inspiration, to my mum, for telling me to get started and Elis, for her sunny strength. To my children for putting up with the cranky bear in the study, and to Dave, for his constant faith in me, especially when mine is at its lowest.

If you enjoyed

She Be Damned

then look out for the next book in the

HELOISE CHANCEY series

For more information, please visit:
www.PanteraPress.com

M. J. Tjia has a PhD in Creative Writing and Literary Studies. Her novella *The Fish Girl* won Seizure's Viva la Novella, 2017. She has been shortlisted for the Josephine Ulrick Short Story Prize, Overland's Neilma Sidney Short Story Prize, Fish Short Story Prize, and the Luke Bitmead Bursary and longlisted for CWA dagger awards. Her work has appeared in *Review of Australian Fiction*, *Rex*, *Peril* and *Shibboleth and Other Stories*.

She be Damned is M.J. Tjia's debut novel, and is the first instalment in her Heloise Chancey historical crime series.

M.J. lives in Brisbane, Australia, with her family.